# SMOKE
## AND
# MIST

# SMOKE
## AND
# MIST

### KATE HALL

Lost Window Publishing

For Jacob, who sees the magic in everything, even me.

# CONTENT WARNING

THERE IS SOME CONTENT IN THIS BOOK THAT MAY be triggering for certain readers. This content includes:

Animal Harm: Page 9, 10, 131-132, 186-188, 231-232, 241
Animal Death: Page 12
Violence Against Young Women, Including Injuries Similar to Self-Harm Practices: Page 96-98, 142, 239, 264-266, 296-302, 312-314, Ch. 42
Depictions of Human Death: Page 50, 98, 113-114, 142, 241

Many of these instances are in italicized portions, but some are not. Throughout the book, the main characters also deal with mental illness such as depression, anxiety, and other trauma. Please use caution if you may be triggered by any of the listed items.

"My drops of tears
  I'll turn into sparks of fire."
    William Shakespeare, Henry VIII

# CHAPTER ONE
## Sarah

GROWING UP IN A RURAL TOWN, SARAH HAS seen hundreds of videos explaining what to do if she sees or hears a wild dragon. Living in the midwest means you have to be cautious in case of a dragon attack, however rare they may be. The inhuman scream is just like the sound bytes she's heard in the safety of a classroom—metal twisting and groaning through her head, all the animals in the summer woods burrowing or flying or quivering with fear.

The week after her parents died, she had to watch one of those videos, and the sounds, so close to the sound of a car crash, had her covering her ears, unable to scream as she envisioned the semi plowing into the front of their pickup, the crushed metal echoing the dragon's call. She was sent out of the room to the counselor's office for the first of many incidents that year.

Now, alone in the forest, she is completely frozen. The

sound is worse than any informational video can describe. This scream is all-encompassing, echoing through the trees and causing any flying animals to take to the sky, and for those who can't fly to burrow deep into the warm, dark earth. She covers her ears, but the sound isn't just through the air: it's in her mind. The creature screams again and again, and she realizes that the cries are not a warning; the dragon is calling for help.

She doesn't know how she knows. She doesn't understand why she's the one the scream is meant for. Something terrible is happening, something so horrific that it's making a wild dragon, the ultimate predator, call out in pain. She collapses to her knees, the sound digging into her eardrums like knives, and once it's punctured them, it digs deeper into her soul. Her brain is going to melt out of her skull, her eyesight dotted with spots of white. She collapses to the ground, her knees scraping against the leaves and rocks and needles along the ground.

Then, as suddenly as it begun, the sound is gone. An emptiness flushes into the space, unnaturally quiet for August. Where there should be a breeze rustling through the leaves, there is an all-encompassing silence. Where animals should be scampering through the underbrush, there is a hollowness. She's only ever heard this kind of quiet in the dead of winter, when everything once living is either frozen, hibernating, or escaped.

Her head throbs, blood pounding through her like a

song, and she blinks away the lights. She reaches for her phone to call someone, perhaps the police, for help, but it isn't in her pocket. Of course, the one day she's left her phone on her night stand, she needs it. She left it at home this morning because she got sick of waiting for Penny to text her back. Now, she regrets that decision.

The light in the forest is going from a bright white morning to a sickly green, the sky above the trees filling with the dark clouds of a summer storm. She should get back to the house before she gets drenched. The idea of spending yet another day stewing in that house is hard to bear, though. Since her Uncle John ended up in hospice care, Sarah has been living with her mom's cousin, Elizabeth, on the outskirts of St. Louis. She doesn't know anything about Elizabeth or her husband, Mark, just that Uncle John didn't like them being married.

Just as Sarah is turning toward the last ribbon she tied—these woods are faerie woods, and she never risks getting lost—an image flashes into her mind.

Deep in the woods, further than she's gone on her daily hikes these past two weeks, is a cave. Even if she's ever seen it, she wouldn't have noticed—it's hidden behind the waterfall of a small tributary that empties into the Missouri River. The vision comes with the feeling of desperation, a need that sinks down into her stomach and keeps her from running away.

The woods remain silent—she is the only living thing

in the world. The animals stay in their burrows, and the air hangs still in anticipation of the storm. If she listens close enough though, there's one faint sound. The slow trickling of water.

She flinches at the crunch of her feet against the discarded pine needles as she stands.

She should text Penny, to thank her for being such a good friend all these years, but without her phone, she can only hope that Penny will forgive her for moving. They've been friends since right after Sarah's parents died, no matter what. Except now, something is different. They've always had one thing in common—neither of them has had more than the barest of affections. When Sarah sent a message to talk about her new guardians' overbearing kindness, she'd received a final message from Penny.

*Good for you,* it said. It's the last message she's received from any of her friends back in Sedalia. She's completely alone.

She might die alone.

She swipes the pine needles off her knees and arms, and her nostrils itch at the sharp smell. When her stance is steady enough to walk, she follows the sound of the river. The waterfall can't be that far; the dragon's call was practically right next to her. Surely it couldn't make that sound loud enough to span miles.

The river is easy to find—she's surprised she's never seen it before, but that's the way of faerie woods. She could walk for miles and miles without seeing or hearing the river, but now that she knows it's there, it takes her mere minutes to discover it, water clear and fast, the complete opposite of the lazy Missouri River that cuts St. Louis in half. A clap of thunder rumbles, and she startles at the sound, a small scream escaping her. She's too tense. The anxiety hovers like the storm on the horizon. The dragon's desperation is needling into her heart, but she can't help it racing as she walks to her possible death.

She walks upriver, carefully picking her way through the underbrush. The trees are thicker now, tall evergreens that caress each other and cover her in shadow. When she looks up, the gray-green clouds are shrouded by the woods. The persistent sting of pine needles attacks her arms and legs as they try to steer her away from her goal—they hug her torso enough that she has to either shove through or duck beneath them.

When she finally makes her way through the thick copse of trees, the sound of the waterfall slams into her. It rushes down and breaks on the craggy rocks below, blackened by the constant barrage of water.

There is no cave. In the vision, she'd been able to make out a small sliver of it around the edges of the falls. Now, though, there is nothing.

She turns to walk back. This entire hike has been futile, and she's lost track of the ribbons she usually ties to keep from losing her way in this faerie forest. The woods wanted her to get lost, and now she is.

A low rumble stops her before she makes it past the first branches. It could be thunder, if not for the fact that it reaches deep into her soul and drags a ragged breath from her body. Her heart sinks.

She looks back at the falls, and something moves that didn't before. A small ripple in the air—not the river pounding down, but a shimmer close enough to touch, the air crackling with static.

When she steps through the film that sticks to her skin like sweat, her eyes widen. There, fifteen feet up, right in the center of the wide waterfall, are the flared golden feathers at the end of a forest dragon's tail. She'll have to scale the wall to get to it.

The climb is more than she anticipated. The rock wall is completely vertical, the stones sharp as they cut into the palms of her hands. She boosts herself up, whispering her lessons from a long-ago rock climbing class to herself. It isn't reassuring, as water splashes along the wall, and she has to be slow and precise to keep from slipping. Yet, her instincts tell her to hurry. Her heart pounds, and her eyes sting with tears.

Halfway up, there's a shelf etched into the wall, just wide enough for her to stand on so long as she clings to the rocks in front of her. She shuffles her feet along, keeping her eyes pointed toward the tail sticking out of a cave, still too far away. When she tries to rush, though, she slices her hand open on a particularly sharp outcropping. She sucks in a breath and has to desperately cling with the other hand. She begins to tilt, and she can picture herself falling down onto the jagged rocks that are ready to catch her broken body if she falls.

Her hot blood mixes with the cold, slimy liquid coating the cave wall, and now her hand. She should wrap it or clean it or something, but she can't do anything but bite her bottom lip and ignore the sting of tears welling up. Although nobody is here to see her, a jolt of shame bursts through her, her face flushing. Here she is, her short hair plastered to her face from the sprayback and blood pooling into her cupped palm as she tries to find a deadly dragon, and she's embarrassed by her tears.

After a moment of collecting herself, she continues on. She stares at her feet, leaning forward so that she doesn't slip and fall to her death. When the rock wall opens into a huge cave, she almost falls on her face. She rights herself and looks to the long, feathery tail that hangs out the edge and gently splashes through the water.

With the bright white falls to the left, she can't see anything past the black cave entrance. Her heart slows now that she isn't hanging precariously onto the side of a cliff, but her sense of security doesn't last long. There is a dragon attached to that tail, but it's hidden in the pitch darkness. She takes a few slow steps into the cave. She can't see, but a sharp metallic smell assaults her, and the air is damp and hot. Something heats her cheeks, like a campfire gently burning her face in waves.

No, not waves.

Breaths.

Nausea rolls through her. The waterfall is drowning out all sound in the cave, but the tiny hairs at the base of her neck raise with a primal fear. Something her ancestors must have developed to keep them from accidentally stumbling into this exact situation, which she has freely strolled into. Her heart races and her stomach clenches.

Another puff of breath against her left cheek pushes her hair into her eyes and open mouth. The stale, fishy taste of the river coats her tongue, and she fights the impulse to bring her hands up to fix her hair. Any move could mean her death.

She turns her head as slowly as she can. Yet another fetid breath wafts over her, the rough, leathery snout of the dragon close enough to touch now that her eyes have finally adjusted. The head itself is as long as her bed, and the rest of the body comes to shape as her eyes trace along in the darkness. She's half tempted to reach out, to feel the skin on its nose, but her hands remain frozen at her sides.

Again, a sort of desperation runs through her, and tears prick at her eyes. A ragged gasp is dragged out of her, and she stumbles with the weight of this despair that is not her own.

She gathers herself and looks back to the dragon.

Its golden eyes are open, staring directly at her. They shine bright and alive, the morning sun watching her from this creature's face.

She takes another step toward the dragon. Her feet are icy from the river water, but when she steps forward, warmth seeps in, soaking into her shoes and banishing the cold.

It could be the dragon's body temperature heating the water. She's read that when dragons are stressed, their entire body heats up the air around them.

But the water suddenly feels wrong. Heavier. Thicker. She looks down. Scarlet streams along the cave floor. She'd stepped directly from a puddle of clean water and into a pool of whirling blood. A shiver runs through her, her body trying to get her to vomit, as none of its other warnings seem to be working.

She will not throw up. She clenches her jaw and swallows.

Her hands are shaking as she tentatively brings one up to the dragon. Its body is a mountain of gold and brown feathers, the plain colors of a female forest dragon. Its wings, tucked against its body, scrape against the high ceiling. So long as she doesn't focus on its eyes boring into her, she can do this.

"It's okay," she whispers, mostly to herself.

The dragon presses its snout against her hand, its skin surprisingly soft, like a horse's gentle muzzle. A low moan rumbles out of its throat, along with a swift, palpable relief that makes Sarah's stomach finally loosen and her heart slow. A huge gash wraps around its neck, the feathers matted and the skin shredded. Her eyes focus on a piece of skin that's hanging down, stripped right off the muscle. Once gold feathers have been dyed crimson, and she traces the path until she sees a single white feather resting gently in the pool of blood.

She stumbles backward and heaves, the contents of her stomach burning in her throat and tears rushing out of her eyes. She hasn't thrown up since she was twelve, living with her uncle John and sick with the flu. The time away from illness has made her forget how absolutely horrible it is. She tries to catch her breath, but she chokes as she heaves once again, bile intermingling with blood on the ground.

It takes her a moment to catch her breath, but the tears don't stop.

"I don't know what to do," she rasps out. "I can't save you." She considers begging, but it wouldn't do much good. Her skin has broken out into a cold sweat. A memory flashes through her mind, but it doesn't belong to her. The wind on her face, the sharp pain as she flies through steel cables tied between a copse of trees, the desperate clawing to get away, a red-headed woman tearing a single fang from her bleeding gums. Sarah's mind sticks to the woman for a second too long, but the face is obscured. Something important is tugging at her own memory, but, in this moment, she can only feel what the dragon feels.

Resignation.

The dragon knows it won't survive. So why did it bring Sarah here today?

Its mouth opens just enough that Sarah can see something shining inside, a twinkling opal that reflects the waterfall behind them. The opal is the size of a watermelon, and it glows dully in the dim cave. The walls glitter with the light emanating from it, dancing with color to displace the darkness of the day.

Sarah has never seen a forest dragon egg before. Some people raise smaller breeds, like fairy dragons that stay the size of a house cat, or even five-foot-tall field dragons that burn farm fields when it's time to switch out the crops, but forest dragons are extremely rare; only a few live in captivity across the world.

It takes a moment before it clicks.

The dragon is going to die. Nothing Sarah can try will change that. Without a mother, though, the egg will die, too. There isn't a choice, really. She steps forward again and holds her hands out.

The mother opens its mouth wider. Sarah should be afraid of sticking her hands between those glistening teeth, but a sense of calm envelopes her. This is the right decision. She reaches in, her arm hairs prickling at the hot, labored breaths of the dragon. She carefully wraps her fingers underneath the egg, making sure she has a solid grip before lifting it out. When she's holding it to her chest, the dragon lays its head on the ground, another breath shuddering out. Its jaw goes slack, and it doesn't breathe in again. The connection that's been barraging Sarah's mind is broken, and she's suddenly empty.

A warm energy thrums beneath her fingers, and she looks back at the shining opal. She imagines a baby dragon, twisting and turning beneath her fingertips.

Her jacket is moist, but she has nothing else to cushion it. Before she leaves the cave, she wraps the egg in her hoodie and buries it in her old brown backpack.

Climbing out of the cave and back to the ground is tedious. Her hand stings even worse from earlier, so she has to be careful when grabbing her handholds on the way out. She nearly falls halfway down the cliff wall, her foot slipping on a particularly slick stone, but she's able to keep her balance, her shoulder burning with effort. She probably wouldn't die if she were to fall, but landing on her back would definitely destroy the egg.

When her feet finally hit the ground, a clap of thunder sounds. The clouds are nearly black and swollen with water, ready to burst. She turns around, and the thick pines that she'd walked through to get here are nowhere to be seen. The forest has rearranged itself, so she'll have to guess her way back. Before she can make a decision, the clouds give way, and she is instantly drenched.

The walk in the sheets of rain gives her a chance to consider her options. Mark and Elizabeth are usually gone until late in the afternoon, so she should be able to sneak in unnoticed like most days. She doesn't think they're bad people, but she doesn't know them. She's lived with her great uncle since her parents died, and when he was put into hospice last month, she'd been sent to St. Louis to live with his estranged daughter.

Lightning streaks across the sky, blinding her for an instant. The trees hum with energy; wild faeries, the ones who don't want to live with humans, love storms. They love to trap people in their woods, wandering for years and years, and the sky's music makes it easier to get people turned around.

Nobody approaches her, though. She's glad she remembered to put on her woven iron cross this morning—she isn't religious, but it's the only piece of iron she owns. It used to adorn her dad's neck, and she found it hanging on the key hook by the back door when she was given a chance to pack a bag. It had kept him safe from the faerie woods behind their old farm house, and now it keeps her safe from these eerily-similar trees.

She turns in a circle to look for anything recognizable, but at this point, even the river has disappeared into the trees and shrubs. Safe enough, she reasons. They may try to confuse her, but at least they can't touch her without getting burned.

After trudging through the thick, pelting rain, she finds

one of her blue ribbons tied to an oak.

It takes a minute of searching to find the second ribbon. Another moment for the third.

She eventually makes her way out of the woods, and she sighs with relief when she sees the house, an amalgamation of a building, part stone colonial and part paneled suburban home. The main portion was built way back in the early eighteen hundreds, but the rest was built less than fifteen years ago to expand it into a four bedroom rather than one. An ancient iron fence surrounds the whole thing—that's the one part that has never changed. If you live in faerie woods, you have to be safe from those who want to steal your children away.

She sneaks through the house, dripping water along the hardwood floors toward her room. She curses under her breath, wishing she'd paid enough attention in her home economics class freshman year to remember the spell that cleans muck off the floor. She isn't great at magic, but something that basic should be ingrained in her memory. She doesn't have much time to dwell on it, though, because the garage door begins to clank open on the other side of the house.

She locks herself in her room, the last bedroom at the very corner of the original structure. When she'd arrived, Mark had informed her that they only had the one spare room, as the other had been turned into an office. His voice had been slow and careful, like she was a wild animal he might scare off. The Halacourts don't have any children of their own, and they clearly weren't expecting to get one thrust on them at any point.

*At least they're trying*, the voice in the back of her head reasons.

Her room has a fireplace, surely built to keep residents warm two hundred years ago, but now comes in handy for something else. She snatches her cell off the charger and pulls the egg out of her bag, Googling how to start a fire. She knows the basics—dragon eggs need high heat to incubate. Female dragons can heat their bellies to hundreds of degrees while they roost, but orphan eggs can sit in a fire or even embers.

Instead of risking magically summoning a fire, she digs up the lighter Penny had stolen from a twenty-year old boyfriend and lights a magazine page, shoving it under the logs in hopes they'll catch. She lays the egg on top of the haphazard pile of logs, and white smoke starts to emanate from beneath.

A knock sounds at the door.

"Dinner will be ready soon," Elizabeth calls, her voice hopeful. There's a pause. "Is something on fire?" She doesn't seem as concerned as she perhaps should about their home burning down.

Sarah's throat goes dry. Elizabeth works at the zoo, so it would only be right to come clean now. "I wanted to try out the fireplace!" The excuse is flimsy at best, but, after a momentary pause, Elizabeth's feet creek on the floorboards as she leaves.

She was entrusted to take care of this egg, and she doesn't want it to be raised by some clinical hands and a robotic mother. Forest dragons are at least a little illegal to keep, though, so nobody can know about this.

# CHAPTER TWO
## Alex

WHEN ALEX RETURNS TO ST. LOUIS, HIS RELIEF is palpable. The drive to campus takes seven hours from his parents' squat ranch house in Kansas, and he makes it overnight so he doesn't have to drive right after an emotional goodbye. Instead, he sneaked away into the night the moment everyone else was asleep.

Every bigger city is more magical than his tiny hometown of Winfield, Kansas, but St. Louis always feels like more. The sun glistens off the arch, illuminating it gold as he comes up over the interstate in his late grandmother's old green Ford Taurus. His fingers twitch and spark, not enough to start a fire, but enough to singe the musty fabric steering wheel cover. His heart soars at the sight, and not even his shining orange and yellow aviators can keep the brightness out of his eyes. The light is no longer blinding when he takes the exit that leads him back to St. Merlin's

Academy, his car tucked into the long shadows of the tall glass and stone buildings that adorn downtown.

There's an excruciating amount of traffic this morning, but he should've expected that when arriving at the same time as everyone is headed to work. He's stuck at the same light by the art museum through three different cycles, creeping ever closer, and his car goes at a crawl through Forest Park, an expanse of green and trees and women jogging by with strollers. Finally, though, he's able to turn off into the back driveway of the school. He has to swipe his student ID to get into the dorm parking lot, which is mostly empty this early in the day. By the end of the afternoon, though, it will be packed with overpriced cars owned by the affluent teenagers that stay here for the year.

Students keep the same dorms their whole high school career, so he parks his new-to-him car in its new-to-him assigned spot and hauls his hefty duffle bag up four stories, the white steel and concrete stairway echoing every step. Halfway up, his eyes begin to droop from the exhaustion of staying up all night.

Freshman and sophomore year, his parents dropped him off, and although he didn't think he'd miss their incessant affection this time, now that he's here, standing in front of the pale wooden door to his room, his throat closes up with emotion. He brushes away the tears that have begun to well up before unlocking the door and walking in.

The room looks just like it did when he left, including the

nerdy decor hung all over the walls. Both of the twin beds have Star Wars sheets, Alex's featuring the Empire insignia and his roomate has the Rebel symbol.

He isn't the only one to arrive early. David, another py-romancer, is already lying in his bed on the right side of the room, a book featuring a girl with white hair in hand. When Alex walks in, he looks up and uses the inside of the book jacket as a bookmark.

"Hey, I was wondering when you'd show up!" David says, a grin spreading across his face as he gets out of bed, still in his dinosaur pajama pants. He must have arrived yesterday. They've been close since they were assigned to-gether the summer before freshman year—neither of them knew anyone in the city, so it had been easy for them to bond.

Alex drops his duffel bag and holds his arms out, and David, a few inches taller and fifty pounds heavier, pulls him into a bear hug.

When Alex pulls away, he asks, "Where've you been? I haven't heard from you half the summer."

He unpacks his duffel bag as David goes over his vaca-tion, which he spent backpacking across Europe. His par-ents own a wireless internet company somewhere in Flor-ida, so they're always going on huge expensive vacations and buying new cars. Unlike Alex, David doesn't need a scholarship to attend St. Merlin's.

Once he's finished unpacking, Alex flops down on his

bed, wrapping himself in the throw blanket his mom had packed. The entire room smells musty and unfamiliar, the result of sitting for three months with no residents. The rough blanket, though, smells like home. David doesn't make fun of him for it, and Alex doesn't make fun of the stuffed Ewok that David has had since he was a baby. Alex's eyes prick with tears once again—he's too tired to care, and David has seen him cry more than anyone else, anyway. When he'd first moved here, his first real time away from his family, he'd cried himself to sleep almost every night for two weeks.

"Wake me up before lunch," Alex says, his voice heavy with sleep and sadness. He's asleep before David can reply.

HE'S BEING POKED IN THE SPINE BY SOMETHING. A broom handle, maybe. He forces his eyes open and sits up, his body aching with protest at his nap being cut so short. A clatter makes him turn to David.

Their dollar broom is lying on the floor; it definitely wasn't there this morning.

"Thanks," Alex says, hopping off the bed.

He should've taken his medication before leaving Kansas, but, by the time he'd realized, it had been packed toward the bottom of his duffel bag. He grabs his toiletry bag and goes to the bathroom they share with two other suitemates, neither of whom have arrived on campus yet. He doesn't talk to Mike or Will often, but they usually show up late at night the day before classes start after every break.

He fills a brand-new syringe with testosterone before giving himself the shot—he used to flinch at it, but he's been taking it once a month since he got off hormone blockers at fourteen, and the fear has long since worn off.

"What are you thinking for lunch?" David asks when Alex is back in the bedroom. He's finally out of bed and is halfway changed from his pajamas to actual clothes—a pair of blue jeans and a violet t-shirt that illuminates his obsidian skin. Alex has always been envious of David's muscle tone—they spend a lot of time together at the gym, yet David has always managed to be more toned than him. Alex has always been lean, but it's an even more stark contrast now that David seems to have bulked up over the summer. It isn't until the shirt is completely on that Alex realizes he's been staring.

"Imo's. Definitely Imo's," Alex replies. It's a tradition for them to eat at the St. Louis pizza staple their first day back—freshman year, Alex's parents had noticed that David was all alone in the dorm. His mom and dad had sent him from Miami to St. Louis on a plane, and tears were beginning to glisten in his eyes when Alex's family was getting ready to go to dinner. Even without Alex's parents today, they fit themselves into the tangerine Corvette David brought back from winter break last year.

The nearest Imo's is just on the other side of Forest Park, a miles-long expanse of land that cuts through the middle of St. Louis like a scar. Some days throughout the school year, Alex walks from his dorm over to the science center or the zoo just to get out for a while. It's a nice day out, cooler than usual for summer, but they don't walk. They used to justify it by saying they didn't want to hike the mile back to campus with leftover pizza, but the truth is, the Corvette is achingly cool, and Alex likes feeling like he belongs at St. Merlin's, if only by association.

They split the biggest pizza on the menu, and, as usual, there are no leftovers.

As they step outside to head back to campus, the faint screech of a dragon reverberates throughout the city. He isn't in any immediate danger—it must be miles and miles away, but the sound still roots him to the spot. Back home, he has to deal with cat-sized prairie dragons occasionally trying to burn down their hay fields, but he's never heard a larger dragon screech outside of television. He feels bad for whichever farmer is losing a cow or two this afternoon.

He's about to ask if David heard it when he spots a curvy blonde girl getting out of the passenger side of a black Mercedes.

"Hey, guys!" she says when she notices them, a grin spread across her face. Kendall is the third pyromancer at St. Merlin's, and she's a year younger than them. Her older sister, Heather, tall and slim in comparison, steps out of the driver's side. The only similarity the sisters have is their blonde hair and their shared apartment near Washington

University, which nestles into the West side of the park.

David plasters a huge grin across his face and jogs up to her, wrapping her in a hug that lifts her off the ground. Alex ambles up slowly behind, hands shoved deep in his pockets. Ever the third wheel.

"How was your summer?" Kendall asks. Before either of them can respond, Heather clears her throat and lifts her eyebrows.

"Are we gonna eat or not?" she asks. Heather is a senior at Washington University, and since her parents decided that Kendall should live with her instead of on St. Merlin's campus, she's been bitter toward her younger sister.

Kendall doesn't seem to notice the hostility. "Be right in!" She turns back to Alex and David and wraps them in a group hug. "I'm so happy to see you guys again," she mumbles before releasing them and following Heather into the pizza joint. Her eyes linger on David just a moment longer than necessary.

As bitter as Heather acts, Alex knows that she cares deeply for Kendall. Otherwise, instead of coming halfway across the park to this Imo's, the one where David and Alex can almost always be found, she would've gone to the one two blocks from her apartment.

"This is gonna be the year," David says, watching Kendall retreat into the restaurant.

All last year, he said he would ask Kendall out. He had a date planned, which he would describe to Alex in detail every time Kendall looked especially adorable. The plan is to take her to the zoo because she loves the sea lions and the Abadas—a small breed of African unicorn—before going out to dinner at Kemoll's, one of the finest restaurants in town.

"I just have to up my game," he says once they're in the car on the way back to school. "Did you see her today?"

Alex had. Last year, she'd been shy and kept her appearance toned down. Today, though, she'd been wearing a dress that accentuated her full figure and makeup ready for a night out.

David talks about Kendall the entire way back, and then pulls out his notebook—yes, an actual notebook—dedicated to planning the perfect first date for her. It would be creepy if Alex didn't know that Kendall cared about David just as much.

Alex enjoys listening to David talk about Kendall, especially because he sees the way she watches him in class, her eyes filled with longing. He is genuinely excited for the day they finally end up together, but he can't help but wonder if anyone will ever look at him that way. Not just with lust or curiosity, but with the longing that comes with falling in love.

He's kissed people before. When he was twelve, he would hang out with a boy named Kyle who was a year older. Alex liked him because he was older, he wore all black, and he drank alcohol. All things that made him seem dangerous, like the sly leading man in the R-rated movies he watched with Dad when Mom wasn't home. When Kyle was visiting his dad's house next door to the Locklears' on weekends, he and Alex would go behind the shed and kiss. "I'll kill you if you tell anybody," Kyle warned. Boys kissing boys wasn't okay in their town. At least not if you were in middle school and wanted to have any friends.

When Alex was fourteen, gearing up all summer to go to St. Louis, he had a girlfriend named Brittany whose mom would drop her at the end of the street and peel away in a station wagon. His parents were rarely home—they were both working more to save up the extra money to send him to St. Merlin's—so he and Brittany spent a lot of time in his room making out. Once, though, she tried putting her hand down his pants, but he protested. She was gone soon after, and his social status plummeted as she spread rumors about him.

David is his best friend, but he blushes when he considers asking what it's like to be in love. Instead, when they get back to the dorm, he packs his satchel in preparation for his first day back at St. Merlin's.

# CHAPTER THREE
## Sarah

DUE TO HER EVERLASTING INSOMNIA, SARAH HAS already been awake for a couple hours when her alarm finally goes off, doing more research on dragon eggs. When the alarm rings on her phone, she simply closes out of it and continues to read her fiftieth article on dragon care—this one is titled "What to Expect When You're Expecting A Dragon," a play on the popular parenting book about half-mer children.

She lazily changes into her uniform, eyes on her phone the whole time. The next article suggests adding oxygen to make the fire even hotter; "Blue fire can be the determining factor on if your hatchling is quiet or active." She skips past that one, as there's no way she could sneak an entire oxygen setup into her room without there being some serious questions.

She pokes at the flames, trying to adjust the logs so they'll burn longer, when Mark knocks. She whispers a quick in-cantation—a shield to hide her illicit activities. Uncle John was always quite vocal about his dislike for any and all above-G-rated content, so Sarah had had to hide her extensive movie and book collection in plain sight. Although Elizabeth and Mark hadn't even blinked at her teen romance novels and R-rated action movies when they helped her move in, they probably won't be quite as understanding about an endangered species being hidden in her bedroom, so the flimsy spell comes in handy.

Mark is standing at the door in a pair of black slacks, a teal button-up shirt, and a coral bowtie, a tweed jacket hung over one arm. He yawns and tousles his curly red hair—whether he means to fix it or make it more of a mess, Sarah isn't sure. His entire aesthetic is rather lax for what she imagines a St. Merlin's professor to look like, but she gives him the benefit of the doubt, although he teaches the least magical class, math. She glances down the hallway nervously—Elizabeth always seems to know what she's thinking, but the tall, ethereal woman is nowhere in sight.

"Ready to go?" Mark asks, not making eye contact. He's been like this since Sarah moved in—afraid to upset her, perhaps.

"Yeah," she says, grabbing the brand-new black satchel by the door and slipping out before he can get a good look inside—the fire may be hidden behind a spell, but her old backpack is crumpled on the floor by the bed, streaked with mud.

"Liz had to work early, so she won't be able to see us off on the first day of the semester," Mark says. Sarah is only able to attend St. Merlin's because of his position, but that also means that she has to ride to school with a teacher.

"Great," she says, masking her nerves by feigning excitement. She's certain she did the spell right, but her hand twitches toward the doorknob as her mind tells her to peek in and check on it one last time. She resists. It would only make her look more suspicious.

The school is supposed to be a thirty minute drive from Chesterfield, but Mark's classic Pontiac makes it in twenty. To avoid talking about anything that may lead back to the dragon egg, Sarah puts in her earbuds and stares out the window, absorbing the sight of the unfamiliar city as the skyline rises ahead of her, and then disappears again when they pull off the exit toward her new school.

St. Merlin's Academy for Talented Students is one of the most prestigious high schools in the country, and it's obvious that they want to look like it. Mark types his employee code into the keypad by the wrought-iron front gate, which is held up by two huge stone walls, topped by statues of hunting dogs taking down an elk on one side and a boar on the other. The elk's body is stretched out, its neck thrown back and eternally frozen as it tries to escape the pack of dogs.

"The gateway was imported from Germany," Mark says

as he follows the traffic leading up the drive. His car may be stylish and classic, but it pales in comparison to the parade of vehicles ahead—a Rolls Royce with blacked-out windows is directly in front of them. "It was taken from a hunting castle somewhere in the mountains."

She nods at the information, but the gruesome scene makes her stomach flop. It reminds her too much of her uncle's dogs, hungry beasts who would tear her apart given the slightest chance. Her heart twinges, wondering if the animals he'd trained to attack would have to be put down for their owner's bad behavior now that he can no longer care for them.

When she looks up, her heart races, a hissing noise growing in her ears. The grey stone-faced building scrutinizes every car that passes, its windows dark; nothing can be seen past them, but they're not reflecting back the golden morning light, either. The freshmen being dropped off in the circle drive wear form-fitting uniforms, but they all seem so young to Sarah. She's probably the only upperclassman being driven by an adult instead of driving herself here.

When they pull around to the faculty parking lot, she looks back at Mark. "It's not too late to send me to a public school," she pleads. She twists the ring on her right hand—her mother's engagement ring that was given to her at the hospital when the doctor explained that Sarah would never see her parents again. They wouldn't have wanted her at this posh city school—she was homeschooled before they died, and then she ended up in a public school.

Back at the front entrance, the boy getting out of the Rolls Royce is covered head-to toe, sleek leather gloves adorning his hands and a parasol over his head. His eyes are covered by a pair of pitch-black Ray-Bans, which surely hide his red eyes from the sun. Back in her hometown, vampires only go to school at night, so seeing one being dropped off in the daytime is the shock her body needs to clamber out of the Pontiac and onto the sidewalk. Instead of following Mark into a teacher door that needs his key, she moves to where everyone else seems to be entering.

Standing at the foot of the steps, she can't help but stare at this building as it judges her. Some of the other students glance at her in passing, and her throat closes up. Elizabeth and Mark made sure to buy her a uniform, and Elizabeth had even had the black skirt and navy blazer tailored to fit her, an unnecessary expense on their part, but she's still an outsider. They can surely sense it—she's too old to be a freshman, and the phone in her hand isn't even close to the newest model.

When someone clears their throat behind her, she moves up the steps, making her way inside. She wants to take a moment to inspect the scenes carved into the ornate wood doors, but the sea of students carries her on, into a foyer with cavernous painted ceilings. According to the website, the main hall used to be a cathedral.

Before she can be swept away completely, she moves to a

side hall so that she can dig out her schedule; the sooner she can find her class and be away from this crowd, the better.

When she finds her schedule, she notices that all the class numbers have a letter written next to the number. She flips the schedule over to see if there's an explanation, but she finds none. She flips it again, but of course nothing has changed. Her hands start to shake, her throat pinching. The words on the page blur. What if she doesn't make it to her classes? She looks around for a sign that gives her any information, but she can't find anything. None of the signs are legible through her dizziness. She takes a breath, but it doesn't seem to make it to her lungs. She looks back to her schedule, desperately hoping that more information will pop out at her.

"The letter is the building code," a silky voice says just as tears prick at her eyes. She lifts her eyes from her class schedule to see a girl standing in front of her, her expression sympathetic. She's in the process of putting her curly mass of black hair into a ponytail, but her golden-brown eyes are on Sarah. "And the number is the room, of course."

It takes Sarah a moment to respond. "Building code?"

The tall, dark-skinned girl continues, her voice almost melodical, "Yeah, so you know which building your class is in." When her hair is up, she regards Sarah. Without saying anything else, she takes the schedule from Sarah's hands, skimming her holographic manicured fingernails over the list of classes. She moves to Sarah's side, holding the schedule in front of her. "Okay, so your first class is in Terrance Hall. That's the one straight across the courtyard."

Sarah nods. "So," she says, considering her words, "there are more buildings than just this one?" Her old school had been a long building crouching in the middle of a field. The classrooms were numbered from one to forty, stretching from one end of the building to the other. The cafeteria was on one side, the gym on the other. She hadn't thought to look up a school map when she was checking out the website.

She expects the girl to laugh at her, but she just slaps a hand on Sarah's shoulder and says, "Welcome to St. Merlin's." Her smile falters for a moment when she sees Sarah's discomfort. "Hey, you're not doing too bad. I got here in the middle of last year. It took me two days to realize I was in the wrong building for half my classes. I thought the letters were for seat assignments."

Sarah laughs a bit at that. She's sure she would make the same mistake, or worse, if not for this girl's help. "Well at least I have you," she says.

The girl's grin returns in full force, and she loops her arm through Sarah's. The scent of flowers and citrus floats over to her, the same perfume that Elizabeth uses. "And we have Literature together first hour." She pulls Sarah through the steadily thinning crowd of freshmen, aiming at a pair of glass doors that lead outside.

When they step out, Sarah takes in a lungful of air, the

outdoors giving her a chance to finally breathe.

The courtyard is a huge patch of grass, concrete paths winding their way through. The smell of freshly-mowed grass wafts into her nostrils, but she doesn't see any evidence of maintenance—she's used to seeing grass shavings on sidewalks after someone's trimmed, but everything is pristine here. Magically cleaned, something her old school didn't bother with. A clocktower sits in the middle of the courtyard, and she sees that her anxiety attack had her standing in place longer than she thought. She's fairly certain that they'll both be late to class.

There are only a few students out here, most of whom are rushing to any of the four buildings that enclose the area. The buildings to the left and right have the same stone facing as the building they just left, but the one across from the main building is more modern, a square stack of concrete and glass and wooden rectangles.

"I'm Gabby, by the way," the girl says. "And if we don't want to be late, we're gonna have to make a run for it."

GABBY AND SARAH ONLY HAVE FIRST HOUR TOgether, but Gabby directs Sarah to her Potions classroom before bounding across campus to health class.

The potions lab is a plain white room, the stark decor contrasting greatly with her Literature class. Instead of having posters with educational charts and famous quotations like her Lit room, there are a just a few laminated signs plastered on white-painted brick walls to ensure lab safety. The one that catches her eye has a faded image of a red stick-person fleeing what appears to be a red toilet on fire, and there isn't a caption to explain what students are supposed to be avoiding. Is there a haunted toilet somewhere on campus? Somewhere in this room? She looks around but finds no such thing.

The tables have slips of paper with names on them, so she searches the room until she finds the sheet that says "Sarah Jackson," which is right next to one that says "Alexander Locklear." As soon as she's scooted in to the shared two-person table, the stool next to her screeches backwards. She glances over to see a boy, a few inches taller than her, shoving his black satchel under the table.

Her face flushes warm just a little as she notices how absurdly hot he is. His jawline is sharp enough to slice right through her inhibitions, so she says, "I'm Sarah. New here."

He turns to her in surprise, his nearly-black eyes widening. "You can see me?" he whispers, glancing around.

Sarah's blood turns cold. She's never met a ghost, and she didn't consider that she might run into one as a student here.

Then, he breaks out into a sloppy grin. "Kidding. Totally human." He leans back in his chair and says, "Alex."

She smiles at his easygoing disposition and is about to ask where he's from—when she was researching the school, she discovered that a large portion of the student body comes from out of town—but the teacher arrives, out of breath, just as the bell rings. He explains that, for the first day, they'll be going around the room and saying a fun fact about themselves. Sarah sighs; these games are never as fun as teachers hope they'll be.

A few of the students say something interesting. "I'm one-third wood-elf," a stunning, tall girl with huge green irises says. Most of the students, though, are less interesting and more of braggadocios. "I spent my summer in Vienna," one says, and another, "Paris!"

When it's Alex's turn, he stands up, hands in the pockets of his uniform black slacks. He's no longer the self-assured boy from a moment ago. Now, he keeps his head down. "I'm Alex, and I'm a telepathic pyromancer."

Telepathy is fairly common, but it's usually a power that stands on its own. Penny had telepathy, but she wasn't adept at controlling it, so she would often blurt out others' thoughts in public. Pyromancy, though. That's nearly unheard of. Being a fire mage alone makes Alex someone worth reckoning with, but telepathy being added into the mix? He would be unstoppable if he decided to join the military, and rich and famous to boot. Of course, he's probably already rich. Sarah bites her lip.

"I'm Sarah," she says, straining to keep her voice above a whisper. Everyone in the room is looking at her with interest. At her old school, nobody would be paying attention, but here, the students' eyes twinkle as they appraise her, and, probably, find her lacking. "I just moved to the city to live with Elizabeth and Mark Halacourt, my aunt and uncle."

Apparently, this was the wrong thing to say, because half the room looks shocked, and those who aren't are whispering to each other with sly smiles. She should've guessed that the name would garner interest since Mark is a teacher here.

By the time lunch rolls around, it feels like half the student body has introduced themselves to her. Her stomach is rebelling with hunger, but it takes twenty minutes to get through the lunchline because people keep trying to talk to her, mainly asking if she can get answers to midterms ahead of time. Along with this, she has to navigate the buffet, which contains things labeled "Foie Gras" and "Spanakopita." She fills her plate with the only thing she recognizes, three sushi rolls, and rushes into the cafeteria.

The entire school has lunch at the same time, so there's a crowd of students at heavy mahogany tables. She always imagined rich kids having sophisticated discussions over lunch, but, just like back home, there are cliques, just harder to sort out with the unanimity of the school blazers. One table has a bunch of short, muscular boys who already have beards to their collarbones—dwarves, maybe—laughing boisterously, and another has students all wearing sunglasses and drinking out of thermoses—vampires, for sure. She even recognizes the boy from this morning.

Since her parents died, Sarah could usually be found eating lunch with the outcasts in the cafeteria. She kept to herself while they talked about their weekend exploits, ranging from video games to breaking curfew to doing cocaine at a college party. Being at a table of abnormal people meant that, despite being an orphan, she was pretty normal among them. Now, she's not sure where she should sit.

A familiar voice shouts from her left. "Ka-caw!" it says in a distinctly feminine, not at all crow-like tone. Gabby is standing on her chair and waving her arms in the corner, drawing eyes, and Sarah ducks her head and goes to her.

She slides into a seat without getting stopped by anyone else, which she's thankful for. Gabby talks over her matching plate of sushi. "Can you believe I've got homework in Spiritual Magic on the first day? I mean, it's just questions out of the textbook about spiritual mages and how they ended Florida's Magical Wars in the 1880s, but still! Day one is supposed to be dumb introductions and name games."

Sarah picks at her sushi and lets Gabby vent, and she doesn't mention that she has Spiritual Magic next. Before lunch ends, Gabby puts her number into Sarah's phone, making a quip about the broken screen, but Sarah doesn't take offense to it like she might with the other students who've been prodding her for attention all day whilst simultaneously looking down their noses at her.

It isn't hard to find her Spiritual Magic classroom—she passed it on her way to Calculus earlier, so she traces her way back across campus. When she arrives, there's only one vacant seat, and it's next to Alex, his lithe form stretched out in his seat, hands behind his head.

"We have to stop meeting like this," she says quietly when she pulls back her heavy wooden chair, a coy smile playing across her lips.

It takes a moment before recognition dawns on his face, making a smile play across his lips. Before he can respond, the teacher begins the lesson. He straightens up when Ms. White, an actual ghost, speaks, his attention leaving Sarah.

She bites the inside of her cheek, heat flooding her face. She isn't sure what made her say something so flirtatious, but she doesn't have any way to take it back or judge his response until class ends. By the time they're released to their next classes, though, Alex has his bag packed and rushes out the door. When he's about to pass the threshold, he turns his head back to look at Sarah, half a smile across his face and mouth open to speak when their eyes lock together.

Suddenly, she's no longer in the classroom. It's night, and a chill whips around her as lights flash in front of her closed eyes and her ears are bombarded with a haunting tune. She forgets, momentarily, that she's supposed to be in a classroom getting ready to go to US History, and instead focuses on the boy she's kissing. His warm arms are wrapped around her in a tight embrace, and she gently runs her tongue along his honey-flavored bottom lip, eliciting a soft moan.

When Alex pulls away, she smiles.

A ragged gasp drags itself out of her, and she's back in the now empty classroom, Ms. White staring at her, head tilted with concern. "Are you alright, dear?" the not-quite-dead woman asks gently.

Sarah opens her mouth, but no sound comes out. She shakes her head, gathers her bag, and leaves for her next class.

# CHAPTER FOUR
## Alex

$\mathbf{A}$ LEX'S HANDS WON'T STOP SHAKING.

After class, he rushes to the restroom and locks himself in a stall, willing himself to not catch on fire. Heat rushes to his hands, his fight or flight response activated by the sudden vision. The hairs on the back of his neck prick, but there's nobody else in this restroom activating his senses.

The vision hadn't belonged to him, that much is for sure. That doesn't change the fact that he felt it, that he was there with this vision coursing through him.

He's had visions before. Almost everyone at St. Merlin's takes Divination at some point, and everyone has at least one vision from the herbal tea they're given. Alex's vision was that he would break his foot while playing soccer in the courtyard. Two weeks later, the nurse had to repair his broken foot after an impromptu game had broken out. He didn't even get extra credit for his vision coming true—the day before, someone else had forced their vision by slamming their head into a wall to receive a broken nose.

He braces himself against the sink and works on the breathing exercises that he learned in his freshman year pyromancy course. He sucks in a breath, holds it for ten seconds, and then pushes it out his nose. He ties his hands together with his fingers and lifts them with each breath, lowering them as he breathes out.

*What the fuck just happened?*

He has had visions, sure, but he's never had someone else's vision. Random thoughts and feelings will float to him on occasion due to his telepathy, but he's never received something so vivid.

It's still reverberating through him, looking for a place to escape. Because it's magic, it tries desperately to escape using his fire. Because he doesn't want to burn the bathroom down, he suppresses it, and it keeps playing over and over again.

In his mind, Sarah's body is still pressed against him, her body cold with the unseasonable chill. Her lips are taut and desperate as they crush against his. They're at some sort of party, and he has to pull away to gather his thoughts. His hands are knotted in her short brown hair, and her freckles stand out on her pale skin. She's tall for a girl, only a little shorter than him. Kissing her is so easy, and he wants nothing more than to keep doing it.

He keeps breathing, slowing it until he's holding his

breath for over a minute at a time before releasing it.

Gradually, the vision goes spotty, fading into memory. It's a powerful piece of magic, but not more powerful than his willpower.

Sixth hour passes in a blur—he can't focus on anything while his thoughts are on the vision, but by the time the class is over, he's regained complete control over his mind.

His final class of the day is Pyromancy, and he's relieved to be here. Normal subjects like Spiritual Magic or Potions don't interest him in the slightest, and he's not well suited to Math and History.

He was born to be a pyromancer. Dad says it's because Alex was conceived at a bonfire, and Mom usually slaps him on the shoulder for saying that.

"He knows how babies are made, Mary," Dad will say in defense, and he laughs when Mom whacks him again. Neither of them were as good-humored when Alex nearly burned down the barn when he was thirteen, the same year he'd been offered a partial scholarship to St. Merlin's.

Phillip Lionel is the youngest teacher on campus, and the only one imported from Belgium. He has a black beard as thick as his accent, probably to make up for the lack of hair on his head. A lot of the freshmen are afraid of him, as he's one of the four live-in professors, the one in charge of ensuring that students are in their rooms with the lights out no later than ten at night before a school day.

"Who actually did the homework this summer?" Phillip

asks when all three pyromancers—Alex, David, and Kendall—are in the room. The desks have all been magicked somewhere else, so they must be practicing today. A large rubber mat has been rolled out across the floor, and the air is charged with a familiar charm that keeps them from burning down the classroom.

They all turn in their thick essays—each of them had to spend the summer researching a famous fire mage and write a five-thousand word essay over them. Phillip tosses the papers in the air, where they disappear with a *crack*, presumably to the work desk where he grades homework in his apartment.

To David's obvious delight, he and Kendall are grouped together to begin their warm-up drills, while Phillip works one-on-one with Alex. Phillip casts a doppelgänger with a swish of his hand, which Alex assumes is the best way to teach multiple pyromancers at once and not have anyone fall behind. The doppelgänger is a wispy version of the teacher who goes through drills with Kendall and David, adjusting their stances as needed. David's movements are aggressive, his fire hot and sharp. He's a grease fire running out of control, while Kendall is soft and graceful, candlelight on a starry evening.

The real Phillip joins Alex at the other side of the room. He explains and demonstrates a few new maneuvers, and then tells Alex where to incorporate them into his current drills. He follows along as Phillip does them, ensuring that he understands exactly what it is he's meant to be doing.

Alex goes through his standard warmup, which is a sort of tai-chi used to balance a pyromancer before starting to use fire. Apparently, he's lost his touch, because the movements that were as familiar to him as breathing last year are being picked at and adjusted by Phillip.

After going through the warm-up twice, he starts on the drills, which mainly consist of Alex producing different types of fire using different motions. In reality, the motions are unimportant, but pyromancers have found that it's easier to focus one's energy when there are specific maneuvers to follow.

He trips up on the second motion, one of the new ones that Phillip demonstrated. He's supposed to stretch his torso out in a straight line that extends through one leg, balanced on the toes of the other. Instead, he falls forward and catches himself with his hands, and everyone in the room stops what they're doing when they hear a loud snap, like a twig underfoot.

A sharp pain shoots up his right arm, and he curses under his breath.

"What have I told you about landing on your hands?" Phillip chides, but he helps Alex up nonetheless. The hand stings and throbs, and his wrist is already starting to swell. When he tries to bend it, the pain shoots through him again. "Ah, off to the nurse with you."

Alex cradles his hand to his chest and curses himself for

being so stupid. He knows how to use his momentum to keep from hurting himself when he falls, but he didn't do it this time. "It will keep you alive in a battle," Phillip often explains. He always laughs at Alex when he responds that he doesn't plan on battling anything at any point in his life.

He passes Gabby Savalza in the hall, and she waves a lavatory pass at him, a green slip of paper. He waves back with his working hand, and she raises an eyebrow at the broken one. When they get close enough, her hand clenches and unclenches in front of her. "That's a good break you've got there, Locklear," she says. "How'd you manage that?" From the whispers in the student body, Alex knows that she's an empath, but he had no idea that her abilities were strong enough that she could feel someone else's pain without trying. Impressive. They have US History together this year, and they had the same literature class last year. Other than that, they don't really know each other, though she seems friendly enough.

"I thought it would be fun," he jokes with a careful shrug as they pass each other and continue on their way.

It only takes the nurse a moment to repair his wrist, although it hurts worse than the initial break. To heal him, she has to hold his wrist tightly, and her magic radiates ice-cold deep into his bones. He tries to focus on a poster about preventing the spread of Faerie Flu, but he still cries out after a few seconds of healing. When she releases him, his wrist as good as new. The icy sting is already fading.

"Hasn't Phillip told you that you shouldn't catch yourself with your hands?" she asks condescendingly as she puts away the oils she uses to focus her healing powers.

"Yes, ma'am," Alex replies. "I'm just talented enough to forget and then break myself on a rubber practice mat. Really, I should get an award."

She rolls her eyes. "I'd better not see you in my office again for at least another month."

He salutes her sarcastically before heading back to class. "You'd miss me too much," he says, shutting the door behind him.

Last year, he had an injury or illness from one class or another every week until school let out. Once, she had to repair both legs and an arm after he fell off the roof of one of the smaller buildings while trying to catch a baby griffon that someone let out during a magical creatures class.

Back on his family's farm in Kansas, he's usually quite careful, but something about the energy at St. Merlin's makes him reckless.

# CHAPTER FIVE
## Sarah

BACK HOME, AFTER TEXTING GABBY ABOUT THE Spiritual Magic assignment, Sarah stares at the dragon egg. She had to add more logs to it and stoke the embers to create a flame, so it's back to being a steady crackle of flame. The orange light causes the opalescent blues and pinks and greens to twinkle brighter, but there's no indication of what's going on inside the egg. For all she knows, it died on her way back to the house in the pouring rain. The internet has been no help in that regard—all she's found have been pictures of the mystical shell pieces after hatching or eggs being incubated.

She runs her finger over her lips, bringing back the memory—no, the vision—of Alex's lips against hers. She can still feel the light stubble on his chin brushing against her, and she closes her eyes to bring back the full thing. He'd mentioned that he has telepathic powers, but she hadn't considered that meant psychic visions, too. Psychics are exceedingly rare, and some people consider them to be dangerous. Sarah has never believed that any magic is more dangerous than other types, although she is wary of blood magic.

She crawls into bed after casting the shield back over the fireplace, curling up tight under her comforter. She only leaves a small hole to the room to let in fresh air.

In moments, she's asleep.

*H*ER EYES OPEN WHEN THE TRUCK STOPS, FAERIES *singing from the trees surrounding Aunt Helen's house. She was trying to sleep, but the dirt roads had bounced her around, her head occasionally slamming against the window. Besides, she doesn't want to have another nightmare, which her parents have been doing their best to quell all week. The drive here was long; it had taken hours to get to Helen's house in the Northwest Arkansas hills.*

*"I'll get the mare if you get Sarah," Mom whispers, her door opening and flooding the cab of the truck with light.*

*Sarah closes her eyes, still feigning sleep before her parents notice she's up. Dad turns the truck off, the roar of the engine suddenly silent in the quiet winter night. His keys jingle as he exits the vehicle, and he closes the front door as quietly as possible. She rolls her head against the seat so that she doesn't fall when he opens her door, and she lets him collect her, his arms warm in the frigid night. It's been a long time since her dad has carried her anywhere, but tonight, he does it without hesitation.*

# SMOKE AND MIST

*When he steps onto the wooden porch of Helen and Dad's childhood home, the screen door squeaks open. Sarah opens her eyes just enough to see her aunt, but not enough that anyone notices she's awake.*

*Helen is two years older than Dad, and her freckled face is weary from the cold night. She's wearing thick, stained tan coveralls and a somber expression. When Sarah was younger, Mom had to explain to her that that's just how Helen's face is. Her mess of red hair is tied back in a braid, a few strands escaping in an attempt to curl their way to freedom.*

*"How was the drive?" she whispers, her voice gentle, the same as the voice she uses to calm frightened horses. Every winter break, Sarah's parents bring her here to celebrate the holidays, including her birthday. One of her favorite things to do is watch Helen train horses that nobody else can, hands steady and feet planted with even the most difficult of animals. Helen's gentle hand brushes Sarah's scalp.*

*Dad tells Helen about the long ride, about the unicorn mare rocking the trailer with anxiety. He carries Sarah into the dim, warm house while he speaks. She can faintly smell something sweet, probably a cake. Helen makes the best chocolate cake, which they eat for breakfast on her birthday before Sarah's parents wake up every year.*

*A loud whinny pierces the night, and she hears Aunt Helen curse, footsteps bounding off the porch. After Dad lays Sarah on the couch, he, too, is out the door. She hears metallic rattling — the unicorn must be spooked at something, its hooves pawing at the trailer walls and shaking the doors. Even the house seems to shake for a moment.*

*She considers opening her eyes to see if she can spot the calamity, but her eyelids are too heavy, like the sticky darkness is holding them shut. Mom is yelling something to Dad, her words jumbled, and then the trailer door clatters open and slams into a gate, the sound ringing through the winter night.*

*She forces her eyes open at the noise, but all she can see now is the white semi truck headlight shining into their cab, her mother's hand tight around her own. She tries to hold on, but her eyelids droop shut, her hands repeatedly slipping out of Mom's bloody one.*

SARAH WAKES UP IN A COLD SWEAT, CHECKING her phone to see that her alarm is about to go off.

She hasn't had a dream about Helen's house since she was twelve, and even then, they were usually nightmares. This time, it was almost a memory. Her only thoughts until now had been related to her parents' accidental death, but now, she remembers more things about her aunt, like the way she'd make sure Sarah's birthday and the winter solstice were always separate days. A couple of her friends had birthdays near winter solstice, and they always whined about how the two were sort of merged together into one celebration.

But Helen had been kind. She didn't want Sarah to feel unimportant, so on her birthday every year, they would eat chocolate cake for breakfast and go horseback riding throughout the sprawling property. Then, in the afternoon, they'd eat pizza for lunch and Sarah's parents would join them with birthday gifts.

Her heart lurches thinking about it now, and her memories turn dark, Helen's eyes turning black and her hands becoming slick with blood, like the blood of Sarah's mother that had covered Sarah's hands in the accident. She slams the door on this train of thought and gets ready for school.

WHEN SHE MAKES IT TO THE BUILDING, SHE'S surprised to find Gabby waiting for her near the front entrance.

"Let's grab breakfast before class," Gabby says. "I left before I remembered that food existed, and I'd rather not starve until lunch."

Sarah agrees to join her, although Elizabeth had prepared breakfast this morning, which she found ready on her bedside table after getting out of the shower. She considers bringing up her nightmare the dragon in the woods, but that would mean bringing up the the egg. And, although she can see becoming close with Gabby, she just isn't that type of friend.

The cafeteria isn't the only place to get food at school—there's also an atrium near the student parking lot that serves breakfast in the morning and snacks throughout the day. It's out of the way of pretty much everything, though, so Sarah didn't even know it was here. The early-morning sunlight streams in through the floor-to-ceiling windows, glittering over the tabletops that swirl with moving galaxies.

While they wait in line, she studies the other students who are milling around, some sitting at the circular wooden tables, others lounging on the plush leather furniture near the windows. She recognizes a few of them from her classes—the dark-skinned girl reading Jane Austen is in her Biology class, and the slender white boy with blonde hair who's slouching in the big armchair is in US History, the seat behind her's.

Gabby loads up on breakfast foods and leads her over to one of the nearly empty tables. Across from them, there's a small blonde girl reading a book about vampires—not a textbook, but a cheesy supermarket romance novel like the ones Penny's always reading.

"Hey, Cynthia," Gabby says, and the girl blinks at them, falling out of a stupor.

"Hey, Gabby," she replies, her eyes sad. Sarah tries to read the description on the book to find out if it's supposed to be depressing, but she can't see it from across the table. *That's just what her face looks like*, her mom's voice rings in her head. The memory is so quick and sharp that Sarah barely has time to register it.

"Any cool visions lately?" Gabby asks, trying to make conversation, but Cynthia simply gives a sad smile and continues on with her book.

They do their best to not intrude on Cynthia's space, and Gabby explains some of the dynamics of St. Merlin's to Sarah. She goes over the campus layout, including buildings that Sarah doesn't have classes in.

"You'll have to check out the library at some point. It's huge, and a great place to get some actual work done." She gestures to the loud atrium, students all clamoring for their voices to be heard over one another, which has only resulted in a low roar. "You can book private study rooms, which are all shielded so that you can practice your magic."

Sarah considers mentioning that she doesn't have a specialty to practice, and that she can only do basic spells, but Gabby continues on. "The gym is alright, if you're into that sort of thing. Some people go to the pool on the weekends. It's usually for swimming laps, but on Saturday afternoons it's more of a recreational area. They even have a volleyball net!"

"Good to know." Sarah doesn't mention that she's really terrible at every sort of magic and all sports.

Cynthia looks up at the door when a group of towering, muscular boys comes in, laughing raucously. One of them, who has blonde, curly hair, scans the room, and when he spots her, he ducks his head to hide a shy smile and a blush. The girl goes back to reading her book, her lips tilted upward with a secret. Yet, for some reason, her eyes are still sad. Sarah looks down at her lap, as this feels too much like intruding on a private moment.

She wants to talk to Alex.

She does not want to mention the kiss to him. By now, she's convinced herself that her hormones have turned her imagination toward love, and she thought too much about the cute boy that she sits next to in two of her classes. She tries to shake it off, but she still feels drawn to him. Maybe after she talks to him, she'll see that he's actually a stereotypical rich asshole, and she'll want nothing to do with him. That way, she can focus on school and the dragon egg at home.

She's distracted all throughout Literature class, deciding what she's going to say to Alex. When the teacher asks her a question, she gets the answer wrong, and he looks at her sternly. As soon as class ends, she rushes straight to potions class, her anticipation of seeing Alex palpable. She's here so early that the class is nearly empty when she arrives. Luckily, the opportunity to talk is clearly labeled on the desk in front of her. In advance, Mr. Thompson has laid out materials and cauldrons at every table, including a worksheet that explains what they'll be doing today.

A love potion. How appropriate. She scrubs her hands over her face in an attempt to banish the blush creeping up her cheeks.

Alex glances at her when he enters, his dark eyes darting away when he sees that she's looking at him, too. She has no reason to be embarrassed, but her face heats up anyway.

He takes his seat beside her, tilting his head in a polite nod, but he doesn't speak. She looks to his hands, his fingers woven together on his desk. His veins cross like rivers in a vast landscape, and, in this moment, she wants nothing more at this moment than to trace them up along his arm. Instead, she aggressively doodles a meaningless pattern on the margins of a sheet of notebook paper to keep her hands occupied.

Mr. Thompson is almost late again, and, this time, when he enters, his tie is on backwards. He seems flustered, but he's at the whiteboard at the front of the room in an instant. When Sarah glances at the door, she sees a frazzled librarian leaving his office across the hall, adjusting her shawl.

"Today," he says, his voice breathy, "we will be brewing up some love spells." One of the boys on the other side of the classroom lets out a whistle, and Sarah rolls her eyes. At least some teen behaviors don't change when moving to a private school. "Thank you, Mr. Gregory, for your evaluation. Yes, love potions are one of the more sought-after potions, and today, we will be brewing them."

It takes him twice as long to explain the process as it should, as he says everything twice, only slightly reworded. Sarah isn't sure if it's to engrain the information, or if it's just how he talks, but she eventually spaces out and just reads the instructions on the page.

When he tells the class to get started, she mumbles, "Great idea to hand love potions to a bunch of sixteen-year-olds."

Alex snorts at that, and her heart thrills with success. When he smiles, his eyes soften, and it isn't until then that she realizes that they have a naturally stern set to them. He looks more approachable with a smile.

They go over the instructions and take turns adding the ingredients. "Can you pass me the rose petals?" Alex asks,. Sarah drops in the mermaid scales one at a time, then he does the unicorn hair, and they mix in a bunch of liquids she can't pronounce, although Alex's tongue turns the words over easily.

"So are you local?" she asks, her hand moving in circular motions as she stirs the mixture. It mostly smells terrible, but every few seconds, she catches a hint of the scent of hay, and it takes her back to living on her parents' farm, feeding the animals twice a day.

He shakes his head. "I'm from Kansas. I stay on campus during the semester." There seems to be more information behind his words, but Sarah can't discern the meaning. Maybe if she brushes her thumb against his lips, he'll spill all his secrets. Her hand tightens on the spoon. Her mind is out of control, and she wishes she could take out that part of herself and give it a stern talking-to. She just might do that when she can escape to the bathroom before her next class.

"I used to live in Sedalia, but I had to move in with my aunt and her husband when my great uncle got put in a home," she explains. "Mr. Halacourt is my aunt's husband," she adds as an afterthought. She's never been afraid to tell people that she's an orphan, but that's because she's gotten used to the looks of concern or sympathy. She used to get angry at their gazes, but now, she lets them wash over her.

Alex gives her neither, just nods. "The city is quite a change for you, too, then?" He takes the wooden spoon to stir for a bit, his fingers brushing against hers. At his touch, heat runs up her arm, and she feels like she's burning from the inside out. She jerks her hand back at the touch, and his eyebrows scrunch together. A flash of longing surges through her, and she wants to rest her hand on his, just for a moment, to see if it happens again. "You alright?" he asks.

She says, "Static electricity," shaking her hand to prove the point. It's a lie, but one that's easier to explain than the truth.

"Nobody drives their tractor to school here," he points out to steer the conversation away from her minor shock, and she laughs a little too loud at that. She ducks her head, her face flushing with heat when half the class turns to look at her, including Mr. Thompson.

After a moment, she adds, "Fewer lifted trucks."

He nods. "No confederate flags."

They go on like this for awhile, and the ten minutes of stirring passes easily. She's careful to not touch him again, lest she feel the heat from before. She doesn't want to find a new way to explain it in case it happens again.

Now, they just have to set the potion on a high heat and wait for it to set for another twenty minutes. They've grown closer and closer as time passed, and she parts her lips to ask about the vision from yesterday, but the sound of a textbook falling and slapping the ground breaks her out of her stupor. She scoots her chair a foot away, and he straightens up and pulls out his Calculus textbook. She notices that he hasn't started the homework from yesterday, and, while they aren't in the same class hour, they have the same assignment.

She wants to offer to help, as math is one thing she's actually good at, but their easy conversation is as far as the vast space now between them. She takes out her young adult novel and opens it, but she can't focus on the words.

Now that everyone's potions are sitting, Mr. Thompson strolls around the room, commenting on what seems right and wrong with everyone's.

"Too much rose in yours. You see, too much rose can make your potion too thick," he tells one group. "Not enough unicorn hair in this one. You should use more unicorn hair in the future," he says to another.

When he makes it to Alex and Sarah, he lifts his eyebrows, looking between them. She tenses up—she's never been good at magic, so she expects that theirs is beyond saving. "Very good. You've done well," he says before continuing on.

When class ends, Mr. Thompson collects everyone's love potions—"Some of these," he says, "are more like death potions. They could kill you." He isn't serious, of course.

Nothing in a love potion is similar to the ingredients needed for a death potion, but a few students still laugh nervously. She waves at Alex as she leaves, but he's either not
paying attention, or he doesn't care.

SHE MEANDERS TO SPIRITUAL MAGIC AFTER HAV-
ing lunch under the clocktower in the courtyard with
Gabby. She's trying to get to class at the last possible minute. She drops her homework in the tray by the door, right
over Alex's. She tries to ignore the fact that he got the second question wrong.

When she sits by him, the bell rings, and the teacher immediately begins speaking, drawing up a chart about different levels of Spiritual Magic on the board and walking
them through it. Sarah takes notes as she goes, although
she's not sure how she'll use the minute differences between telepaths, empaths, and psychics. It all seems pretty
obvious, anyway. Her mind trails to the kiss she'd imagined, the feeling of Alex's lips on hers.

Her eyes dart to him, and she's half scared that he'll look
back at her and know about her thoughts from yesterday.
However, he's staring at the board, his pencil hovering
over his sheet of paper. His eyebrows are bunched together,
and he's squinting in confusion. She wants to laugh at his
caricature of an expression, but she notices that one of his
hands is shaking when the teacher finishes explaining the
complicated genes that give a person Spiritual Magic over

Physical Magic.

"Does anyone need me to explain it again?" Ms. White asks. Alex's hand twitches like he's going to raise it, but after glancing around to see that nobody else has a question, he keeps it down. Sarah looks away from him when his head turns toward her, but her eyes are back on his paper as soon as he looks away. She notes the point where he obviously got lost, and shoots her hand in the air.

"Yes," Ms. White looks at the seating chart on her very tangible clipboard, "Sarah? What part has you confused?"

Sarah glances at Alex, who's looking at her, his mouth parted slightly in surprise. He looks to her perfect notes, a question piqued somewhere along his eyebrows but remaining hidden behind his lips.

"Sorry," she starts, her voice slow with nerves. She never speaks up in class if she can avoid it. "But I honestly got totally lost around the part about Telepath versus Empath DNA. Can you go over that again? I meant to stop you, but I didn't want to interrupt."

Ms. White smiles gently. "Of course." She addresses the entire classroom. "And nobody should be afraid to interrupt. If I'm going too quickly for you, please let me know."

Alex isn't the only one to let out a relieved sigh when Ms. White starts over.

# CHAPTER SIX
## Sarah

SARAH HAS FOUND HERSELF, INEXPLICABLY, AT the zoo.

After classes let out, she went to Mark's office, and Elizabeth had been lounging elegantly across his office loveseat, a creature of whimsy despite her khaki uniform. Her raven hair is spilling over her shoulder in beachy waves, her green eyes patiently studying Mark's movements as he grades papers. Sarah briefly wonders if her aunt might be descended from mermaids, but it would probably be rude to ask. Besides, how could Uncle John have possibly enticed someone who was even part mermaid?

Elizabeth had stood up upon realizing that Sarah was there and dragged her excitedly to the car, driving the few miles across Forest Park to the St. Louis Zoo where she works.

"I mainly do training," she explains, "but I'm writing my

dissertation on Forest Dragon familial bonds." Forest Dragons. Too close to the secret in Sarah's fireplace. Thankfully, she continues on, "This is where we do most of our research and rehabilitation. Many of the dragons we receive are sick or injured, and others are transferred here from other facilities. You see, St. Louis has the most sophisticated dragon program in the Western Hemisphere, and we pride ourselves on our care-taking."

This would be the perfect opportunity to bring up the egg. Sarah opens her mouth to speak up, but before she gets the words out, they've already reached the aviary. It's a tall half-sphere, white-painted steel woven through foggy glass that renders everything inside completely invisible.

"Have you ever been?" Elizabeth asks, but she must know that Sarah hasn't. She'd said so her first week living in St. Louis.

"I've always wanted to," Sarah offers.

The moment they walk into the little brick building attached to the aviary, a balding man in a business suit says, "Miss Halacourt, I wasn't aware you were working late."

"Oh, I have the afternoon off. I thought I would bring my niece in to meet Hawthorne." It isn't until she mentions Sarah that the man's eyes slide over her in appraisal. "Sarah, this is Victor Phillips. He leads the dragon program here."

Sarah wanders through the exhibit for a few minutes while they chat about work. The small building is a miniature museum with interactive areas: *Can YOU Identify Dif-*

*ferent Dragon Calls? Dragon Scales — Tougher than STEEL! Fire,*
*Acid, and Ice, OH MY — the Different Dragon Classifications.*

She meanders through, all the while itching to walk
through the aviary. The informational area is dim and
crowded, and Sarah has never seen captive dragons before.

Finally, after escaping her boss, Elizabeth leads Sarah to
the dome's entrance. There are three separate gates to get
through, and each one has to be latched before they're allowed through another. The final gate is guarded by a zoo-
keeper, a girl matching Elizabeth in a khaki zoo uniform.
She can't be much older than Sarah.

"Elizabeth, always here, even when you're off," she jokes.

"I'm here on an educational trip," Elizabeth replies, clap-
ping a hand on the girl's shoulder. "I thought my niece
could learn something from meeting Hawthorne."

Elizabeth clearly knows everyone who works here, closer than a lot of coworker relationships Sarah has seen in
the past. While she's conversing, Sarah wanders down the
path, which is blocked on either side by ropes. She reaches out, but her hand is barred from going any further by a
rubbery barrier spell. Before she has much time to consider
the logistics of the spell, she hears a whooshing noise, and
the light is blocked, a sudden frigidity taking the air around
her. She jerks her head up, and a silver and blue creature
is hovering above her, its head craned down and tilted to
the side with curiosity. Its wings, which cover the sky, push
gusts of icy air toward her, and she welcomes the coolness

after the heat of the August day.

"Hello," she croons. "Nice to meet you."

The dragon huffs, and a sprinkling of snow melts as it falls through the barrier. The water droplets land on Sarah's face, still cold.

"This is Keida," Elizabeth says, her voice gentle behind Sarah. "She was rescued in Alaska after a hunter mistakenly killed her mother. I was lucky enough to raise her from an egg. She's turning seven this year."

"Hi, Keida," Sarah says, reaching a hand up as if to touch her, although she knows the barrier will keep that from happening.

Keida lets out a gentle chirp and startles back, apparently offended at Sarah's audacity. She chirps again and flies away—from here, Sarah the ceiling of the dome is obscured. It's been enchanted to look like the sky, and the room must have been expanded on the interior, because it seems that there are miles of sky for the dragons to frolic through.

If she squints, Sarah can see the forms of a few species in the distance—a red Mountain Dragon that glistens like a shiny new car under the artificial sunlight, a violet African Drake with leathery wings and soft fur.

They keep walking, occasionally coming across smaller species, such as brown feathered prairie dragons no bigger than a small dog, and fairy dragons that look like hummingbirds at first glance as they flit from flower to flower, their long tongues lolling out to sip lazily at the dew inside.

Elizabeth's eyebrows squish together as they draw closer to the exit. She pauses and then turns to look around, searching for something while they stand in a copse of trees.

"What's wrong?" Sarah asks, trying to find whatever it is she's looking for.

Elizabeth purses her lips. "I was hoping to meet Hawthorne, our forest dragon. He was brought in recently when a hunter found him with an injured wing."

While Elizabeth squints at the sky, Sarah bores her eyes into the forest surrounding them. After a few moments of intense focus, something prods at her mind. The air cools, not like Kaida's icy glade, but like the woods at dawn.

A familiar presence slips into her mind, so subtle that she almost misses it. It isn't quite the same as the dragon that she met in the forest earlier in the week, but it feels like a kindred voice. Her breath is drawn out of her, and her heart races with excitement, which may or may not be her own. She'd felt the female's emotions before, and the emotions had been difficult to discern as separate.

Sarah snaps her head around to a set of trees, and a slight movement makes the forest dragon visible. His dark green feathers are dotted with pale green and yellow, disguising him in the sunspots of the woods so that she doesn't find him until he moves toward her. Interest piques in her mind, and she tilts her head with curiosity at the same moment as the dragon.

Elizabeth doesn't notice him until he steps closer to the

path, pulling his wings close to keep them from scraping against the foliage. His motions are so quiet that a gentle breeze would mask his movements.

"Hello, Hawthorne," Elizabeth whispers, her hand coming to rest on Sarah's shoulder. "He's healing up extremely well. We expect that he'll be flying in just a couple more weeks."

Sarah steps closer, reaching her hand up to touch the barrier. Hawthorne takes only a moment to evaluate Elizabeth before looking back to Sarah.

He tilts his head down, his green-feathered forehead resting against where Sarah's hand is pressed on the barrier. His metallic gold horns spiral a few feet up, and she wishes she could go through the barrier and touch them to find out if they're as soft as they look. She rests her face against his, and she imagines that she can feel his feathers brushing against her cheek, but it's just the gentle thrum of magical energy.

A desperate need to protect something courses through her veins, her skin practically aflame. The image of an egg just like hers flashes across the back of her eyelids. He can smell it on her, the scent roiling off her in waves. Keep it safe, keep it safe, keep it safe. Her fingers twitch as she suddenly feels the urge to take her egg into her arms and hide it from the world. It's hard to figure out what is her and what is Hawthorne.

"I'll keep it safe," she promises, her voice the barest of

whispers.

With that, he pulls away and dives back into the forest, the rush from his movement enough to stir a few leaves from the trees.

When Sarah turns around, Elizabeth isn't the only one staring at her.

# CHAPTER SEVEN
## Alex

FRIDAY NIGHT, ALEX TAKES ADVANTAGE OF ST. Merlin's lifting the curfew for the weekend. St. Merlin's prides itself on being the best of the best, and what would that be without—they claim—the best students? Someone invited Alex to a party earlier, or they told him about a party they were invited to. These things aren't always the same, but sometimes they aren't very different, either. He considers attending—he has no other plans for the weekend. He makes it so far as to put on his favorite jeans, a dark pair that David jokes make his ass look amazing, as well as a plain black t-shirt, and a flannel button-up with the sleeves rolled up.

He makes it to his car, and the engine starts on the first try. He weaves through the Friday night traffic, his car groaning against the effort of going the speed limit. When it comes time for him to take the exit off the interstate toward his friend's party, though, he keeps going.

He loves St. Merlin's. It's filled with opportunities that he wouldn't get anywhere in Kansas, and he has friends he wouldn't trade for the world. David and Kendall are like the siblings he never had.

Some nights, though, when he's sitting in his tiny dorm room and contemplating being here for the next two years, he wants to scream. Staying in one place that long feels like an eternity.

To release this feeling, he drives.

He passes through downtown St. Louis, ogling at the lights of the city, and he can't help but be awed at the masterpiece that is the arch. The one time he went up it was with his parents, and he had to quell a panic attack in the elevator. When they got to the top, the view was worth the fear. The city glistened in the late morning sunlight, and he pressed his face right against the glass while Dad pointed out the different sights.

When you're a giant, everything else feels so small.

He passes the arch, and Cardinals stadium, and his car makes its way through downtown and out the other side to Illinois. Almost as soon as he's on the other side of the river, the city disappears and turns into fields of wheat, lit only by the stars and the half-moon. He could drive into the middle of one and lie on his roof, sleeping with the stars as his guardian until morning, when he'd probably go back to St. Merlin's.

He keeps driving.

He drives until his preset stations don't play music anymore, and then he just changes the stations and keeps going. A faerie hums through the speakers, her song springing tears to his eyes. The thrum of magic should, logically, be higher in the city, amplified by the thousands upon thousands of users. In the country, though, on a dark interstate under the night sky, he feels so alive.

He stops off at an exit to fill up the Taurus's nearly empty gas tank, and he picks up a few snacks while he's inside to pay. A faerie boy is working the front counter, his eyes dark with rectangular pupils like a deer, his face freckled. He has messy brown hair, and moss is hanging gently off his antlers, swaying just a little when a breeze comes through the door. Alex considers asking if the moss is natural or just an accessory, but it's probably rude to ask.

"Drive safe," the boy says, his voice a melody that Alex almost remembers, like a song he heard once on the radio when he was little but never learned the words to. He's tempted to pull himself on the counter and kiss the faerie until the sun comes up over the horizon, but that's just the draw the fae have on humans. He learned to quell those types of feelings long ago.

Alex grew up in one of the few communities that is equal parts faerie and human, the two groups interacting as equals rather than dancing along the boundary between the two worlds. This town, wherever he is, must be another one of those.

"Have a good night," the boy says, half waving as Alex walks out with his bag of snacks and bottled water.

It's incredibly late, and he is not tired. How could he ever get tired when the night is so alive, calling louder with every mile under his tires?

Eventually, the call is too loud, too electric, for him to go any further. He takes an exit, and the call pulls him along, down back roads and hidden highways. He parks his car in the middle of a field, and he understands.

He digs through his center console for a bracelet Mom made for him before he moved away. It's simple, just a few pieces of yarn and a strand of iron woven together, tying in the middle. "Not all faeries are like the ones you know," she warned, pressing the bracelet into his hand.

He ties it around his right wrist and makes sure that he doesn't have anything with his name on it in his pockets. He's glad to find a small salt packet hidden in one pocket. Then, he finds the entrance to the faerie party.

A faerie party is fluid. It does not belong in just one place, through the doorway of a collapsing barn in a field in Illinois. It could be anywhere and everywhere. He knows this, so he takes note of the entrance he's come through and casts the easiest tracking spell he can on it. No matter how tonight goes, he has to be able to find his way home. With that, he takes a breath and heads into the crowd.

# CHAPTER EIGHT
## Sarah

THE NIGHT IN THIS CITY IS ALIVE. SARAH CAN feel it with every breath she takes.

Breathe in. The wind dances gleefully around the puzzle pieces that make up her new home, taunting her. It can't get past the iron fence, though.

Breathe out. A song cradles her, taking her by the wrist and leading her to the window.

In. There are lights dancing through the woods. They twirl like fireflies, but she knows better. Far away, the revelry of the fae teases her ears.

Out. She climbs out her window, careful not to rip the screen as she removes it, to join the party.

The walk to the party takes no time at all, and the sound is coming from a dilapidated castle, something that shouldn't be in the middle of a forest in Missouri. Still, there is no party. Not that she can see, anyway. The breeze is warm and comforting as it pulls her inside. Her mind is a fog; she's still half asleep, although she should be wide awake by now. The pine needles along the forest floor don't prick her feet like they should, and her hands don't sting with the scrape of bark and thorns as her fingers reach through the brush to find her way in the dark half-moon night.

As soon as she steps over the stone threshold, everything changes. One moment, she's in deep blackness, and the next, she's bathed in the color-changing strobes of the party. It's as though a curtain has been lifted—her drowsiness floats away, and her senses return.

Before she can get distracted by the sudden pain in her hands and feet, a beautiful faerie boy with green cat eyes and curled ram horns pulls her into a dance, his body tempting hers as he presses against her to the tune of the music. He grins as he feeds her a plump red strawberry. There's something wicked about him, but his body distracts her, and she runs her hands along his chest, and then down, down, dow—

"Sarah," a voice shouts in her ear before she can continue.

Annoyed, she turns to Alex, who is standing much closer than expected. The heat of his breath is on her cheeks, and she tries to look into his eyes, but he's not looking at her.

"Mind if I take her for a dance?" Before the faerie boy can protest, Alex wraps his hand around Sarah's and pulls her away.

Fury rises in her, hot and sudden. She wants to go back to that boy, to kiss him and touch him and lie with him until the sun rises. "How dare y-"

"Did you eat something?" he interrupts, his eyes finally finding hers.

She scoffs. "So what if I did? You're not the boss of me." She tugs her hand out of his grasp, but before she can spin around to get away, he runs a thumb gently over her bottom lip. The touch is electric, and, without thinking, she bites him.

He jerks his hand away, but not before the taste of salt clears her mind. The rage dissipates, and her body hurts. How long had she been out there, pressed against that boy?

"Oh my god," she moans, crouching to the floor where she stands, in the middle of the dance floor surrounded by faeries and lured humans. She should be more concerned about getting kicked in the face, but at the moment, she's too nauseous to care. How naive does she have to be to fall under a faerie spell so easily? The lights and music pound through her skull, the sound amplifying as she takes shallow breaths and the figures close around her.

"Hey," a gentle voice says in her ear, cutting through all the sound. Alex is kneeling beside her, concern flooding his beautiful dark eyes. She can hardly stand to look at him. "Are you gonna be okay?"

She sucks in a lungful of air and lets it out slowly, bracing one hand on his shoulder to keep from losing her balance.

"Let's get you out of here," he says, helping her to her feet like a newborn foal. Her legs are a bit shaky, but at least her head has stopped spinning. So long as she's looking into Alex's eyes, it'll be alright.

"Can we go sit down?" she finds herself asking, the words trembling out of her mouth before she can stop them. He nods and pulls her to the side, through the other party-goers until they find a fallen stone wall just the right height for sitting.

He waves his hand and a plastic convenience store bag appears. "Water?" he offers, pulling out a new bottle, the seal unbroken.

"Thanks," Sarah says, taking a long swig. The icy drink is invigorating, clearing some of the remaining fog from her mind. She watches the forms writhing around them to the beat, and she's glad to be sitting on the side. For now.

"What brings you out here?" Alex asks after a few minutes of comfortable silence.

Sarah shrugs. "Just felt like I should. You know?"

He nods and takes another swig of his own water. A drop trickles from his lips and down his chin, and, before she can stop herself, Sarah reaches up and brushes it away. The contact with his skin is electric, and she doesn't remove her hand.

His eyes dart down to her lips for just a split second, but it's enough for her to lean forward, her heart racing. He rests his spindly fingers ever-so-gently on hers, and a breath catches in her throat.

A frigid wind rips through the castle, shaking her out of her stupor. She yanks her hand back and looks away from him and toward the party. "So why'd your parents send you to St. Merlin's?"

She can feel his gaze prodding her, but she keeps her eyes on a couple of human boys that are dancing twenty feet away.

"I got a scholarship, and it's about a thousand times better than the high school in my town," he says. She turns to him in surprise.

"So you're not rich, then." It isn't a question. It makes sense, of course. Rich people don't talk reverently about tractors being ridden to school, and they probably have better things to do on a Friday night than attend a faerie party. Like run for office or something.

"Nah." He drops his empty water bottle back into the plastic bag, and she follows suit. The instant he dematerializes it—she has to learn that spell—the song changes from an unbearably mournful solo to a more upbeat pop song that's been on the radio all month. "Wanna dance?" Alex asks, helping her back to her feet.

She's more sure of herself now. Oriented. Her head is clear. The grass within the castle walls is gentle on her stinging feet, grounding her. "I'm here, aren't I?"

They walk side by side to the dance floor, his hand hot against the cold sweat on her back as he guides her to an open space.

He holds his hand out, and she takes it, her face warming incrementally.

The air is sucked out of her in a laugh as they careen back and forth, earning a dirty look from a pixie girl with violet and magenta skin. Sarah goes out in a dramatic twirl before Alex pulls her back into a dip. She tilts her head back and absorbs the moment, her eyes on the stars that shine clear as ever despite the flashing party lights.

When she jolts back to standing, Alex has a goofy grin on his face. Before she can think too hard on it, she moves closer to him so that their lips are mere inches away.

"I'd like a kiss," she suggests, taunting him. Daring him. He closes the gap without hesitating, and her mind explodes into a thousand stars brighter than anything in the sky. Their lips are desperate as they press together—it's the type of passion that could be misinterpreted for hate or love. Her veins burn dry with his fire, and she licks his bottom lip to feel the almost campfire taste of him.

She is absolutely absorbed in this magic, a sparkling electricity that wraps around them both, and it isn't hard at all to imagine falling for him.

She pulls away, a contented sigh falling out of her before she can catch it. They're the only two not dancing, and she bites her bottom lip.

"Looks like your vision came true," she says, her voice husky.

"What?" His eyebrows are just starting to bunch together in confusion when a redheaded woman catches Sarah's attention just behind him—she's the only other being not moving. The woman begins to turn toward them as if in slow motion, and Sarah's blood goes cold. Before the woman's face appears, Sarah runs. It's all instinct, an iciness that runs through her veins and keeps her moving. All she can picture are black eyes and bloody hands. There's something wrong with the red-haired woman's face. She knows it. Her body carries her away as fast as possible.

She can't be sure, but it sounds like Alex's voice is calling for her as she goes.

# CHAPTER NINE
## Alex

THERE'S SOMETHING WRONG WITH ALEX.

Not in the "I just made out with a girl I met this week" sort of way, although that is unusual for him. No, this is something else entirely.

He vaguely remembers the party—the kiss with Sarah is the only crystal clear moment, but after that, everything is indistinct. After she'd run off, something had prick in his arm, like a bee sting, and then a heaviness had fallen over him.

Now, he's lying on his back in the grass, and when his mind returns to him, he's lying half beneath his Ford. He has a serious case of cotton-mouth, and he can't salivate enough to fix it.

When the feeling starts to come back to his limbs, he slowly drags himself out from under the car, the prickly grass scraping at his bare skin, giving him pause.

He sits up slowly, his head spinning and the sun stabbing his eyes out. He tries to summon his convenience store bag, but the spell isn't taking, so he has to stand up. Pins and needles stab through his legs and feet, but at least he can stand. He brushes what feels like dirt off his chest, but when he looks at himself, he finds that he's covered in blue and gold glitter.

*Please don't be drugs.*

He takes the last water bottle out of the trunk and chugs half of it in one go before dropping into the driver's seat, mourning the disappearance of his favorite shirt. His car takes a few tries to start, but after some prompting, the engine wails to life. He digs around the glove compartment for his phone, but the battery is dead. He plugs it in to the cigarette lighter and, once he's determined that he's not inebriated, directs his car to the interstate.

He stops for gas on the outskirts of the city, taking a few extra minutes to go to the restroom and wash up after tossing on the hoodie that was squished under the passenger seat. His face still looks like a wreck, but at least he's no longer covered in faerie powder. He's fairly certain the streaks aren't drugs, but it's better for him to be cautious about the whole situation.

It's mid-afternoon by the time he gets back, and David is just walking through the parking lot toward their dorm when Alex pulls in to his spot. He was hoping to come back unnoticed, but it seems like this is going to be unavoidable as David stops and lifts his arm in a half-wave.

Alex cuts the engine at the same time as opening the door, and David's eyebrows shoot up. "You look like hell," he says after a quick appraisal. "Where were you last night?"

He could lie. There's a good chance that whatever happened to him won't have any lasting effects. It won't matter in another hour when he's taken a hot shower and changed into clean clothes.

"I think," he says slowly, "I messed up."

David walks him up to their floor and even makes sure the coast is clear of Phillip before waving Alex over to their bedroom door. Just as Alex is about to step over the threshold, though, he hears a booming, accented voice.

"Locklear," Phillip calls. "My office." Alex groans and turns toward him. Phillip doesn't have an actual office— that's just what he calls his apartment living room. There are four staff apartments, one for each floor of the building so that the residents are monitored properly.

"Where have you been?" says Phillip. He switches on one of the many antique lamps sitting on the cluttered coffee table, and takes a closer look at Alex's face in the light.

"I'm sorry," Alex whispers, pretending to be fascinated by the paperweights on Phillip's ancient roll-top desk to avoid eye contact. He picks up a mail opener and fidgets with it, looking anywhere but at Phillip.

"You're going to have to do better than that." Phillip fumbles over his words, and that's how Alex can tell he's upset. Usually, his English is impeccable.

The only clean thing in the room is the floral eighties couch, and that's because, otherwise, it would have to be cleared off every time a student enters the apartment, which is often. Alex trips over a stack of newspapers that's at least a decade old, and, although the stack doesn't budge, he's confident that he's going to have a bruise on his calf. He collapses on the couch, pressing his hands into his eyes, and a dull throb knocks in his head, he hopes from mild dehydration and not whatever substances he can't remember consuming.

"You were gone overnight. I figured you were out on one of your....things.... But now you come back looking like shit, and I don't know what to think."

Phillip doesn't curse. Alex sits up slowly, his entire body protesting. Now that he's laid down for a moment, his muscles don't want to move ever again. "I didn't mean to. I just..."

He could get kicked out of St. Merlin's if he took anything. He's seen it happen with more privileged students than himself—rich boys whose parents have endless pockets to save their asses. Alex, though, is an investment, and the school wouldn't hesitate to drop him at the slightest mishap.

"I was at a faerie party," he says, his voice rough. He feels his chest tighten, and tears make their way into his eyes. He doesn't usually cry easily, but he hasn't slept since

Thursday night. "I think I may have been drugged. Or taken something. I can't remember anything, but I was careful. I don't know what happened. I'm sorry."

Phillip's anger subsides, and he takes a seat next to Alex. He runs a hand over his face and across his bald head.

"Are you okay?" he asks, his voice now gentle.

Alex nods, not trusting himself with words right now.

Phillip puts an arm around his shoulder and squeezes gently, then drops it. "Take a nap here. I will get a test kit to see if there are any drugs or spells in your system." Alex buries his head in his hands to keep Phillip from seeing the tears now falling from his eyes, but his shoulders are trembling. "We don't have to tell the dean. For now." Phillip pats his shoulder before retreating, and Alex hears the apartment door close. When he looks up, he's alone. He leans back on the couch and falls into a fitful sleep.

# CHAPTER TEN
## Sarah

SARAH WAITS ALL WEEK FOR ALEX TO TALK TO her, possibly to confront her about running off at the party, but he says nothing. They don't even talk in class, other than the bare necessities for making potions. Other than that, silence. Her heart drops lower the days go on, tangling itself up in her intestines.

She dreads going to class, fearing that he won't tell her why he refuses to have a conversation with her, or worse, that he will. How does she explain the anxiety attack that had encapsulated her just by seeing a woman with red hair?

It shouldn't matter to her that he doesn't want to speak to her. She turns cold, removing all hope from her tone. She stops trying to start small talk, and she stops making jokes under her breath for his benefit. At home, she pushes him out of her mind and focuses on the egg. She read an article over the weekend that explained how to tell if an egg is still alive, so she'd cast the basic spell and delighted over the momentary pulsing light emanating from it to show that she is, in fact, going to have a dragon.

Friday afternoon, Gabby and Sarah are eating lunch in an abandoned classroom that's hidden up a circular flight of stairs at the end of the main building. Sarah is reading an informational eBook she'd spent some of her meager savings on, *How to Raise Your Dragon*, when Gabby asks, "Are you going to the fall formal?" Gabby is sitting cross-legged on the dusty old teacher's desk, her mouth full of pasta.

Sarah shrugs. "I don't really like dances. Too many people." She puts her phone away and tries to force one of the antique windows open—when they discovered the room and started eating up here, this became her project. Today, she has a can of WD-40 she found in Mark and Elizabeth's garage so she can try to loosen the hinges. So far, she hasn't had much success.

Gabby nods while she chews. After swallowing, she says, "I feel that. I just enjoy having a chance to dress up."

Sarah oils the hinges again, waiting a moment for it to soak in before yanking it, and it budges about a quarter of an inch. "Ha!" she cries victoriously, bouncing and pointing at it. Gabby raises her eyebrows and nods at the accomplishment, although she suggested yesterday that Sarah just use magic to open them. "Told you that you don't need magic for everything," Sarah says smugly.

"Kelly is coming," Gabby says, holding up her phone to

show off the text from her girlfriend in Chicago. "I know you said the other day you wanted to meet her."

It takes Sarah a moment to remember that they're talking about the dance. Gabby pulls up a photo of the red floor-length gown she designed over the summer just for the formal.

"I'll think about it," Sarah relents. "But I'd rather not be a third wheel." She hits her palm bluntly against the wooden window frame, and it goes just a smidge more.

Gabby considers for a moment. "What about Tyler from first hour? I'm pretty sure he has a crush on you."

Sarah makes a face. "Tyler is obnoxious," she objects. "All he talks about is his dad's solar energy company."

"Right," Gabby says, nodding. "And we all know you're more of a wind-farm girl."

Sarah laughs. "Precisely. If you're gonna do clean energy, do it right."

Gabby finishes her salad quickly and pulls out a note-book. "Okay, give me a list, then."

"A list?" Sarah asks, raising an eyebrow at her, the window project forgotten.

"A list of all the attributes you want in a *beau*—" Gabby waggles her eyebrows at that old-fashioned word "—and we'll figure out who you should ask."

Her freshman year, back in Sedalia, Penny had asked Sarah who she liked, but Sarah didn't really have feelings for any of the boys at school. In fact, her true love at that time was Aragorn from the Lord of the Rings movies, which her neighbor introduced her to. Penny did not know that Sarah was in love with a fictional character—Penny was the type of person that believed in a strong divide between fiction and reality, and having a crush on a fictional character just didn't make sense.

Sarah had sighed and relented, picking the first person that popped into her mind. "It's Will. From science class."

There'd been nothing wrong with Will. He was a tall, skinny boy with more limbs than he knew what to do with, although it was an average number of limbs for a human being. He'd been short at the end of eighth grade, but when they came back to school, he'd grown at least six inches, and he was due to grow more before he graduated. He also liked to play his guitar in the cafeteria before school, although he only knew two songs—Master of Puppets by Metallica and The Thunder Rolls by Garth Brooks.

"You're bi, right?" Gabby asks. After Gabby had shyly mentioned her girlfriend earlier in the week, Sarah had given her this information about herself. When Sarah nods, Gabby quizzes her, although the questions about her zodiac sign don't give her a lot of confidence.

Sarah sighs and hopes that she won't have to fake-like somebody for this friendship to work like she had with Penny. Gabby has insisted on a slumber party at her house this weekend, and Sarah will have to mention her kiss with Alex. She's already dreading that part.

At the end of the day, Gabby slaps a piece of paper across Sarah's chest.

"I've narrowed down your specifications to five people," Gabby whispers, her voice conspiratorial.

"Why are we whispering?" Sarah asks, her voice hushed as they walk out to the student lot.

"Because it's more fun," Gabby replies.

*Raul Venados*

*Wendy Whatshername (from first hour? You know?)*

*Sam Foster*

*Catherine Harvey*

*Daniel Williamson*

Alex isn't on the list. She can't help but slump her shoulders in disappointment, so she's glad that Gabby is walking ahead of her. Sarah's overnight duffel bag is already in the backseat of Gabby's black Cadillac Escalade, so they leave as quickly as possible to avoid St. Louis's rush hour traffic. The leather is hot, but Sarah is too charmed by the crystals and stuffed dog and National Parks lanyard hanging off the rearview mirror to care.

Gabby and her family live on the southeast side of town, in a suburb called Kirkwood. Their house is a tall, brick faced building with white Grecian columns guarding the front door, and the neighborhood is filled with matching tall, brick faced buildings with Grecian columns. Of course Sarah knew ahead of time that Gabby is rich, but she's still thrown off-kilter by the mansion. The car gets parked under an overhang between the house and the separate three-car garage, and they take their shoes off just inside and hang them on a rack next to the washer and dryer.

"This just in," Sarah says, "the rich are just like you and me. They, too, do laundry!"

Gabby laughs. "No, those are just for show. We have to burn everything as soon as it's been worn once."

They banter like this as Gabby weaves them through the house, all dark wood floors and ivory walls. When they've gone up three flights of stairs, she leads Sarah to something completely out of place—an wrought-iron spiral staircase that climbs up to the attic.

Sarah wants to mention how awful it is that Gabby has been relegated to living in the attic, but she gasps when they go up the stairs.

She immediately falls in love with Gabby's room.

One side of the attic, which has a magical window that allows stargazing on the ceiling, is filled with star charts and astrology information, all surrounding a huge bronze telescope. There are notes scribbled obsessively on most of the charts, and Sarah hopes that she gets a chance to look them over.

Another corner holds Gabby's bed, where a king-sized mattress rests on a rustic pallet frame. There are wall tapestries that have mandelas and stars and woven trees draped across the ceiling and the walls, overlapping each other. Fairy lights surround the nest of comforters and fleece blankets and faux fur throws, and pillows are strewn every-where. Dozens of pillows. Sarah would love nothing more than to bury herself in that bed and never come out.

The corner adjacent to the bed contains a study area—an office computer desk with a brand-new computer, and bookshelves piled high with books that spill out onto the floor to the sides. The slatted wood floors are covered with what must be fifteen antique rugs, some soft, some itchy, all intricately woven. A golden chaise lounge sits along one wall, so Sarah sets her duffel and school bags there.

Sarah's room is bland and boring, the guest room of a house she's merely visiting, but Gabby's room feels lived in, like it truly belongs to the girl who occupies it. Maybe Sarah should attempt to decorate her own. While she gapes, Gab-by changes into an ivory bohemian dress with lace shoul-ders and linen that scrunches at the torso and flows gently to her knees. She even puts a flower crown on her head and sighs gently with satisfaction as she sinks into her fluffy bedding. This is the first time Sarah has seen her out of uni-form, and the change is dramatic yet fitting.

Sarah changes into the ratty sweatpants she sleeps in and a plain black tank top, wishing she could look as ethereal as Gabby.

"What's wrong?" Gabby asks, concern flooding her face when Sarah collapses next to her on the bed. "I have more flower crowns if you want to match."

She starts to get up and go to her armoire, but she stops

when Sarah mumbles, "I kissed Alex."

Gabby gasps and sits back down immediately. "What? Alex Locklear? The pyromancer? Don't you have a class with him? When did this happen?" Her eyes are wide and inquisitive, but not judgemental like Penny's would've been. Penny would have taken one look at Alex and called him a weird emo.

Sarah's lips tug into the tiniest of smiles despite being ignored by him all week. "Last weekend." She can't exactly tell Mark and Elizabeth that she snuck out; she's already keeping the dragon egg from them. It feels good to let it out, to have someone to confide in. She starts with the feeling that she needed to be at the party, then mentions Alex pulling her out of the spell, and ends with the kiss. She doesn't bring up the red-haired woman that had freaked her out.

"How was it?" Gabby asks, a grin spread across her face. She's like a mermaid, her attention caught by this big shiny thing, and she has to know everything.

"It was...nice." Sarah reaches up and brushes her fingers against her lips, remembering the softness of Alex's. "Magical."

Gabby sighs and lies down. "So I guess you aren't going with Catherine or Raul to the fall formal, then."

Sarah shrugs. "I don't know. Alex hasn't said a word to me since we kissed. I think he probably regrets it."

She wants to talk about the vision she'd accidentally shared with him, the connection she feels when they joke around, but she doesn't know how to put it into words without seeming like a naive child. "Let's talk about something else. Anything else."

They should be doing their Spiritual Magic homework, but instead they end up watching the Lord of the Rings series since Gabby has the extended editions. "Eowyn is so much hotter than Arwen," Gabby argues at one point. "I knew I was gay because of her. That whole 'I am no man' thing."

"I knew I was bi because of Arwen and Aragorn, though," Sarah says.

Gabby purses her lips, then concedes. "Fine. Maybe Eowyn and Arwen are equally hot."

Towards the end of Return of the King, Sarah drifts into sleep. Before losing consciousness, she realizes, for the first time, that Penny was wrong to abandon her.

Maybe she can be happy at St. Merlin's.

# CHAPTER ELEVEN
## Alex

MONDAY MORNING, A CHANGE IN THE AIR wakes Alex in his dorm. At some point in the night, he kicked his blankets to the floor, and he wakes up shivering before the sun has even considered rising. He gets down and searches in the dark for his comforter, but it doesn't help to dispel the chill when he wraps it around himself. Magic doesn't work in the dorms, probably because they'd be burned to the ground if it did. The communal microwaves already cause enough grief.

It had taken all of last week, but Phillip pulled him aside after class on Friday to inform him that he'd been dosed with some sort of love potion. He'd taken him to the nurse to get it reversed, and Alex spent all weekend sick in bed from the side effects. Now, though, he feels quite a bit better. Instead of trying to fall back to sleep, he changes into his uniform and decides, despite the early hour, that he's awake for the day. He sneaks out of his room, careful to not wake David, and waves at the desk attendant, Ms. Quaker, who laughs. "Go back to bed, Locklear. It's too early to be up."

"No such thing," Alex replies, his voice quiet as he notices her six-year-old twins sleeping on the floor like a pair of puppies in a pile of blankets and couch cushions. They usually occupy her first-floor apartment, but they must have followed her the twenty feet to the desk when she got up for her shift.

The air is brisk, a slap in the face as soon as he opens the door, so he half walks, half jogs to the library, the only other building on campus that's always open. He allows his hands to heat themselves, just not enough to be set ablaze. He's sure the librarian wouldn't be so willing to let someone in the library after seeing their hands on fire. Magic can do a lot, but books are quite flammable.

His eyes catch a woman on the other side of the courtyard. He only notices her because it's abnormal for someone else to be out right now, and he doesn't recognize her from the staff. She's dressed in all black, the only color on her a mane of red hair. He wants to point out to her that the other buildings aren't open yet, and they won't be until seven. When he considers calling to her across the courtyard, though, another sharp wind cuts at his eyes and cheeks, so he rushes inside.

The library is the biggest building on campus, stretching five stories into the night. One side of it has an entirely glass wall, only interrupted by steel framework. The lights are lower at night than in the daytime, but, with the lack of stars, the library is the brightest thing in the world. When he was younger, he would sometimes hide in the depths of the reference section well into the night, which is hidden away in the basement. There, he would pretend that he wasn't a pyromancer. He could act like nobody was interested in him, like he didn't have everyone's expectations on his shoulders.

When he enters, warm air envelopes him, and he's embraced by the scent of books. The main entrance is grand and modern, all sleek dark wood desks and white shelves. A cart of books rolls by on its own, the books shelving themselves. Dazzling silver lights float through the air, tiny stars and moons enchanted to follow the time of day. Crickets chirp and a stream bubbles somewhere in the distance, although it's impossible for either of those things to be anywhere in here.

The librarian is lounging at the dark wood front desk, a Stephen King true-crime novel in hand. Clown demons and black shucks—omens of death that take the form of a dog—don't usually attack people, but the novels are a sensation because they make people wonder if it could happen to them. She nods at Alex before getting back to her book.

He wanders through the stacks, tracing his fingers along the spines of books that interest him, and they whisper to him, begging him to pick one—or all—of them. He eventually ends up in the basement, a warm, cozy hovel with rich browns and golds and endless hot cocoa and espresso for anyone that knows where to look. Plush armchairs surround a fake roaring fire. He caresses a biography about Norman Claire, a famous pyromancer from the nineteen-thirties.

Alex has read most of the books on pyromancy that this library has to offer, but they've brought him no closer to understanding why he is one. It's supposed to be genetic, but neither of his parents are pyromancers. They're both only mildly interested in magic at all, and, although they support him living a state away at St. Merlin's, he sometimes feels as though they'd prefer it if he were normal. If he were to settle down with a nice girl, making an honest living, they'd be just as content, but without the barrage of questioning from friends and relatives about what he's going to do with his gift.

When he gets past the introduction of the biography, he feels a sudden charge in the air, the electricity of a storm. The spark of a spell. The hairs on his arms raise in anticipation, like lightning is going to strike him down at any second.

Someone else is in his mind.

*What's going on?* He thinks, pushing his thoughts toward the presence. It doesn't seem hostile, but he keeps his guard up.

*I'm so sorry, Alex. I just don't want to be alone.* It takes him a moment to place the voice. He's only had one class with Cynthia, but now that he recognizes her, the connection gets stronger. If he closes his eyes, the basic colors blur around her, dark, desaturated greens of the trees and grass at night.

Before he can ask what she means, a sharp pain digs into his right arm, burrowing deep into his bones. He grits his teeth as a gasp is dragged out of him.

*What the hell is going on?* He demands, but she doesn't answer. Instead, he can only take her pain, her fear. He has to find her, to stop whatever is going on.

He drops his book and runs to the stairs, but he stumbles when another cut streaks through. There should be an upside-down star when he looks at his upper arm, but there's no blood coming through his button-up shirt. He sucks in a ragged breath and gets up as many stairs as he can, bracing himself for more pain.

When he reaches the front door, he has to hold the handle tight as something else is carving over his collar, the invisible knife scraping into the bone. His blood is cold with fear, but he keeps going the moment he can stand it.

When the cold air hits him, so does a single sharp image—a wall with a stag atop.

He runs to the front gate, a shout ripping through him as another slice goes into his left arm, and the front gate is in sight when he feels the fifth motion on his left wrist.

*I'm coming,* he tells Cynthia. *It's going to be okay.*

*Thank you for not letting me be alone,* she replies. By the time he gets to the gate, he can no longer feel her. The sky has gone from grey to pale gold, and the light shines on the slick blood that now adorns the pavement.

Cynthia is worse than he could have imagined. She's tied to the gate by gleaming silver chains that bite into her too-pale skin. A figure leans toward her, obscured by swirling black shadow. The person turns to look at Alex, so he twists to throw what little flame he can at her, but she disappears in a dark cloud of smoke before the meager fire hits her.

He runs over to Cynthia, lifting her head. His eyes are drawn to a series of symbols that have been drawn across her body, spanning from her right arm to the end of her left.

"It's going to be okay," he says, this time out loud, a whisper. His eyes blur with tears as his hands melt the chains so that he can bring her down. The crippling pain that consumed him moments ago is already fading, like the ache of a once-broken bone. Her eyes are distant, her body cold and unmoving. Still, he holds her close until sirens assault his senses and someone pulls her away from him.

# CHAPTER TWELVE
## Sarah

DESPITE THE FIREPLACE RUNNING, SARAH wakes up to a frigid morning, and the hot water isn't working during her shower. Mark shivers under his tweed jacket when they pull out of the driveway, so he suggests picking up a hot breakfast before school. Sarah doesn't object, assuming they'd just pick up fast food before jumping on the interstate.

Instead, they end up downtown, the car crawling through early-morning traffic while they eat bagels from Mark's favorite coffee shop.

"Why did you guys take me?" Sarah asks, watching men in black and gray and navy suits rush along the sidewalks to enter different glass-and-steel buildings.

Mark looks away, she thinks to avoid the question, but then she realizes that he's just trying to merge into the left lane. After his move is successful, he answers, "When Elizabeth found out about your parents, she wanted to vie for custody."

Sarah is stunned at this information. Her hands freeze, her bagel halfway back to her lips. Her parents were never close with their extended family, and Uncle John had rarely spoken about his daughter and her husband, so finding out that they knew anything about her before she moved in with them is a shock. She looks at Mark and studies his face, searching for something in it.

"We weren't in a situation where we could take care of a kid, though. We lived in a tiny one-bedroom apartment, and we weren't even married yet. I thought you'd be better off with John, so we held off." He makes a left by an out-of-place cathedral before continuing, "Then, last month, John had a stroke, and we have a house now. Not a great house, but a house. I can't have biological children, so I guess it sort of worked out." His eyes widen when he says that. "Not that I'm glad about John getting sick. It's just—"

Sarah interrupts him before he can ramble too much. "No, I get it. And yeah, John is a huge dick. Anytime he mentioned you guys, he was a huge transphobe about everything."

Mark seems stuck in a shocked silence. "So I guess you know about that, too."

Sarah shrugs, letting her eyes fall back to the sidewalk. Since they're talking about family, she wants to mention last weekend. She's almost certain that she'll get grounded for sneaking out of the house, but she needs to tell someone about the woman she keeps seeing. Maybe Mark and Elizabeth will find her a good therapist. Or even a mid-range one.

When they come to a stoplight, Sarah is caught by a tangle of red hair atop a woman in all black. She's facing away from the Pontiac, waiting to cross the street.

Sarah keeps her eyes on the woman, and when the light turns green, she waits for the car to get far enough past to see her face.

Sarah has to crane her neck around as they pass, and she's only able to get a short glimpse. However, she instantly recognizes the square jawline that runs on her father's side of the family, and her nose, like Sarah's, is slightly too large for her face. There are no bloody hands, no black eyes.

"Stop the car," Sarah says, but the sound isn't much more than a whisper as her blood runs cold. She says it again, louder. She looks at Mark, and she can feel her throat bubbling with emotion.

"Why?" he asks, his neck turned to try to see whatever she's looking at. He has to slam on the brake to avoid hitting the car in front of them, and she takes that opportunity to leap out, narrowly avoiding a silver Mercedes in the right lane. "Sarah!" Mark yells, but she's sprinting to the sidewalk. Although Sarah is tall, she can't see past the crowd of business people. In her desperation, she trips over the curb, and someone's heel crushes her hand, either because they don't see her, or because they don't care.

Someone lays on their car horn as she shoves her way along the now crowded sidewalk, caressing her hurt hand to her chest. She takes a good look at every stranger's face before continuing on. Mark is still calling to her, but she ignores it. "Have you seen a redheaded woman?" she asks a few of the suits, but nobody answers besides a puzzled stare.

The woman had been so close, but Sarah can't find her. Her fingers are going numb with the morning air, and the wind tears into her, a shudder making its way down her body. She moves over to the edge of the sidewalk, right at the corner. If she can get higher, she can see where the woman went.

Just as she grabs the wide pole that holds up a stoplight, a hand wraps around her upper arm. She twists around, ready to defend herself against an attacker, or perhaps demand an explanation from the woman she's searching for, but Mark is standing there, his eyebrows bunched together, his breathing labored.

"What are you doing?" he demands. It takes a moment for him to realize that he's got a tight grip on Sarah's arm, and he releases her as though she's on fire. Her throat tightens. She looks around the street, which is suddenly close to empty, only a few people walking down the sidewalks—a woman in a pencil skirt and navy blouse, a gay couple with a stroller rushing toward a Starbucks, and a man in an ill-fitting black suit yelling at someone over the phone.

She continues to search for the woman, but the only redhead she can see is Mark. She opens her mouth, looks around, then closes it again.

"Sarah, what's going on?" Mark asks, his tone shakey. He wraps one arm around his torso as the cold air embraces them, and he looks around to find whatever she's searching for. A siren sounds somewhere in the distance. "I'm sorry I grabbed you. Can we please get back in the car?"

A lump forms in her throat, and she lets out a breath to deflate. Mark's car is parked in front of a fire hydrant, one tire propped up on the curb—she's almost surprised he didn't hit any of the people who had been crowding the sidewalk just moments ago. She'd been in such a rush to find the woman that she hadn't even shut the door. She looks down, and the pavement at her feet is speckled with teardrops.

"I saw..." She pauses, unsure if she should say anything. The woman has been missing for seven years, but Sarah knows that she didn't imagine it. She has to take a moment to breathe so that she doesn't choke on her own words. Finally, she says, "My aunt Helen was here. But she disappeared the same night as our accident. Everyone said she was dead."

THE ENTIRE WAY TO SCHOOL, MARK IS ON THE phone with the police. If he didn't have to work, she's certain he would have turned around and driven her straight home, but he pulls into the parking lot at seven-thirty. A police officer waves them away from the main road that goes into the school, so they have to enter the parking lot through the side gate by the dorms. Instead of walking around the front of the building by herself once they're parked, Sarah huddles close to Mark through the employee entrance and then weaves back to the front to tell Gabby what she'd seen.

Gabby is waiting just inside the front entrance, her knuckles white as she grips her backpack straps. She's wearing a long black peacoat, the collar up to block out the wind that comes in every time the doors open. Sarah gets her attention from the side hallway where they first met.

"You're late," Gabby says, her voice coming out with a rush of relief. "I thought you'd been murdered."

Sarah barks out a laugh, but the sound is a bit off. Her heart is still racing from seeing Helen, and she finds herself looking down a corridor, waiting for her aunt to appear in the throng of the morning rush. There's nothing except students milling around as they avoid going to class. About half of them are wearing layers over the school uniform, scarves around their necks or jackets on their shoulders to keep the abnormally cold early September weather at bay.

"No, really," Gabby insists, not humored. She moves closer, and her amber eyes penetrate Sarah's. "Didn't you hear? A body was found near here this morning."

Sarah stops in her tracks. It takes her a moment to comprehend what she means. Death isn't uncommon in St. Louis, but there's something about the way Gabby said it that makes Sarah's shoulders tense and her throat dry. The combination of the out-of-season cold, seeing Helen, and now a body renders her unable to move. A shiver runs down her arms, and the hairs on the back of her neck stand on end. There had been a police officer blocking the front entrance.

"A body?" she asks, her voice hushed, and her ears begin to catch hints of the conversation around them. It's only now that she realizes that it's too quiet here. Normally, the halls are a cacophony of sound, her senses bombarded with voices. Today is a stark contrast; everyone is whispering, their eyes darting around as they discuss the body.

Gabby lowers her voice, sensing Sarah's apprehension. "Alex Locklear found a girl hanging on the gate. A St. Merlin's student."

Sarah's vision goes spotty, her head spinning, and she grabs at Gabby, but she's too far away. The fall seems eternal before Sarah crashes to the ground.

Her ears are ringing, and Gabby's voice seems far away when she says, "Oh my god!" Her voice rises in pitch as she continues. "Sarah, are you okay?" Sarah has to blink a few times to see Gabby leaning over her, hands fluttering like she doesn't know what to do.

Sarah tries to speak, but her mouth is dry and doesn't want to move right. She slowly sits up, trying to ignore the twenty or more pairs of eyes watching her, the conversation now at a complete halt. When she's taken a few steady breaths, she mumbles, "I don't think I've ever fainted before."

Gabby helps her stand, and Sarah has to lean on her friend to make sure she's not going to fall again. Her head is spinning, and lights gently dot her vision. She waits for the nausea to pass before letting go.

"Sorry," she breathes.

Instead of speaking, Gabby runs her hands over Sarah's hair, smoothing it down from the fall. When she's done, she says, "We'd better go." Sarah expects her to spin on her heal and leave her behind, but she takes Sarah by her still slightly sore hand and pulls her past the gawking freshmen and across the courtyard. Instead of going to Literature class, they spend the hour in Mark's office so that Sarah can breathe and explain her experience seeing Helen this morning.

# CHAPTER THIRTEEN
## Gabby

GABBY DOESN'T SHOW IT, BUT SHE IS PANICKING hard by the time the school holds an assembly rather than second-hour classes. Rumors have spread throughout the school in that short time, and nobody, not even the teachers, seem to know whether the murder was real or not. It's as if the whole place is under some sort of spell—it just isn't real if the adults don't acknowledge it.

Students are crammed like cattle into the auditorium, and Gabby is separated from Sarah before they make it in. She sends Sarah a text to let her know that she'll meet her afterwards if possible. The crowd pushes in, and she gulps in deep breaths. She can get through this. It will be fine.

It takes a few minutes for everyone to take their seats, and the dean takes a spot at the podium for his speech. By then, anxiety and fear and, from a few students, boredom, are all vying for attention in Gabby's head. She tries to shove them out, but the more she tries, the more they filter through.

A squat man with a receding hairline and bushy eye-brows walks on stage, his usually pristine suit ruffled like feathers. Gabby has only ever seen Dean McKinley at official school hosted events, like the benefactor dinner her parents made her attend before the start of this semester. "I'm sure you have all heard the rumors," he says, his voice reverberating throughout the auditorium without even needing a microphone. "It is with a troubled heart that I confirm that Cynthia Rowell was murdered on campus this morning." His voice shakes as he says this last part. Dean McKinley has never sounded unsure of himself, but right now, while Gabby focuses on his voice, she feels her heart stop and a lump form in her throat. He's terrified, and now, so is she.

Every voice in the auditorium goes up at once, and Gabby covers her ears and duck down to get them out. It doesn't work. Anguish, fear, and nervous energy all flood through her, and it takes all of her self control to not claw at her skull and pull her hair out.

When the Dean tries to speak again, everyone goes silent. Everyone wants to know exactly what happened, although he doesn't go into any detail. Gabby is already nauseous enough, so this is a small mercy. "The family has been notified, and we will be working with the police to ensure the safety of every student here, but—"

A shout in the front row interrupts him. Gabby shakily sits up to see the commotion; Hannah Murphy is standing up. "This is your fault! You knew it was happening! You could have stopped it! She wouldn't be dead if you weren't such a coward!" The boy behind her is Alex Locklear. She throws something at him—a spiral-bound notebook. He doesn't flinch, but he closes his eyes for a moment when it hits him. His face is stoic, his eyes planted on the stage while he's being screamed at. When Gabby is finally able to focus on him, pain crashes through her, crippling her. She wants to scream, to apologize, to run away.

Alex doesn't defend himself—he lets Hannah take her anger out on him. He just sits there, his face a statue, the perfect essence of calm.

Gabby's ears ring, and all the voices around her fade while Hannah gets dragged out of the auditorium by the counselor.

*You're just as afraid as anyone else!* Gabby wants to shout at the counselor as he tells Hannah that she needs to calm down. *Liars! You're all liars!* Instead, she stays quiet like everyone else. She has no idea how Alex isn't shattering in front of everyone, though.

The dean goes on for another thirty minutes about school safety, new rules, and mentions that St. Merlin's will be bringing in a team of psychologists that anyone can speak with about this incident. He doesn't say her name again, but Gabby is picturing that morning in the breakfast atrium, the one where Cynthia was pining for Vince Palmer. She'd been sad. Desperately sad, but resigned. Gabby had assumed it had to do with Vince, but now, she isn't so sure.

Cynthia was a psychic. Had she known she was going to die?

INSTEAD OF GOING BACK TO CLASS, GABBY AND Sarah hide out in Mark's office after the assembly. Since the teachers' offices are far from the noise and bustle of classes and students, Gabby uses the opportunity to lie down on the couch, and Sarah sits in Mark's office chair. Instead of talking about anything going on, they sit in comfortable silence. After a few minutes, Sarah's breathing gets slow and heavy; somehow, she was able to fall asleep in the cramped chair.

Gabby wonders if her parents will even notice the disturbance. They're too busy fawning over Jasmine, who's about to get a law degree from Yale, and worrying over Rudy, who's in a mental health facility in Chicago since he had a breakdown in college that ended with getting found and returned by Toronto police after a week-long disappearance. It isn't hard for Gabby to see why they ignore her. The moment she came out to them, told them she was in love with her best friend, something shifted in their emotions. Instead of getting angry, they just gave up. There was more important stuff for them to focus on.

She wonders if they might have noticed if she had been the one to get murdered on the front gate. The thought of nobody showing up to her assembly, her funeral, makes her nauseous.

She's starting to spiral, so she scrolls through Instagram, the monotony of her feed helping to slow her heart rate. She mostly follows National Park rangers and full-time travelers, the hipsters who live out of vans and take photos over cliffsides or in front of mountains. If she doesn't think about anything stressful for long enough, then maybe she will melt back into the ground. She offhandedly thinks that she would be a much better tree than she does a human. She'd want to be one of those giant trees in a west-coast forest, untouchable by man or nature. Trees don't have much to worry about, and they're a great deal more important than her.

She double taps on the post of a park ranger in Calaveras Big Trees State Park—the girl is reading a book at the base of a sequoia with a bigger radius than the length of Gabby's massive car.

Maybe she'll move there when she graduates. There's sure to be a college around there that will let her become a park ranger. Mom says that's a waste of the expensive St. Merlin's education, but Gabby didn't want to go to a private school in the first place. Mom was too busy caring about her siblings to push it.

She orders Chinese take-out for herself, Sarah, and Mark when it gets close to lunch, and on the way to pick it up from the side entrance, she passes Alex in the hallway. She tries to ignore his puffy eyes or the way he curls into himself just a bit more whilst sitting on the floor by a row of lockers. His pain, though, radiates into her.

Sequoias don't feel pain the way humans do—when she was a child, before her sister was expected to become a premiere lawyer and before her brother couldn't bear the world, their family took a roadtrip in their old, beat-up station wagon that Dad refused to sell, all the way to California. She got to walk through the redwoods, her soul calm from the presence of the ancient giants.

She texts Kelly a link to an art college in San Francisco. It's right along the forests, and Kelly can get her degree in animation while Gabby hides among the trees, away from all this pain.

HALF THE SCHOOL IS AT CYNTHIA'S FUNERAL on Saturday. Gabby didn't want to go, but when she decided not to yesterday, she had a nightmare that she died and nobody showed up to her own funeral. She texted Sarah to find out if she'd be attending, but she'd replied that it wouldn't feel right to attend the funeral of someone she never knew. She said it would feel too much like an intrusion.

So, when Gabby goes to the funeral, she goes alone.

There's a service at Cynthia's family's church, a huge cathedral smack dab in the middle of downtown. Gabby is early, as she always aims to be for this sort of thing. The emotions of others are easier to sort through when she doesn't take in too many at once.

The day is sunny and hot, and she almost regrets wearing her long black gown with thick lace sleeves and huge black hat that obscures her features. The church is air conditioned, but after the service, she'll be standing out in the sun in all black.

She enters the cathedral, and the force of Cynthia's family's emotions makes her stumble. She already wants to scream, to cry out in anguish as her heart fills with the heavy weight of tears. The casket is at the front of the room, open so that anyone can see her one last time.

Gabby approaches slowly. Cynthia's parents' sadness weighs down her dress, trying to drag her back, down the aisle and out the door into the humid parking lot.

She hates funerals.

The steps she takes echo throughout the otherwise empty building, half stone and half colorful windows, which depict different stories, most with Jesus in the center. Somehow, all of them seem sad. How can anyone survive in a building filled with such constant sadness?

She has to take two steps up in order to face Cynthia, who is lying in a bed of lavender and wildflowers. Her hands are resting gently on a bouquet of pink peonies. Gabby has never believed in Catholicism, but at this moment, she desperately hopes that she's wrong, that Cynthia gets to go to heaven.

Her eyes are shut, and Gabby's mind tries to convince her that she's just sleeping, delicate arms crossed over her.

Gabby will not cry on the pretty green dress, the same one Cynthia wore to the graduation ball last year—long-sleeved, probably to cover the dark symbols carved into her arms by her murderer. Her skin has an unnatural blush, and Gabby wants to slap the mortician who used such a bright shade of pink lipstick on her cool-toned skin. She can't help but think that she could've done better by her, but these thoughts aren't allowed. Of course, she looks beautiful, an elven queen who's laid down for a nap in this casket of flowers.

With the wrong shade of lipstick.

*Fucking mortician.*

Gabby almost reaches out to touch her, to see if she's warm, in case she's really asleep and nobody has noticed yet. What if she wakes up a moment after she's put in the ground? Gabby ties her hands together behind her back and turns away to approach the family.

Cynthia's mother is staring straight ahead, and she reaches out to shake Gabby's hand automatically, which are clad in black satin gloves—she's certain that if she were to touch this grieving mother directly, she would go to the highest point of this building and dive off of it, leadened with the weight of a mother's sadness. Gabby has no idea how she has the strength to stand here while all these strangers stare at her with sympathy.

"My condolences," Gabby mutters as she shakes her hand. The woman nods and continues to stare right through her. Gabby can't blame her.

When she gets to Cynthia's father, he whispers, his voice catching, "Are...were you a friend of hers?" She can feel that saying her name would shatter him. Although she only talked to Cynthia on a few occasions, she nods. He smiles weakly. "She had so many wonderful friends," he whispers, a tear escaping his eye.

By the time she makes it to a seat near the back of the church, she's shaking, fat tears falling out of her eyes and onto her dress.

# CHAPTER FOURTEEN
## Alex

HE'S AT THE CEMETERY BEFORE ANYONE ELSE. THE air smells like fire, and he has to check to make sure his hands aren't catching. The smell isn't his familiar campfire smell, though. This fire is a forest dying in the night, the funeral pyre of a child taken too soon, a house burning to the ground with the family inside.

He doesn't want to be here, but he feels obligated to pay his respects. He was the last contact she had before dying. He was the closest thing to comfort she found, and she held onto him until her final breath. He has to be here.

*There's nothing I could've done*, he tells himself. His heart races, a lump forming in his throat. Tears sting at his eyes, threatening to fall.

The first vehicle there is the hearse, followed by a long black limousine carrying her family. A line of cars pulls slowly into the cemetery, stopping along the thin road that weaves along the graves. When there isn't enough room in the cemetery, people pull over on the street and abandon their cars.

He stands behind a mausoleum; if he can avoid being seen, he will. He's here for nobody except Cynthia and himself. He owes it to her to see her put in her final resting place. He's not really the religious type, but he whispers a prayer that her soul makes it to heaven. It's the least he can do, even if God doesn't want to hear him.

The sky is too bright, the sun bearing down on everyone as they stand in a half circle around the grave. His pale, sensitive skin is burning before they even start the sermon. It's never ending as they bow their heads in prayer five times and go through what feels like every scripture about death and perseverance.

Before they start the final prayer, Alex moves to the back of the crowd. Still, a few people from St. Merlin's notice him and shoot him dirty looks. Those who would force him to leave, however, are closer to her casket and don't see him skulking around. That's how they would probably describe him, although he tries his hardest to not skulk often.

He wants to scream at those still glaring at him, *I felt her pain! You have no idea what she went through. You have no idea what I would've done if I could!* Instead, He keeps his head bowed low to avoid their gazes.

Gabby Savalza joins him at the back, gently making her way through the crowd. Whenever someone makes an attempt to shame her, she seems to know what they need to hear. Vince Palmer shoots her a dirty look, but, instead of returning it, she puts a hand on his cheek and whispers back, "It's okay to be hurting. I know you loved her." After she walks away from him, his face crumples, and a sob bursts out of him with agony that Alex didn't know was possible. There are so many other people crying that nobody judges him, although a few people shuffle over to give him space for his grief.

When Gabby makes it back to Alex, she takes his hand in hers, lacing her fingers through his own. He's not short, but in her heels, she's half a head taller than him, so he rests his head on her shoulder, mussing his styled black hair. He's caught her watching him a few times since Cynthia's death, and he suspects that she's been tuning in to his emotions.

"You did what nobody else could," she whispers, watching ahead as they lower the pearl white casket into the ground. He wishes he could speak up, tell everyone how Cynthia stayed proud, how she found a way to not be alone in her last moments. "You took some of her pain so that she wasn't alone. That's more than anyone else did."

*You could've done better*, he wants to say, but everyone has grown silent as the casket finishes its descent.

Before Cynthia is buried, he lets go of Gabby's hand and walks back to his car. He doesn't want to hurt Cynthia's close friends and family by existing too near their pain. He weaves his way through the cemetery, letting his tears fall freely. Usually, when he's really upset, he has a tendency to catch fire. Today, his hands feel like ice. The spark in his heart is all but gone, and he wants to go back to his dorm to curl up and cry alone.

When he turns to look at the crowd of mourners one last time, he's not the only one leaving early. A middle-aged woman with red hair and a square jaw is looking right at him, but after catching his gaze, she turns around and strides away.

He knows this exchange is important, but there's something in his mind, a wall that prevents him from knowing why.

# CHAPTER FIFTEEN
## Sarah

SARAH COULDN'T BRING HERSELF TO GO TO THE funeral. Since Mark is at the service and Elizabeth is working at the zoo all day, Sarah spends Saturday morning lying in bed, catatonic. She can only think about her parents' funeral, like a movie playing over and over again in her head, until she falls asleep, her thoughts only on death.

*IT SHOULD RAIN AT EVERY FUNERAL. THE BEST WAY to cleanse one's pain is to mask their tears with raindrops, the cool water pulling away all the hurt.*

*Mom and Dad always told Sarah that rain is purifying. "Unicorns play in the rain," Dad prodded late one summer, which convinced her to sprint out to the pasture in her boots and her favorite dress. She danced until the sun went down, but she didn't see any unicorns. "You'll have to try longer tomorrow," Dad said to her frown.*

# SMOKE AND MIST

It didn't rain at Mom and Dad's funeral. It was too cold for rain, so sleet pelted her in the face—she had to squint against the wind to not get stabbed in the eyes. Her fingers were numb before anybody else got there, but that's because she walked. Uncle John had passed out drunk deep into the night, so when she woke up, he was practically comatose. Luckily, his house was only a few miles from the one cemetery in town.

While she sat in a cheap folding chair in the front row, waiting for someone else to show up, a hand rested on her shoulder, and she spun around. An elven woman stood over her, her dark face gentle and soft. Her golden hair was a fluffy halo around her despite the weather.

"Where's your Uncle?" Winifred asked. Her sheep farm backed up to the far end of the Jacksons' pasture, and she was always the one to find Sarah when she ran off and fell asleep in a pile of the woolen creatures. It was only appropriate that she found Sarah at the funeral, shivering next to an empty grave.

Tears welled in Sarah's eyes, and she wrapped her arms around the familiar woman.

The rest of the neighbors showed up after the hearse. There weren't enough people to carry the caskets, so someone levitated them over. They hovered there while the preacher spoke, his words too loud over the tiny gathering.

The thick wooden caskets holding her parents' remains fell into the ground with a finality she hadn't felt until now. As people dropped fistfuls of dirt over the grave, Sarah was buried, piece by piece, until there was nothing left of her heart.

*"I'll drive you home," Winifred said gently. She lead Sarah to an older pickup truck and bought her fast food, which her parents only rarely allowed. Sarah cried over her hamburger, and she cried when Winifred carried her back to the truck.*

*When they got to the cold, unfeeling house, Winifred walked Sarah to the door. Sarah clung to Winifred, begging to go with her.*

*She looked at Sarah with large, sad eyes. "I wish I could, darling."*

*The door swung open, and Sarah's uncle dragged her into the house by her lower arm.*

EARLY IN THE AFTERNOON, THE SOUND OF THE doorbell wakes Sarah up. She wanders through the house, peeking into the kitchen and then her Aunt and Uncle's bedroom before determining that they haven't made it back yet. When the bell rings again, she pads over and looks through the peephole to see Gabby standing on the porch, huddled under an enormous hat and slim black dress.

She opens the door and notices Gabby's hulking black SUV, which seems to suck in all the sunlight pouring onto the driveway rather than reflecting it. The grille grins at Sarah as if it's waiting for her to get a joke it's just told. Whatever it is, it isn't funny.

Gabby leans forward and puts her head on Sarah's shoulder, a feat due to their height difference, which is dramatically larger because of Gabby's high heels. She's shaking, so Sarah wraps her arms around her friend and pulls her into the house and onto the vintage couch in the front sitting room. The keys in Gabby's hand dig into Sarah's thigh, but she bites her lip and ignores the pain. Her chin rests on Gabby's coconut-scented hair as she waits for the anxiety attack to abate.

They sit like this for a few minutes, until Gabby catches her breath and sits up. She rubs her eyes, somehow not smearing her makeup. "Oh, god, I'm sorry," she says, laughing shakily. "It's been a long fucking day." Sarah scoots over to give her some breathing room and notices the Cadillac emblem now imprinted on her own thigh, which she traces her finger over.

"Funerals suck," she replies, not sure what else she should say. These things are never easy, and she can't find words to get rid of Gabby's pain, especially when she can't keep her own away, still clinging to her from the dream.

"Tell me about it."

After digging around the kitchen for coping snacks—mostly chocolate—they go to Sarah's room, which is a complete mess. She rarely remembers to toss her dirty clothes in her hamper, so they're strewn all over the floor.

"You do know that floors exist, right?" Gabby chides, and Sarah shoves her shoulder against her as they sit cross-legged in the center of the bed. Gabby waves a finger, and all the clothes fly over to the hamper. Sarah has to dodge a St. Merlin's blazer so that she doesn't lose a chunk of her face to one of the buttons.

"Thanks," she says. "I, uh, don't know that one." It's a lie—she knows the spell, but she's never been able to do it.

They snack in silence for a few minutes, then Gabby asks, "Why do you have a fire going? It's a million degrees today."

Sarah freezes. She hadn't put the spell up before answering the door, so her secret is out there for anyone to see. She opens her mouth, but she doesn't have a good response lined up before Gabby jumps out of bed and strolls over, bending down to look in the fireplace. Sarah tries to stop her, but she ends up dumping a bag of Doritos all over the bed, and while she's distracted by the mess, Gabby finds what nobody was supposed to.

"Ho. Lee. Shit." She spins around to face Sarah. "Where the hell did you get a forest dragon egg?"

"I dont—It's not -," Sarah sputters, her heart leaping into her throat.

"I'm not gonna tell anyone. It's just....this is super illegal."

Sarah flinches. "It can't be that bad."

"I mean, you technically can get a permit, but it's super strict and expensive," Gabby continues, kneeling down by the fireplace. "They're considered exotic animals. I think some director in Hollywood has one, but that's just a rumor. How are you gonna keep it a secret after it hatches?"

Sarah joins her on the floor, taking a large pair of tongs

to twist the egg around. Every time she adjusts it, the fledgling's life energy thrums through her fingertips. She wants to take the egg and hold it in her arms, but her body temperature isn't nearly high enough to sustain the still-fragile life inside.

"I have an idea," she says, hopping to a standing position.

GABBY PARALLEL PARKS HER ESCALADE BEHIND a silver car on the shoulder of the road along the park, and she puts anything valuable in her small black leather backpack before joining Sarah on the sidewalk. The warm air has brought flocks of visitors to the zoo this Saturday afternoon, so they have to walk nearly a mile from their parking spot to get to the front gate.

Gabby is now wearing a borrowed pair of Sarah's galaxy leggings and a black tank-top, plus a pair of flip-flops that were buried in the backseat, and Sarah is still in the ugly shorts and t-shirt she'd been in when Gabby showed up to her house.

The zoo is crowded, and Sarah and Gabby have to weave their way through packs of slow-moving women with strollers to get to the Aviary. On the way here, Sarah had texted Elizabeth to let her know she was coming, and Elizabeth had been quite excited to know that Sarah was bringing a friend.

She probably wouldn't be so excited if she knew about

the dragon egg in Sarah's room.

Sarah recognizes Victor as soon as they walk in, and he raises a hand to catch the girls' attention when they step into the almost chilly educational area.

"Elizabeth's niece, right?" he says upon approaching them. He shakes both of their hands, and Sarah is thrown by how he's treating them like people. All of John's colleagues and friends had treated her like a toddler until the moment she left. "Your aunt told me you'd be coming."

At the exact same moment, Sarah's phone dings. When she looks at it, she has a text from her aunt.

*I have a surprise for you!*

"Miss Halacourt informs me that, last time you visited, you had quite the connection with Hawthorne," he says, leading the way through a door labelled "Staff Facilities."

The room they enter is a concrete hallway with another door at the end. The girls follow Victor through the dim corridor, and they have to blink away the brightness of the fluorescent room they walk into. While he tells them the different things they do with the dragon program, Sarah takes in as much as she can. At one point, she sees an artificial nest filled with opal and onyx and rose quartz eggs, and Gabby has to drag her by the arm to keep up with Victor's spry pace.

They come up to another door, this one heavy reinforced steel.

"I'm going to hand you off to your aunt. You'll be in the

best hands, but I'm sure you knew that already." Sarah expects a keypad to appear for him to type top-secret codes into, but he simply turns the doorknob and lets them in.

This room is much like the first, all concrete, except there's a line of chain-link fences along the left side going up to the top of the twenty-foot ceilings. Elizabeth is leaning on a gate at the end of the hall, somehow managing to look like a cover model in her khaki and green zoo uniform and black rubber boots.

"Who's a good dragon? Is it you? Are you a good dragon?" she says, her tone babyish as she speaks to something Sarah can't see on the other side of the fence.

"Miss Halacourt," Victor calls, and she straightens up and rushes to them.

"So sorry, Victor," she says, her voice hard. "I'm working on training exercises." When her gaze moves to Sarah and Gabby, she beams. "I'm so glad to have you here. I've been trying to convince Victor for weeks to bring you into the training area." While she's talking, Victor waves and goes back through the door, leaving them all alone.

Sarah is unsettled by this entrance. She had expected to walk Gabby through the aviary, and perhaps get a glimpse at Hawthorne again so that she could explain that he somehow knows about the egg. She'd been thinking that, maybe, if she gets close enough, she can find out more about him. She had not expected to be greeted at the door and taken to see the training area.

Elizabeth swivels around and walks away, leaving through one of the chain-link gates without another word.

Gabby and Sarah look at each other and then look back to her.

"Come on, girls. Can't leave gates open for long when you've got dragons about."

They rush over, following her out the gate and through a thin aluminum door, and they're suddenly in the aviary. The transition is jarring; they'd gone from a long concrete room and into what seems like an open field in a mountainous valley.

"Holy crap," Gabby whispers, craning her neck to look at the infinite sky that stretches above them. Sarah smiles at her amazement.

They're standing in a patch of thin grass outside, and if they squint, they can see the guest pathway in the distance.

"This place is magical," Sarah says.

"It has to be," Elizabeth replies. "We have over two hundred dragons in one building, and a good deal of them are not small."

Gabby's eyes widen. "Two hundred?"

Elizabeth tilts her head. "Two hundred thirty-six, actually."

She strides off through the field, her pace brisk, probably due to her mile-long legs.

"Hawthorne!" she calls, cupping her hand over her mouth. She elongates the first syllable before sharply cutting the second upward.

A red and black mountain dragon lands in front of her, heaving his glowing, lava-like chest plates. Its amber eyes blink curiously, its pupils adjusting to take in the three puny humans. Sarah shrinks back. She hadn't considered that they were within the magical boundary that protects zoo patrons from the dragons.

"Not you, Smaug," Elizabeth chides, waving a hand at him. Sarah is delighted by his geeky literary name, although she doesn't move closer. "Shoo! Go harass Keida." She makes a "tch" sound as she flaps a hand toward him. He tosses his head, snorts black ash into her face, and then takes off. This motion doesn't phase her—she just wipes the ash away from her eyes and calls again, "Hawthorne!" This is the first time Sarah has seen Elizabeth look anything less than perfect, and it warms her just a bit.

A juvenile prairie dragon crawls up the galaxy leggings Gabby is borrowing, and it burrows itself under her shirt. It's long, furry tail hangs out the bottom, the puff of brown fur at the end wiggling with excitement. She squeals, jumping backward and holding her arms out to her sides.

Elizabeth rushes over to assist her, unabashedly reaching under the hem of the shirt to retrieve the creature. By the time she has a grip on it, faerie dragons are nesting in Gabby's piles of hair.

While this chaos is happening, Hawthorne lands in the field, tilting his head at the scene.

Sarah walks away slowly, Gabby and Elizabeth tangled in a futile dance of removing assorted dragons from her person.

Hawthorne sniffs the air as she approaches, his expression going from quizzical to excited. He dances in place, his huge feet pawing the grass underneath him flat. A previously hidden crown of red and black feathers flares up behind his horns, and she hesitates. The red reminds her of the blood on the murdered female dragon. She'd been terrified when meeting the female dragon a month ago, but now, she doesn't have adrenaline to push her along. She lifts a shaky hand up, trying to appear confident.

He leans his head forward and sniffs, then suddenly presses his forehead against her entire torso, his nose brushing the ground. Sarah almost falls, but she buries her hands in his feathers and tightens her fingers to steady herself. A laugh leaps out of her before she can help herself.

"You're a good boy, aren't you, Hawthorne?" she says, her voice a gentle croon like she used with Keida weeks before. She strokes his shining golden horns, which are surprisingly rough against her fingertips. He smells like fresh-cut grass and morning dew.

"What's going on?" Elizabeth calls, her voice suddenly tight. Sarah turns her head enough to look, and she and Gabby are standing far back and watching.

"I'm fine," Sarah replies, resting her head back against his forehead. When she rubs her hand through his baby-soft facial feathers, the smell of leaves getting ready to abandon branches for the winter springs up. Quietly, just to Hawthorne, she says, "I hope I'm doing the right thing with this egg."

He doesn't move, but a feeling of warmth and affection spreads lazily through her. She lets out a sigh as she realizes that everything will be alright. It's a familiar intrusion in her mind, the same energy as the female dragon's telepathic messages, but an utterly different tone.

"What do I do about Helen, though?" She pauses. "You're a dragon. Of course you don't know anything about that." When she's about to pull away from him, he nudges her, his green eye focused and serious. She puts a hand back on him to steady herself, and another vision hits, this one like a load of bricks.

*S*HE *CAN FEEL A PAIN IN HER WINGS—NO, IT'S NOT her. This is Hawthorne. He's crouched to the ground, hiding as far in the underbrush as he can, restraining from calling to his mate. If she doesn't come to him, she may be safe. The egg may be safe. A human that looks like fire at the top and darkness all over pulls out a light box and puts it to her mouth, and a sound keens out. The sound of another forest dragon. Deceit.*

*He tries to tell his mate not to come to it, to go back to their den and hide. It's no use, though. She's drawn to the call, and she becomes hopelessly entangled in the wires that had sliced Hawthorne's wing open. He tries to get to her, but the human is already stealing something, anything, from her. Scales. Teeth. Blood. It isn't until the human disappears in a cloud of black smoke that his mate is able to escape, not even looking his way. He tries to follow, but he can't get off the ground with his wing destroyed.*

THE VISION GOES SPOTTY, AND SARAH HAS TO blink a few times to see where she is. Right. The aviary at the zoo. Except now, she's lying on the ground. Hawthorne is staring down at her. When she opens her mouth to speak, though, he flies off, his now repaired wing carrying him through the air.

Elizabeth runs up and crouches over Sarah. "Oh my god, are you alright? Did he hurt you? Forest dragons, even wild ones, are usually very docile. I don't know why he would do anything."

Sarah keeps staring into the distance, where Hawthorne is no more than a green and gold speck. "Where exactly did you guys get Hawthorne?"

# CHAPTER SIXTEEN
## Alex

IT'S BEEN LESS THAN TWO WEEKS SINCE CYNTHIA was murdered and strung on the front gate, yet nobody is talking about it anymore. Alex can't get the image out of his head.

It had taken five minutes for a first-responder to arrive. In his life, five minutes had never been long. Practically the snap of fingers.

When you have to pull a dead girl off a fence and hold her so she isn't alone, five minutes is a lifetime.

Cynthia and Alex weren't friends, but he'd had a few classes with her, and she'd always been kind. Freshman year, when another student was diagnosed with cancer and lost all her hair, Cynthia shaved her own head in solidarity. A bunch of others followed suit, of course, but she was the first, and, he thinks, the only one who really meant it. If she hadn't, she probably wouldn't have shaved her eyebrows to match the victim. Nobody else did.

His nights have been sleepless, and he finds himself wandering campus. Sometimes he falls asleep in the grass while gazing at the stars, or curled on a bench by the clocktower. The rest only lasts a short time, as he's always startled awake by the ten o'clock dorm curfew that pulses through him when he isn't in his room. He can't bring himself to sleep in his dorm, though. David doesn't bring it up.

After the funeral on Saturday night, he drove until he ran out of gas. Then, he filled up the tank and drove until the stars were hidden by an early morning sky. He wasn't searching for a party this time, and he didn't find one.

Every time he closes his eyes, he pictures Cynthia, her frail body chained to the front gate of the school. When he can finally get rid of her face, it's replaced by Hannah screaming that it's his fault, that Cynthia would be alive if he'd tried to save her.

He wants to tell her that he tried. He wanted to apologize for not getting there in time. But he couldn't get the words out. He just let Hannah be angry at him.

It's easier that way.

He hasn't been able to concentrate in his classes, and he fails the Spiritual Magic exam on Tuesday. The rest of his classes are easier to keep up with, but he has a hard time with Spiritual Magic on the best of days.

When class ends on Wednesday afternoon, he doesn't get up to leave. He can't bring himself to move. His body feels entirely too heavy, and he has no motivation to get to his next class until the absolute last minute. He isn't sure if it's from exhaustion or from the image of Cynthia being reduced to a black bag, but he just stays in his seat, staring at his blank notebook. He now has five days of blank notes.

Sarah is the last one to go; he vaguely notices that she's putting her bag together slowly, but he doesn't actually focus on her until she stands next to him, waiting for something, or perhaps deciding if she should say something. He doesn't know if he could take another person asking how Cynthia died, and he definitely can't deal with talking about the kiss he and Sarah had shared a lifetime ago.

After a moment of silence, he hears the sound of paper being torn out of a notebook, and the small stack of paper brushes against his arm as she sets it on his desk.

He doesn't look at it until she's gone. He considers just crumpling it up, disinterested in a love letter that demands he speak about the kiss when the only things he can focus on right now are guilt and anger.

It's not a letter, though. There are five sheets, each with meticulously color-coded Spiritual Magic notes in neat, bubbly letters. He closes his own notebook, but not before realizing that there are teardrops on the empty page. He hadn't even noticed that he was crying again.

AFTER CLASSES LET OUT FOR THE DAY, HE changes into his only set of fireproof clothes and goes to the gym.

St. Merlins' gym is an entire building—besides the regulation basketball court, there's a weight room, a gymnastics room, a pool, and a magical sparring room. The sparring room is where he goes—it's been a while since he's used his fire, and he finally feels its power flowing back into his fingertips after a week of emptiness. Something awakened in him when he saw the tear stains on his blank notes, so he's taking advantage of this sudden burst of motivation to get some practice in.

He rolls out a rubber mat, smaller than the one Phillip uses in Pyromancy class. Alex has been skipping Pyromancy all week, sitting in the counselor's office so that it would be excused, although he never says much. He's been afraid that his fire was gone for good, and he didn't want to have to tell Phillip that. If he weren't a Pyromancer anymore, his scholarship would be redacted at the end of the semester, and he'd be forced to go back to Kansas.

He starts with basic stances to warm up. These motions are slow, practiced. By the end of the first set, he can feel sweat beading on his forehead.

Some of the more prominent religions believe that fire is the first gift given to humans by God. That, when God granted humanity with fire, they were cleansing us. People believe that those born with the gift of fire are pure, the only humans able to cleanse their soul in the same way that a wildfire will cleanse land to make space for new life. He isn't so sure about that.

He likes to believe that there's something special to make him the first pyromancer in his family, but he mostly just feels like everyone expects for him to be greater than he is. In public, he's a stoic firestarter, only allowing precise motions and flawless execution. In private, though, when there are no expectations placed on his shoulders, he's restless and sloppy, desperate to discover what makes him special.

After repeating his warm-up a few times, he creates slow, broad strokes of flame, painting the air around him gold and red before the fire disappears in a crackle. He is a phoenix, painting the air with his cleansing fire. Each movement is meticulous, practiced.

A few of the younger students in the gym stop their sparring to watch him when he quickens his pace, the flames going from red to gold to the hottest of blues as he twists and pulls at the energy flowing through his body.

He works through his magic the same way he might work a tight muscle—if he goes too fast or moves wrong, it could tense up, flaring back to hurt him. His longest bout without using fire was the three weeks after Brittany broke up with him, and it became such a furious turmoil inside him that, when he lost his temper working on a fence, it exploded out of him, destroying half a field worth of corn. Thankfully, nobody was injured, but he did have to pay for the damage to his neighbor's crops.

He sees a girl out of the corner of his eye, her blonde hair pulled back in a loose bun, and he almost thinks that it's Cynthia. He turns to look and stumble, but he doesn't stop the flames. He curses at himself under his breath. Of course it isn't her—it's just another freshman coming over to watch his performance. The fire senses his trepidation, licking outward and testing the boundary that protects the onlookers.

Every year, St. Merlin's holds an end of year expo. It's mainly for students to show their parents what they've learned, but a lot of important people show up, too. Alex was asked by the dean to show off his skill with fire, a routine that he'd worked all year to build up. When he got up on the stage, he gave a mediocre performance due to his nerves, but he was still approached by four college scouts and three military recruiters when they found out he was also a telepath.

He sucks in a shaky breath and drops his torso, lifting his leg in a circle kick and creating even more fire. He's supposed to spin back around to pull the flames back into his hands, but he overshoots and fall to the ground, the fire dissipating at once. This time, he's able to make it look purposeful—he uses the momentum to roll and land in a crouch, but he knows that he screwed up.

A few of the students clap halfheartedly, but the small audience he's gathered disperses before he's on his feet. He didn't do as well as he should have, but he still feels immensely better now that he's gone through the motions.

Phillip is standing at the back of the room, watching Alex

with an eyebrow cocked.

"I expect to see you in class from now on, Mr. Locklear," he says after approaching Alex. He pats Alex on the back, exiting the room while Alex's shirt sticks to his skin with sweat.

Alex considers trying again, knowing that he hasn't performed as well as he should, but when he looks at the clock, he finds that he's been at it for nearly an hour. If he goes much longer, he'll probably hurt himself, and the nurse won't be able to heal a broken bone until tomorrow morning.

He puts away the mat before rushing after Phillip. He also texts David, and they all three have dinner in Phillips apartment, a tradition they haven't picked up since last year.

EVEN AFTER THE DINNER, HE CAN'T SLEEP. He roams campus some more, telling himself that he just needs the fresh air. St. Merlin's campus is dotted with strategically placed trees and flowers, and they're in different stages of autumn. Some of the more delicate trees are bright red, leaves floating to the ground in the wind. The piles look like pools of blood dotting the grass and pavement, so much so that Alex wants to pick one up to make sure it's dry, but he keeps his hands in his pockets.

He wanders aimlessly around campus, telling himself that he can't go to the front gate. Last time he was there, a silver chain was still woven through the bars, Cynthia's dark blood dripping off it. It glimmered in the light of the police cars, gleefully strangling the vines that wind their way through the gate.

Still, he ends up at the gate, trembling at the sight of it.

He considers, for a moment, climbing up the stone wall, sitting on the elk whose head is thrown back in a deathly cry; a lot of his classmates have done it. Their Instagram accounts have photos, the tag "RideTheElk" accompanying them. It's sort of a rite of passage for the richest of the rich, teenagers who don't have anything better to do than conquer an eighteenth century statue. He wonders if Cynthia had thrown her head out in pain, unconsciously mimicking the elk in her last moments, or if she'd hung her head and accepted her fate. By the time he arrived, she'd been facing the ground.

Instead of climbing up the rough stone wall, he traces his fingers along the metal bars that lock the school in, the iron cool with the late-September evening. He expects to feel something, a trace of the energy that remains from Cynthia's death, but there's nothing except cold metal. The school must have had someone wipe the entryway clean, clearing all trace of the gruesome sacrifice that tainted it.

He sits down, his back against the bars, and when he looks to his right, he finds a tiny dot of red that's embedded itself in the stone, the last evidence of the crime committed here.

Blood.

Of course.

He knows she had bled, of course. He'd felt the markings being carved into his arms as it happened to her. He'd seen it flowing from her body in the early morning light. Still, the sight of her blood awakens something in him. He should've done something.

Maybe he still can.

Maybe, upon touching that nearly imperceptible speck of blood, he can find Cynthia's killer. When the thought enters his mind, he can't shake it.

Surely, the police had a seer check the scene already.

If that were true, wouldn't Cynthia's killer have been found? There had been someone there that night, but the memory is blocked, buried deep within Alex's mind. All he can think of is the blood pouring out of Cynthia.

He sprints to the library to find a book on blood magic, and, the moment he finds what he's looking for, he runs back to the gate.

*Please let this be enough.*

He whispers the incantation three times and then pricks his thumb with the pale little blue, pink, and white flag pin that he wears on his lapel. Sucking in a breath, he puts his finger to the drop of blood on the stone.

He's thrown back into that night, only this time, instead of hearing Cynthia's thoughts and feeling her pain, he *is* her.

*H*ER HEART TWINGES AT THE FACT THAT IT HAD *to be so soon, but she's known for months that this is where she is to die. The gate of her school, her home. Her stomach drops with guilt as she forces herself into Alex's mind, but she can't bring herself to be completely alone. She thought she was strong, but she isn't. Not for this.*

*The woman in front of her is mumbling to herself, "Blood of a dragon, flesh of a seer, hair of a mermaid, flame of a mage, tears of an empath." The words echo through Cynthia, but she can't focus on them when the woman starts to carve into her skin. For a moment, she thinks she's burning her, but no flames come out. She tries to hold back a scream, but the sound rips out of her, volatile. "She who intervenes must be the last to die."*

*She can't even tell Alex what's happening, although she's sure it's important. She can only hold on to him, desperate to cling to something outside of herself.*

Thank you for not letting me be alone, *she tells him just as her vision starts to fade. She wishes she could tell Vince how sorry she is for leaving.*

*T*HE AIR ALL RUSHES BACK INTO ALEX AT ONCE. The woman at the funeral.

He'd been inches from her, and he hadn't known it. He could have stopped her right then and there, but he hadn't. He shakily pulls out his phone and calls the officer he'd spoken to the morning of the murder.

"Hello?" The woman's voice says after a few seconds,

142

muffled by other voices in the background.

Alex says, "I know what Cynthia's murderer looked like."

# CHAPTER SEVENTEEN
## Sarah

THURSDAY MORNING, SARAH IS INTERRUPTED before she can meet Gabby at the front entrance.

Alex is sitting on the stout wall between the faculty lot and the front steps, elbows on his knees while he sits and messes with his phone. As soon as Sarah pulls herself out of Mark's Pontiac, he puts his phone away and jogs down to meet her on the sidewalk. He's probably here to ask about her Spiritual Magic notes.

"Alex," she says, surprised. "Um. How are you?" Her voice is too cheery. Of course she knows that he's the one everyone is whispering about. Some people are even saying that he killed Cynthia, but everyone knows he didn't—they just want to start shit.

Wind rips between them, and a shiver runs through them both. Alex glances around, and Sarah catches the eyes of other students that dart away from her as they stand on the steps.

"Can we go inside?" Alex asks. "I need to speak with you...privately."

They walk up the steps together, not speaking. Sarah isn't sure what made him want to talk to her now, but it must be important if he felt the need to seek her out. Were her notes really that bad?

Gabby is waiting inside, and her eyes widen when she sees that Alex and Sarah are walking together.

"Hey, Sarah," she says, her voice slow as she evaluates Alex. His hands are in his pockets, and his head is ducked as he tries to avoid the attention of passing students. "What's going on?"

Sarah looks to Alex, then back to Gabby. "Let's go upstairs," she replies.

Gabby leads the way, and Alex seems uncomfortable as he follows. "I really need to talk to you," he tells Sarah, his tone hushed.

"I know," Sarah says. "We're going somewhere more private." She doesn't want to get told about how much her notes suck in public.

A senior crashes his shoulder against Alex, and Sarah could swear that she hears him mumble, "What's up, lady killer?"

Alex tenses up and doesn't speak as they make their way to the stairway, and he doesn't speak as they climb up. In fact, he doesn't say a word until they come to the almost hidden staircase that leads to the unused classroom.

"Where are we going?" he asks, looking over his shoulder to the near-empty hallway they just walked down.

Gabby smiles. "Our secret clubhouse."

Sarah chuckles at that. The room is just a dusty old room with a teacher's desk and a few wooden chairs—it doesn't even have student desks anymore. She and Gabby have done a pretty decent job getting rid of the spiderwebs and the pixie nests, though.

Gabby sits in her usual spot, cross-legged on the teacher's desk, and Sarah leans against her project window, which now opens nearly two inches. This leaves Alex to either stand or sit in one of the rickety wooden chairs—he remains standing.

"What's going on?" Sarah asks, keeping her voice gentle. She'd been mad at Alex for ignoring her, but now, all she could feel for him was sadness. He had gone through something terrible, and it's only gotten worse for him since then. On the way home from the zoo on Saturday, Gabby had told her about the funeral, about the emotions she could feel rolling off of him. Even without Gabby's empathy, though, Sarah could see how much Alex was hurting.

He looks at Gabby, and, after deciding that she isn't leaving, he says, "I need your help with something, but it's going to be terrible."

Sarah cocks her head. "What kind of terrible?" A study group? Tutoring? Does he want her to help him cheat on his tests?

He hesitates and looks at his hands for a moment, seemingly deciding if he really wants to talk to her.

"Your aunt is Helen Jackson, right?"

Oh.

In a million years, Sarah could not have predicted this question.

She freezes, her eyes widening. "How do you know that name?" she asks, her voice coming out hushed and frantic when her voice sticks.

He looks toward the door as if someone might be listening, then looks at Gabby.

"Spit it out, Locklear," Gabby says, not unkindly, over a spoonful of yogurt.

He closes his eyes and sighs. "I did a spell. Last night. To see if I could get more information on what happened to...." he fades off without saying Cynthia's name.

Sarah waits for him to continue. Of course this isn't about school work. How could Alex possibly think about school work—or anything else, for that matter—when he'd watched someone get murdered?

"I saw her. Your aunt. In the vision. I didn't know it was her at the time, but I talked to a detective, and I looked her up, and it was her."

He's rambling, so Sarah interrupts, "I thought it might be."

He stops and collapses into a chair, which creaks with his

weight. "I didn't know who else to talk to. I thought you might... I don't know. Be able to find her?"

Her blood goes cold, and Sarah grits her teeth. "What do you mean by that?"

His eyes widen. "I don't mean anything. I just thought, since you're related, that maybe-"

"That maybe I'm on her side? That I'm harboring a murderer?" Her voice is too loud for this small space, but she doesn't care. She isn't sure why she's so angry, but her face is hot, and her heart is thudding hard in her chest. Of course, none of what she's saying makes any sense. Nobody could possibly think that she's a part of this. She wants to flee, to run out of the room and out of the building, but Gabby still has her hand, and she'd have to get past Alex.

Alex shakes his head, backpedaling. "I didn't mean to offend you. I just thought...." he considers his words before speaking again. "I didn't mean anything by it. I'm sorry."

Gabby is still holding Sarah's hand, and Sarah can feel herself cooling down under her touch. When she's no longer boiling over, Gabby lets her go.

"Come on," Gabby says through gritted teeth. "We have to get to class. Lit test today, remember?"

"What about—" Alex starts, but Sarah lifts a hand to stop him.

"We'll talk later."

IN POTIONS CLASS, ALEX APOLOGIZES AGAIN.
"I really didn't mean anything bad by it," he says while they go over the instructions for today's potion.

Sarah shakes her head. "No, I shouldn't have freaked out. I don't know where that even came from." She thought it over in Literature class while she was doodling on the back of her finished test, and her reaction was definitely unwarranted.

He stays silent for a moment, then changes the subject. "Thanks for the notes in Spiritual Magic, by the way." Every day, Sarah has been transcribing the notes twice. Once for herself, and another set for Alex. Her personal notes are just written with a pencil, but she's been using red and black and blue pens to color code his, hoping that it would be easier for him to follow along. She's even been writing annotations on the side that explain the technical aspects in more detail.

"Yeah, it's not a problem," she says. "I'm good at remembering information. I'm total shit at casting any sort of spell, though."

"Language, Miss Jackson," Mr. Thompson chides as he walks by their table. "No cursing."

"Sorry," she responds.

When their teacher is out of hearing range, Alex says, "I could help you with magic, if you need it."

Sarah tilts her head. Alex has been avoiding her for over a month, and then she exploded at him, and now he wants to help her? "Why?"

He shrugs. "I want to. Plus, maybe you can teach me how to actually learn Spiritual Magic theory so I don't flunk out of school my Junior year."

Sarah smiles just a little. "True. It's always better to flunk out your Senior year."

Alex laughs at that. "Exactly."

Sarah forgot how easy it can be to talk to Alex. She wishes that he wouldn't have ignored her for so long—the kiss they'd shared weeks ago is barely even a memory anymore, and his silence in class has been exhausting. She just wants to be friends with him. He's the only one who seems to truly understand how she feels here.

"Maybe we can study after school sometime." The words just fly out of her mouth before she thinks of them, but it's too late to take anything back.

A small smile plays across his lips, and she suddenly remembers exactly how soft those lips are. "I'd like that."

# CHAPTER EIGHTEEN
## Alex

ALEX EATS LUNCH IN THE ABANDONED CLASS-room with Sarah and Gabby. He doesn't recall being invited, but he feels as though he's supposed to be here.

He wants to talk about Cynthia's death. He wants someone to help him find out exactly what happened. Instead, they talk about classes, and Gabby tells him about their trip to the zoo over the weekend, mostly detailing how terrible it was to get all the faerie dragons out of her hair before they left, but also going over Sarah's bond with Hawthorne, the sassy forest dragon. She acts out her and Elizabeth dealing with her dragon problems whilst trying to make sure Sarah didn't get eaten, and he finds himself invested in the story, laughing at the image of a juvenile prairie dragon claiming someone's shirt as its pouch.

He doesn't want lunch to end—he's having too much fun, and he's able to shed his sadness for the short half-hour. He and Sarah walk to class together, and she clarifies a few parts of the story that Gabby had embellished on.

"Hawthorne was fifteen feet *tops*," she says. "Forest dragons don't even grow to be thirty feet. The females can be as big as twenty-two. He could be thirty feet long, but not tall. Mountain dragons, though..."

Alex is content to listen to her explain the differences between the dragon species. He barely even notices the stares he's still getting, as Sarah's face is aglow with excitement.

They don't get to talk during Spiritual Magic, but it turns out that their sixth hour classes are close to each other, so they walk together once again. Alex talks about his life in Kansas, being raised by both humans and faeries. "I used to swim in the lake with the nymph kids, and one time I almost drowned because they didn't get that I needed air."

Sarah sighs with longing. "That must have been amazing," she says. "I mean, not the almost drowning. The part about having so many people that care about you."

He doesn't have a chance to ask what she means by that, but he doesn't have to be an empath to see how sad her eyes are at that comment.

AFTER SCHOOL ENDS, ALEX WAITS WITH SARAH in the atrium until Gabby shows up. As he's walking away to spend the rest of the evening in his dorm, Gabby calls, "Hey, pretty boy. Are you following us back to my place or are we hanging out at yours?"

The question shocks him. Did the two have a chance to talk about him coming over when he wasn't around? Then, he considers her question. He would be in a good deal of trouble for having guests in his dorm on a school night, so he goes to his piece of crap Ford after figuring out the details with them. When Gabby's big black SUV pulls up to the dorm building, Sarah hops out and joins him in his Taurus.

"She drives like an old lady. But the Florida type, where speed limits don't exist, and neither do blinkers. I don't want you to get lost," she explains, orienting her feet around the junk that's all over the floor.

"Thanks," Alex says with a smile. When he woke up this morning, he'd planned on soliciting Sarah's help. He hadn't expected that he would be absorbed into her friend group and end up going to study with them after school, especially in less than a day.

He has friends at St. Merlin's. He and David hang out often, going to dinner in town rather than eating at the dorms. They even occasionally have lightsaber fights in the courtyard, coating steel poles with fire to be realistic. He counts Phillip as a friend, although most people wouldn't be friends with their teachers.

He hasn't made any new friends in a long time, though, and David is so busy trying to charm Kendall that Alex always turns into a third wheel. He's at ease around Sarah. Perhaps it has something to do with their similarly modest upbringing, or her easygoing humor. He wants to reach across and take her hand in his, lacing their fingers together, but that's not something friends do. He has to forget about their kiss at the midnight party.

Sarah skims through the radio stations while he drives, but she can't seem to find a channel she likes. He wordlessly offers the AUX cable, so she digs around in her bag and pulls out a Zune.

"That thing is ancient," he laughs.

She smiles, plugging it in to the radio. "It was my dad's. He got it when he was in college."

Alex sobers up immediately, and he wants to apologize, but she doesn't look upset by what he said, so they listen to her music the rest of the way. He even sings along to one of the showtunes that comes on, although she informs him that he isn't a musical nerd if the only Broadway plays he knows are Wicked and Into the Woods.

Sarah was right—Gabby is a terrifying driver. She was out of sight within moments of leaving St. Merlin's, and Sarah has to direct him the rest of the way to her house. When they finally pull into the driveway, Gabby is no longer in her car.

"Take your shoes off," Sarah tells him when they walk in the house. He follows her lead, placing his shoes next to hers on the rack.

He follows her through the house, and they wind their way upstairs. He traces his fingers along the black metal railing of Gabby's spiral staircase, amazed at the craftsmanship.

"Hey, guys. I was afraid you got lost," Gabby says, sitting cross-legged in bed, wearing mermaid-patterned leggings, a tank top, and a gold and pink flower crown.

"Nah," Sarah replies, "Alex just doesn't want to kill me, is all. Because he cares." His heart jolts at that even though he knows that she's just taunting her friend.

Gabby laughs heartily at that. He wants to sit, but he isn't sure where. Sarah is already spreading her domain on the couch, which she is obviously the ruler over, and Gabby has her books set all over her bed. After standing there for too long, he opts for the computer chair, setting his backpack on the floor.

"Nice house," he says, glancing at the telescope and star charts taking up nearly half the room.

"Yeah, Dad bought it like the day after he finished his residency. A big private hospital in the city offered him a job as a neurosurgeon, so he makes a ridiculous amount of money," Gabby says.

He nods. Most of the students at St. Merlin's are from rich families, so it makes sense that Gabby would be.

"What are you going to do with your thing?" Gabby asks him, wiggling her fingers to imply that there's fire shooting out of them.

He shrugs. "Most people think I should join the military, but I'm not really the fighting type." He has no idea what he wants to do, although everyone else expects him to have his whole future planned out.

They study for a while, and Alex tries to explain some of the techniques for Sarah's practical magic course, but she doesn't seem to understand them. After a while of failing to hold up his end of the deal, she explains the day's Spiritual Magic assignment to him, walking him through every question until he sort of understands the information. His brain is still a muddled mess, though, especially at the unexpected question about his future.

"Do you need a ride home?" he asks her after they've all given up on studying.

Sarah looks at Gabby, as if gauging her response, but Gabby is deeply entrenched in a book.

"I live way out in Chesterfield," Sarah says, her voice suddenly unsure.

"That's not a problem," he insists. He should be getting back to school, but he desperately wants to spend more time with her.

She looks at Gabby again, but a car horn lets out a short honk before she can reply. She stretches and looks out the window.

"Oh, my aunt is here. How did it get so late?" She checks her phone, then goes back to pack up her bag. "I'll walk you out if you're leaving, though. This house is kind of a maze."

# CHAPTER NINETEEN
## Alex

THEY GO TO GABBY'S HOUSE ALMOST EVERY DAY after school. Alex is delighted that, even after that first day, Sarah sits in his car, their fingers occasionally brushing. Can she feel the electricity that shoots through him every time, or is it just a part of his imagination?

It's best not to mention it. Friends don't talk about their unbearable attraction for each other, their chemistry.

He brings his ancient laptop, the one Dad gave him after upgrading for his graphic design job. Even though its functionality is normally questionable at best, Gabby's incredible WiFi tricks it into working decently. There must be some sort of spell on it, because this computer never lets him so much as edit a Word document without some sort of problem. After homework is done, he searches the web for any hint at why Helen murdered Cynthia. The memory is a knife slicing through his mind, so he distances himself internally to keep from getting hurt even more. The school psychiatrist informs him that it's called "compartmentalizing."

Gabby and Sarah sit together on the bed, hunched over piles and piles of books, some of which are borrowed from the school library, others ordered online. He makes himself small on the edge of the chaise lounge, his laptop hot on his legs.

He's reading an article about the death of Sarah's parents when she walks over and plops down next to him. His neck heats up, and he doesn't look at her. Should he close the tab?

She sighs and leans her head on his shoulder, like he's seen her do with Gabby so many times before. He's frozen, unsure of what move to make. Apparently this is something that some friends do.

"I remember this article," she says. Her voice is flat, emotionless. He can't see her face to evaluate her emotions.

After another moment, she continues, "They spelled Dad's name wrong. It's supposed to be Llogan with two L's."

He doesn't know what to say to that, so he just closes the tab so she doesn't have to look at it anymore.

"Guys?" Gabby calls before he can come up with something to say. Her voice is haunted.

Sarah turns her head, but it remains on his shoulder. Goosebumps raise up on his arm as her hair brushes against his skin.

"Did you find something?" he asks.

She lifts her head from the book, her eyes wide.

"What is it?" Sarah asks, her breath tickling his throat. He has to resist scrunching his neck and laughing at the sensation.

Gabby turns the book around, and he recognizes the symbol on the page instantly. It's a simple design, a circle with a line through it and a V at one side and what appears to be a capital A on the other, the points connecting with the line.

"I've seen that before," Sarah says, standing up and joining her back at the bed. She studies the symbol for another moment, her arms wrapped around her torso.

"What is it?" Alex asks. It's the same symbol that had been carved into Cynthia's wrist. Nausea roils through him, but he keeps it down.

Gabby says, "It's apparently used to summon demons, I think?"

Sarah shivers, but nobody asks why.

"More specifically," Gabby says, "It's a common sigil needed to summon an unholy power."

Sarah has her eyes closed now. He has to ask now. "That symbol was on Cynthia." His throat closes up, but he has to continue. "Where have you seen it before?"

She opens her mouth to answer, but nothing comes out, and a look of confusion comes across her face. "I don't remember."

"What do you mean?" Gabby asks, setting the book down, but not before bookmarking the page.

Sarah blows air out, and she doesn't look at either of them when she answers. "It's like when a word is right on the tip of your tongue, but you're thinking too hard and it won't come out. But with my memory. I know the symbol, but it's like there's a locked door."

"Then it's probably pretty important," Alex says, his voice steadier than his mind. He will never forget seeing this marking on Cynthia, and he can't imagine where Sarah would see it and just forget about it. It's like how he couldn't remember Helen's face after Cynthia died, not until he looked through Cynthia's memory. Something had happened to his own mind to lock it away.

They do more research on that specific symbol and demon summoning, and Alex finds a website that lists different demonic symbols. He instantly recognizes the rest, four symbols used to summon a demon. It specifies that all four are needed.

"Why would she want to summon a demon?" Sarah asks, her voice cracking. She's shivering heavily now, and Alex feels the need to reach out, to wrap his arms around her. He sits on his hands to keep from touching her. No tears fall from her eyes, but she's suddenly distant.

"I think we need to stop," Gabby says, her voice authoritative.

They can't just stop. He has to know what happened to

Cynthia, why she was murdered. He has to do something about it. "But—"

"No. We're done." Gabby's gaze flicks to Sarah for just a moment before her face hardens, daring him to question her. "This is too much. It's too dangerous."

He sighs. "Okay."

He should tell them the rest. That he did a ritual to see what happened. That Helen had been saying something. He can't remember her exact words, but it seemed like ingredients for a spell. Something big if it involves killing a girl. When he sees the look on Sarah's face, though, he keeps his mouth shut. Her eyes are scrunched shut, and her breathing is rapid as she clenches the comforter beneath her.

"Okay," he says again, but this time, he means it.

The police will figure out what's going on. They have all the information he does. This isn't something he can fix. It's not something he should try to fix.

He makes himself useful and goes to the kitchen, bringing Sarah a glass of icy water. When he returns, she's no longer shaking, although she drinks the whole glass in one go.

"Thanks," she whispers, averting her gaze. That avoidance pinches his heart.

"It's no problem," he says earnestly. He wants to ask what's wrong, but he doesn't. He's done enough harm today. He takes a photo of the symbol in Gabby's book, sending it to the officer in charge of the case.

It could be important.

By the time he drives Sarah home, she's back to her cheerful self, the same confident girl that flirted with him the first day of school, the girl who kissed him at the party. He puts everything bad out of his mind for the too-short trip. The whole situation is out of his hands. Maybe it's okay if he actually tries to enjoy being a teenager instead.

He really has to let the kiss go, but he can't help but focus on how she doesn't move her hand when her fingers rest against his on the center console on the drive home.

# CHAPTER TWENTY
## Sarah

WHEN THE DANCE BECAME TOO CLOSE TO IG-nore, Sarah suggested during lunch that they all go as a group. "You're renting a limo anyway," she pointed out to Gabby. "It would be kind of a waste if it was just you, me, and Kelly."

That's why, now, there are six teenagers getting ready in Gabby's house. Alex and David were directed to the guest bedroom downstairs to get ready, and the girls—Sarah, Gabby, Kelly, and Kendall—are getting ready in the attic. Their gowns are hanging up on the sturdy curtain rod, golden evening light trickling in between the cracks. The golden sun dances off the delicate fabrics, a rainbow of col-or lined up.

Gabby is doing everyone's makeup, which is how Sarah discovered the suitcase full of professional makeup in her closet. Sarah was first, so she's waiting on the bed, wrap-

ping herself in a faux fur throw to cover up the special bra
and underwear that Elizabeth bought when they went dress
shopping, a nude, strapless bra and a thin pair of "seamless"
nude underwear. She'd tried putting her jeans back on, but
Gabby had yanked them out of her hands. "You don't want
seam lines all down your legs!" she exclaimed.

Her dress is blush pink, long ivory lace sleeves contrasting with the fact that it only goes down to her knees. On her
shopping trip with Gabby and Elizabeth, she had to assert
herself to keep her feet out of a pair of platform stilettos, so
she has a pair of navy blue kitten heels with ribbons that
weave around her ankles. She wishes she could be wearing
it right now instead of her underwear and a blanket, but
Kelly insisted that the chiffon skirt would wrinkle if she sits
in it for too long.

Sarah is glad to finally be meeting Kelly. She and her family live in Chicago, and, as soon as she got out of school
yesterday, she drove the five hours to Gabby's house. Those
two are going to be wearing red gowns made of the same
chiffon and lace fabrics, Gabby's a floor-length mermaid cut,
and Kelly's a knee-length strapless number. Gabby's black
hair is piled high on her head, decorated with gold vines
and flowers, and Kelly is wearing her box braids down, a
huge gold bow tying it where it meets in the back.

Kendall is excited, practically bouncing in her seat while
Gabby applies her fake eyelashes. "I usually don't do these
kinds of things," she'd told Sarah when they met up at the

house. Her dress has been in a bag since she arrived, and Kelly and Gabby have been buzzing to see it. All she's said is that it's blue.

"Blue must look amazing with your eyes," Kelly says over the bobby pins in her mouth, putting half of Kendall's layered blonde hair up into an elegant bun, the rest cascading elegantly over her shoulder.

Sarah worries at a frayed thread coming off the blanket, her mind trailing to the dragon egg that's been sitting in her fireplace for a month and a half now. Should she give it to Elizabeth to take to the zoo? Surely it would do better under the care of its father instead of a teenage girl.

"Dress time!" Gabby announces, interrupting her train of thought. The dance started five minutes ago, but she's insistant that they can't be there on time. The limo her parents are paying for won't even be at the house for another ten minutes.

Sarah is the first one in her dress, and Gabby laces up the back with a satin ribbon. The lace is luxuriously soft along her arms, which is why she chose it—all the other dresses she tried on were too itchy. She feels like a princess as Kelly puts her into her shoes and Kendall helps Gabby keep the ribbon as straight as possible.

Gabby has her shoes on before her gown, and Sarah stands by as Kelly buttons up what must be fifty small, round buttons up the back.

Kelly's dress has high-necked lace, but Gabby just has to

zip it up in one swift motion. Then, she simply steps into her black platform stilettos.

They all gather around excitedly when it's Kendall's turn. She blushes and unzips the dress bag.

The dress is baby blue, and layers and layers of tulle and chiffon make up the skirt. The bodice is simple, a corset top with long lace sleeves similar to Sarah's. This one needs all three of them—Sarah holds up the skirts so that they don't get stepped on, and Gabby and Kelly hold the back open so that Kendall can step into it.

When they've finally got her laced in, they take a step back.

"You look amazing," Sarah breathes.

"Like an actual princess!" Kelly gushes.

Gabby smiles. "It's perfect on you. Definitely worth the suspense."

The boys are waiting for them at the bottom of the grand staircase that leads to the foyer, a part of the house that's rarely used since they usually come in through the garage. Gabby and Kelly walk down first, and Alex and David hoot and holler and take pictures as they pose like models. From her hiding spot around the corner, Sarah's eyes trace over Alex in his slim-fit navy suit with a pale pink shirt and skinny floral tie. She imagines pulling his face down to hers by that tie for a second kiss. David is in a white tuxedo jacket with black lapels, a white shirt, a black bowtie, and black slacks. She gets why Kendall is so into him. He looks great in his St. Merlin's uniform, but in a tux, he's irresistable.

Next goes Sarah, and David whistles at her, but Alex just stares. She smirks just a little as she takes one step at a time, thankful for her very flat sandals. When she gets to the bottom, Alex holds out his hand to help her down the last step. She takes it, and her skin burns where it touches his.

"You look incredible," he breathes, then blushes when he seems to realize what he said.

Kendall gets to make the final entrance, grander than all the rest, taking the steps carefully. David's jaw drops, and he doesn't comment.

When she gets to the bottom of the stairs, she looks up at him under her heavily-lashed eyes.

"Kendall," he says, his voice quiet.

"Do you like it?" she asks shyly.

Instead of replying, he leans down and places the gentlest of kisses on her pink lips.

Sarah glances away, looking to Gabby instead. At some point, presumably before Kendall came down the stairs, Gabby took out her phone, and now she's taking as many pictures as it will let her.

"Called it," Alex whispers in Sarah's ear, and she has to suppress a laugh.

They pile into the limo, a sleek, stretched out black car that seems too long for roads. Gabby really knows how to do everything in style.

Suddenly, she's nervous. The only dance Sarah has been

to was her freshman year winter formal. Penny had told Will to ask Sarah to the dance, and they awkwardly swayed to the radio-friendly versions of songs their teachers picked out. They didn't talk after that, although Will's brother had to give Sarah a ride home.

ST. MERLIN'S PAYS TOP DOLLAR FOR THEIR EVENTS, so instead of being held in the gym like a normal school, the fall formal is at the St. Louis City Museum, an industrial-aged warehouse transformed into an attraction. The school must have had the option to book a single floor, but instead, the entire building is set up for the dance.

Their's isn't the first limo to pull around to the main entrance, and a line of expensive cars and limousines waits behind them, as well. An employee of the museum opens the door for them, helping those wearing dresses to step out of the vehicle without losing their modesty.

"I feel like a celebrity," Sarah whispers to Alex.

A photographer waits just inside, snapping pictures of them individually and then as a group before they can continue forward. It's all a rush of being pushed from person to person until a pair of attendants open the secondary doors.

Sarah is breathless. Seeing the finery and elegance of everyone at St. Merlin's has been overwhelming, and she expects the same from this building. She's picturing gold crown molding and filigree, and perhaps a fountain of champagne and marble floors. Instead, the interior is a mesh of found things, tiles from different places lining the floors, hand-painted railings lining the bannister up the mosaic staircase. Nothing matches, and Sarah adores it.

"Welcome to the St. Louis City Museum," a woman in an elegant black gown tells them. "We don't provide maps, and we encourage you to get lost. I'd also like to let you know that you have full access to the world aquarium during your visit this evening."

Sarah grins, taking Alex's hand in hers with excitement. When she realizes what she's done, she looks to him, unsure, but he simply tightens his hand around hers with a small smile.

"We're gonna go find the food," Kendall says, craning her neck around David to address the group.

The two make their way up the staircase, Kendall's gown trailing behind her like Cinderella.

That leaves Gabby, Kelly, Sarah, and Alex standing next to the stairs, unsure of where to go from here.

After a moment of silence, Gabby says, "I'm thinking ball pit."

Sarah is confused but curious. Gabby is the only one in their group who's been here before, so everyone follows her through the building and outside, where a crisp wind greets them. Sure enough, there's a giant ball pit surrounded by nets and adult-sized treehouses to climb through. Gabby and Alex jump right in, and Sarah and Kelly look at each other conspiratorially before climbing precariously up the ropes to a ledge, where they have a better vantage point. Sarah is impressed at Kelly's skill in climbing a rope ladder in heels.

There's a tense moment of silence as they all glare at each other, now enemies in the most childish battle ever. Sarah slowly rolls a ball into her hand from her crouch, aiming it right at Alex. When she releases it, it hits him square in the chest.

The war is short—quickly, Kelly and Sarah realize that they don't have enough plastic balls to sustain their position, and they can't seem to catch any that Gabby and Alex are throwing at them. They all laugh as they go back inside, ending up in the second floor ballroom.

The gold-detailed vintage room is a flurry of color as the other students in more expensive dresses than hers dance to the music, and Sarah is completely out-skilled here. She usually enjoys dancing, but that's mainly when she and Gabby are bored of studying and romp around her room to Kesha, not the skilled waltzing that her classmates—and, before long, Gabby and Kelly—are performing.

"Do you want to dance?" Alex asks, holding his arm out for Sarah to take. She looks to him, then to the crowd of skilled dancers. He looks so sure of himself that she doesn't want to disappoint him and ruin his night by embarrassing them both.

"I don't know how," she admits, ashamed.

He laughs. "Neither do I. But we can try."

She grins and takes his arm, and he pulls her to the swirling dancefloor.

Their steps are clumsy, and Sarah steps on his toes more than a few times, but they almost keep up with their classmates as they imitate their movements to the best of their abilities. She doesn't care, though, because either way, her body is pressed up against Alex, his hand gentle on her waist.

After two songs, she drags him back off the dancefloor, out of breath and red-faced.

"Are you okay?" he asks, searching her face, his eyebrows pushed together with concern. She wants to put her thumb right on the crease between them, but she's basically a professional at not touching him whenever she feels the urge. It's not a profession she wants to keep, though. She's seen the way he looks at her, felt the heat when he leaves his hand against her's in the car.

She smiles. "I'm alright. Although if I don't eat soon, I'm gonna starve to death."

They find the food upstairs after getting turned around through an ancient Egyptian-style walkway. Dinner is a buffet with a mixture of pricy rich person food and barbeque.

Sarah tries a tiny spoonful of caviar out of curiosity, and as soon as she tastes it, she loads a plate with ribs, mashed potatoes, and fries instead.

Alex makes up a cheeseburger with fries, and they find that Gabby and Kelly are already at a table, although Sarah never saw them leave the ballroom. She and Alex must have been lost for longer than she thought.

Sarah devours her food, and Gabby has to rush to put a black cloth napkin in the neckline of her dress to keep sauce from getting all over her.

"You do not want to try getting that out of something so light," Gabby says sternly.

Sarah rolls her eyes, and Alex tucks a napkin into his collar—"Like a member of civilized society," he says, putting on a bad English accent and jokingly looking down his nose at her. She wipes one finger across his cheek, leaving a smear of barbeque sauce behind.

"Perfect," she says as Kelly and Gabby laugh as he pretends to be outraged.

After eating dinner, Kelly and Gabby go back to the ballroom, but Sarah and Alex agree to check out the aquarium.

It's not quite what they expect—it's pretty small, and it only takes them five minutes to walk around the whole place, two of which are spent looking at the round alligator tank that takes up the majority of the space.

They go to the first floor, a mosaic ocean area, where an open-mouthed whale statue spans across half the room beneath a kelp ceiling. The mouth of the whale is the entrance to the cave system. The stone caves are fake, of course, but Sarah allows herself to imaging that they're real, that she's a princess escaping the castle after a siege.

Sarah finds herself alone after Alex gets distracted by the

sign indicating a ten-story slide, and she walks through a hidden archway and ends up under a waterfall, tracing her fingers along the teal mosaics. She watches groups of students standing around talking to each other, but they don't seem to notice her behind the fake vines, freshwater aquarium, and waterfall.

A pair of strong arms wraps around her, and Alex's voice is in her ear. "Found you," he says, his voice husky.

She twists around slowly, letting herself stay trapped in his arms. His hair is mussed from all the running around, and he's loosened his tie and unbuttoned the top button of his shirt. He is, at this moment, unbearably sexy.

"I want to kiss you," he whispers, so she stands on the tips of her toes and presses her lips to his, gentle as a butterfly's wings. The kiss is the complete opposite of their first kiss at the party. Where that had been wild and desperate, a moment of spontaneity between near strangers, this kiss is the gentle response to weeks of careful flirtation. When she pulls away, his eyes are closed, and there's a small smile playing across his face.

She leans her head on his shoulder, wrapping her arms around him. She buries her face into his neck so that he doesn't see her blushing.

# CHAPTER TWENTY-ONE
## Alex

A LEX IS UNSTEADIED BY THE KISS.
His friendship with Sarah has been tenuous at best, hanging by a thread after they kissed at the faerie party, the event that he's tried to push out of his mind because of his loss of memory after her leaving. Weeks of growing closer, of small touches and affections here and there, have slipped in, invaded his senses. He didn't realize just how consumed he is by her until he saw her in the grotto, the waterfall spraying her face gently as she watched everyone else at the party.

The kiss had been barely there, the hint of something more, the gentlest press of Sarah's lips on his. Alex can't help but thrill at the thought of it, his heart racing at the possibility of getting to do it again. Whatever they have is far deeper than the gentle flirtations, than the spontaneous kiss they shared weeks ago.

Her breath is hot on his neck, and he holds her tightly to him for a moment before relaxing his arms so that they're just resting against her back. They stand there for what could be an eternity, but it isn't nearly long enough. A shiver rips through Sarah at the gentle spray of the waterfall, so he pulls away. She groans and crushes herself back into him, and he can feel her trembling.

He smiles and presses his lips against the top of her head. "Maybe we should go somewhere warmer."

Her voice is muffled against him when she says, "I am somewhere warmer."

He laughs and pulls away, and this time, she doesn't protest.

He leads her out of the tunnels, their fingers intertwined and they somehow end up on the second floor. Despite being cold, she goes outside, climbing through the connected treehouses until she gets as far from the building as possible. Alex has to hurry to keep up, worried that she's going to trip over her flimsy shoes.

She sighs as she collapses to the ground inside one of the treehouses, and he joins her. Once he's leaning against the circular wall, Sarah rests against him, shivering once again.

He removes his suit jacket, a slow process since Sarah is lying across him, and uses it as a blanket over her.

The music inside is muffled by glass and brick and the brisk October night, and Sarah's breathing slows as she relaxes against Alex's chest.

175

He almost thinks she's asleep, when she whispers, "Why do you like me?"

He's surprised at the inquiry. He's been spending most weekday afternoons with Sarah and Gabby for a couple weeks, and his feelings have been getting ever clearer to him. He should be asking her this question. He's the one who's an unstable mess who was drugged at a party one week and witnessed a murder the next.

He lifts his head to look at her, to see if her face will reveal what she's really asking. He's shocked to find tears streaming down her face, glistening in the faint light that trickles into the treehouse with them.

"Hey, what's wrong?" he asks, his hand fluttering up to wipe the tears away as best he can. His heart races. What did he do wrong?

"I just...I don't know why you like me," she says, her voice hitching. That hitch, the slight tremble, brings him a revelation. That day at Gabby's house. He hadn't recognized the symptoms in her at the time, but he does now. Of course she has anxiety. This fear that she has, the uncertainty of his affection, it isn't real. She feels it, of course, but it's her mind playing tricks on her.

He squeezes her in a hug and kisses the top of her head. "There are a lot of reasons," he says trying to keep his voice reassuring.

She sits up and looks at him, her eyebrows upturned with pain. "But why?"

He sits up, too, realizing that he's slid down the wall a bit since getting here. He lifts a hand and rests it against her wet cheek, and she leans into his touch. "You're funny," he says. "You always make smart-ass remarks in class that make me laugh." The barest hint of a smile makes its way across her lips, but she's still trembling. "And you're kind. You gave me your notes when I was gonna bomb Spiritual Magic after...After everything happened." He sighs. "That's what sort of woke me up. After everything. Gave me a chance to breathe again. I thought you were gonna talk to me about the party, but you didn't. You never pressured me to talk, you just knew that I was hurting, and you did what you could to help."

She buries her face in his chest and lets out a deep breath, and the shaking stops. "I'm such a mess," she whispers.

A short, humorless laugh bursts out of him. "Pretty sure I'm a bigger mess than you. By a mile." She sits up, pulling away from him enough that he can see her face. A streetlight from outside streams in and highlights her curled hair, which is starting to come loose from its bonds. Her eyes still shine with tears, but she accepts the answer, leaning in and kissing him again.

Their earlier kiss had been small, a drop of rain, and now he sees the storm that it had warned of. Much like the first kiss weeks ago, she smashes her lips against his, and he puts one hand around the back of her neck to pull her even closer. He wants to run his hand through her hair, but it's put up with dozens of pins and too much hairspray—he doesn't want to hurt her. Still, he twirls one escaped piece of hair around a finger.

Her hands are resting in her lap, but she uses one to grab his tie, holding him close, as though he might try to escape, but nothing that could happen right now could take him away from her. They sit there, locked in a desperate kiss, consuming each other's energy, their breath coming in gasps as they forget to breathe for moments at a time.

"Sarah?" someone calls from the direction of the building. In the haze, it takes a moment for Alex to realize that it's Gabby's voice.

Sarah jerks away, and Alex lets out a small moan. "Don't," he begs, brushing a thumb over her cheek and leaning forward to kiss her neck.

She pulls back and smiles, tears no longer in evidence as she leans into his warm touch. "I have to."

She gives his jacket back and walks away, but not before laying another sweet kiss on his lips. Instead of going with her, he hides in the treehouse for a few minutes longer. He'll find her when she isn't preoccupied with Gabby. After a few minutes of sitting in a daze, he stands up and stretches to return to the throng of students.

When he gets back to the party, Sarah is gone.

# CHAPTER TWENTY-TWO
## Sarah

SARAH'S LEGS ARE SHAKY AS SHE MAKES HER way across the ropes that lead to the main doors. The night has been cool, but now, a frigid wind rips across the playground, rocking her for just a moment. She grips the ropes lining either side of the walkway, and she's shaking with cold by the time she gets to the other end. She wishes for a moment that she'd kept Alex's coat.

Gabby is waiting for her, eyes wide. Her knuckles are white against the door that she's holding open.

"Sarah," she says, her voice hushed, her eyes darting around. "Mark is here. He says you need to go."

Sarah glances behind Gabby to see that more than a few people are staring at her. She reaches up to feel her hair to find out if it's out of place, but Gabby's words finally sink in. She freezes up, looking back to the treehouse where she'd just been kissing Alex. She wants to call to him, to bring him wherever she's going. He didn't come with me, she thinks, her heart twinging. She looks back to Gabby, setting her gaze hard. Mark isn't one of the teachers who volunteered to chaperone this event.

"Let everyone else know I had to go, okay?" she says.

Gabby nods and leads her down the main staircase, which features the intricate mosaic of a mermaid riding a sea dragon, to the main entrance, where Mark stands, pacing in a sweatshirt and jeans.

"Oh, thank God," he whispers, rushing up and hugging her. She can hear his heart pounding in his chest.

She pulls away. "What's going on? Where are we going?" Her heart thrums with fear—Mark and Elizabeth have been encouraging her to come to the fall formal ever since she first brought it up, and now that she's here, Mark is making her leave early. Something must be horribly wrong. "Where's Elizabeth?" she whispers, her voice breaking.

"Elizabeth is fine," he assures. "She's at home. We have to go. Now." A scream at the other end of the hallway makes him snap his neck around, a hand reaching out to take Sarah's wrist. However, the noise is just a girl, one of the door attendants, laughing and dodging the other as he goes to stick a finger in her ear.

Mark drops Sarah's wrist and rests his hand on her lower back to steer her toward his Pontiac, which is parked right along the curb where the limo had dropped her off earlier.

"We have to get moving," he insists, closing her door after helping her into the stout vehicle. His fear is so palpable that she locks the doors. It only takes him a moment to walk around the car, but she doesn't want to risk whatever is freaking him out so badly. When he gets to the driver door, she unlocks it for him.

He jumps in, locking the doors again before even putting on his seatbelt. So her fear had been warranted. His hands shake when he puts them on the steering wheel, and he has to take a deep breath to steady himself once the car is running.

"What's going on?" she asks meekly.

He peels off the curb, racing through the city streets. Her body is pressed into the seat with momentum, and she grips the handle of the door as hard as she can. He doesn't answer her until the car is flying down the interstate.

"Helen has killed someone else."

"What? When?" she demands. She wants to look online, to check the news and see if she can find a news story that points to her aunt from the past few days.

He glances at her, hesitating. "At the dance."

All of the air seems to get sucked out of the car at this revelation. Her head goes light, and a whooshing sound takes over her ears. She can't open her mouth to speak, but she's not even sure what she would say. Tonight.

"Everyone there is safe," he says. "It seems that she disappeared after she was caught. There's a barrier keeping everyone out of the museum."

"How did this happen?" Sarah says, her voice barely a whisper. She wants to throw up, but she's too afraid of the possibility of Mark stopping the car, of Helen appearing right there on the side of the road.

Mark gives her a pained look, and she can see that he's just barely keeping it together. Forcing himself to be brave, to be the adult. "They think the girl was parked too far away. When she left, she got out of the barrier before getting to safety."

*Someone died tonight.* The thought takes up every ounce of space in her head. She doesn't know who it was—she hadn't looked for anyone besides Gabby. What if it was Kendall? Or Kelly? Then, guilt rushes through her, tears springing to her eyes. She shouldn't be relieved if she finds out that she didn't know the girl. While she'd been busy kissing Alex, someone else was dying.

Every sound, every light that flashes by, is agony. Voices whisper to her in the night. They tell her to run, run as far as she can. *She'll still catch you*, one says as they pass under a streetlight. They're coming from all around her, prodding at her consciousness. The night closes in, and the entire world is condensed to what suddenly feels like an overly flimsy vehicle and whatever can be seen by the headlights. Everything else is just paper, a backdrop of a city that is letting terrible things happen.

*You're going to die*, another voice says, right in her right ear. She can feel its hot breath tickling the hairs at the nape of her neck. She twists around, her heart jumping in her throat, but there's nobody there. Her mind must be playing tricks on her, the thought of Helen's demented form haunting the back of her mind.

Because of this, it takes her a while to realize that the drive is taking too long—Mark isn't going directly home. He goes well past the exit, then turns onto a back highway, across to a different interstate, which he then takes back to the northern side of the city, and then he takes another backroad to get to Chesterfield. Even then, he doesn't go back to the house until he gets a call from Elizabeth.

When he answers, Elizabeth's voice comes over the speakers. His bluetooth must be hooked up to his updated stereo. "Alright," she says. "We've got a path for you." She directs him through the streets, and Sarah's ears are popping as if a big storm is coming in. She has to stretch her jaw to get rid of the feeling, but it only gets worse.

"Cloaking spell," Mark says when he sees her digging a finger in her ear. "It's very powerful, but they have annoying side effects." He speaks louder, to Elizabeth. "We're almost there. Be ready to let us in."

Sarah looks around to see that they're in their familiar neighborhood, and Mark speeds up at the lack of cars. He has to hit the brakes hard to make the turn into the driveway, throwing Sarah against the seatbelt at the sudden loss of momentum. The moment they get through their iron gate, the popping is gone. Instead, the air feels static, charged.

Three police cars are sitting in the driveway, and Mark has to guide the Pontiac carefully so he isn't blocking them in. The lights aren't flashing, but the porch light illuminates two uniformed figures standing by the door.

"Why are they here?" Sarah asks, but Mark doesn't answer. She climbs out of the car, stopping by the officers, but they're too busy with their radios to acknowledge her. When Mark joins, he ushers her inside, where a woman in a suit is talking to Elizabeth. She has a shiny gold badge on a long chain around her neck, but she isn't wearing a uniform like the other two.

When Mark closes the front door, Elizabeth's head turns to them. At the same time, the whispers that have been taunting Sarah the whole time go silent. The sudden quiet is jarring, and she has to pause to steady herself.

Elizabeth rushes up and hugs her, just like Mark had when he saw her at the museum. Since she moved here, Sarah hasn't received physical affection from either of them, so both of them hugging her tonight only heightens her fear.

"Sarah Jackson?" the woman asks, her voice serious. It reminds her of the time she was sent to the principal's office her sophomore year, and, despite knowing she's done nothing wrong, she cringes.

"Yes?"

The officer looks at Elizabeth and Mark, hesitant.

"I need someone to tell me what's going on," Sarah says, her voice firm and louder than usual. Everyone is so careful around her. Her face is heating up, a scream building in her throat, but she keeps her face flat.

"Miss Jackson, I'm Detective Harris. I'm the lead on the case regarding Cynthia Rowell's death." She pauses, but her eyes stay on Sarah, evaluating her. "We have reason to believe that your aunt, Helen Jackson, may attempt to cause you harm."

She waits for a reaction, but Sarah doesn't know what is expected of her. She found out half an hour ago that her aunt murdered a second person after being missing for six years. Both of the girls who died were St. Merlin's students. There have been voices telling her all night that she isn't safe. She'd seen Helen on the street and, possibly, at the faerie party. Is she supposed to be surprised?

"Sarah," Detective Harris says, pulling out a phone. "Do you recognize this image?"

She isn't sure what she's expecting, but it isn't this. There are the same symbols that she and her friends have been researching for weeks. Except, instead of being drawn in Gabby's book or in an online article, these are carved into a piece of pearlescent white hide that gleams with the flash of a phone's camera. The symbols should be difficult to distinguish with all the blood that has soaked into the creature's fur, but she recognizes them instantly.

Detective Harris doesn't wait for her to reply. Sarah's face must say enough. "These images were pulled from Llogan Jackson's phone shortly after your aunt went missing."

Dad's phone. These pictures are from Dad's phone. The memories begin to pull at her, seeping past the wall in her mind. The photos must have been taken at the gas station, moments before the accident. There'd been no time otherwise. Moments after pulling back onto the road, the truck had been hit by a semi. She shudders.

"I need to lie down," she whispers, her head suddenly spinning once again. Elizabeth moves her to the couch immediately, where she curls up. The scratchy old throw pillow is cool against her cheek.

Detective Harris talks to Mark and Elizabeth for just a minute or two longer, then the front door clicks shut.

She falls asleep while Elizabeth and Mark are talking behind the couch in hushed tones. She should be more interested in what they're saying, but she's just too tired to care.

*S*HE ISN'T QUITE ASLEEP WHEN SHE HEARS THE *unicorn screaming.*

*She remembers Dad carrying her in so she could sleep on the couch, and she remembers her parents making their way to the guest room for the night. Despite the past few hours of darkness, it isn't actually that late. The clock on the oven, which she can just see from her makeshift bed, read 9:35. Darkness is early to rise during an Arkansas winter—the sun escaped past the horizon before six was even a consideration.*

*The house is quiet, the old Victorian creaking occasionally with winter winds, a faucet dripping down the hall. She hears a mouse* scurrying away, and then she hears the scream.

Sarah has grown up with horses. Her father taught her how to plant her feet in the stirrups, and her mother taught her how to get back on when she falls. She heard stallions fighting and screeching at each other when they were mistakenly put together in the horrible kill pen at the auction, and she's heard mares keening across sunny pastures for their foals who were venturing too far.

This is not the same thing.

This is a desperate plea, a fearful cry. It calls to her, begging to be saved, for the pain to stop. Sarah bolts off the couch, slipping on her old, muddy boots before sprinting out the front door.

When they were loading it into their old stock trailer that morning, Mom told her to stay away from the unicorn. "That horn is sharp." It has been raised in an expensive stable, fed expensive hay, and worked under the most expensive tack. It only makes sense that the spoiled creature would require expensive training, and Helen is the best in the midwest. Her stables are worth five times as much as her house, the house where she and Sarah's father were raised. In the daytime, it's a bustling network of stable hands and trainers and horses, some less magical than others, but all very expensive. In the dark, though, something else creeps in. An energy that raises the hairs on the back of her neck even on normal nights.

Sarah leaps off the porch, skipping the wooden steps. The barn is mostly dark, but the big metal door has been slid open and left that way. This would be a normal sight during the daytime because of all the foot traffic, but at night, when the stable hands *and trainers have all gone home and the horses are settling in their stalls, the door should be secured shut. Even if someone is out here, they would usually take the normal door to the side. The only reason to take the main door would be if horses need to be moved.*

*Sarah makes it halfway to the barn when she sees the unicorn, which is being dragged out of its stall. Although it's bracing its legs against the ground, Helen is still able to force it out of its stall, across the concrete barn floor, and out the door. It appears to be wearing intricate red tack, but when the redness drips wet and slick across the floor, Sarah gets sick. It's bleeding. There is so much blood, more than she ever thought she might see.*

SHE WAKES UP IN HER OWN ROOM, THE SUN BLARing through the window and her dress bunching uncomfortably beneath her. Her phone is buzzing incessantly, and she looks at it to see Gabby's photo grinning at her—a selfie Gabby had taken and assigned to her phone during their first slumber party. The memory Sarah dreamt is already ebbing away, although her heart is racing.

"Hello?" she croaks, blinking away as much of the morning as she can, and she sees from the vintage clock on her nightstand that it's nearly noon.

"Sarah, are you okay?" Gabby asks, her voice hushed.

The previous night snaps to the forefront of her mind like a rubber band. "Oh my god, I didn't text you." She stands up to go change out of her dress, which feels ridiculous the morning after. She no longer feels like a princess, just a stupid girl in a dress that she could have died in. "Yes, I'm fine. Everything is fine," she lies.

She isn't sure how to tell her best friend that Helen most definitely wants to kill her. She pulls on a pair of forest green leggings and an oversized yellow sweater that Elizabeth had given her, claiming it didn't look as good on her. It was a lie, of course. Everything looks good on Elizabeth.

"Oh thank god," Gabby says. A familiar male voice mumbles something in the background, and Gabby takes the phone away from her face to reply, assuring him that everything is fine. "Alex looked everywhere for you before Kelly found him. He had no idea where you went."

Sarah's heart drops. With everything that happened last night, she'd forgotten to text him, too. The memories of their time together trickle in—the dancing, the exploring, and finally, the kissing. She puts a hand up to her lips and smiles despite the horrible situation. They'd kissed—for real this time, not just a random kiss at a late-night party. Although they'd made out pretty heavily in the treehouse, the kiss that sticks in her mind is the one under the waterfall, his lips gentle on hers as he wondered if it would be alright.

She freezes. What if he's mad at her? She should've texted him as she was leaving, or on the drive, or as soon as she got home. She'd had so many opportunities.

"Can I talk to him?" she asks, suddenly timid.

There's a rustling on the other line as Gabby passes the

phone over.

"Sarah." His voice is exhausted and gruff, but not angry. The sound floods through her, warming her cheeks and pushing away some of the darkness. "I'm so glad you're alright."

She can practically feel his arms around her, comforting her. She still wishes she had his jacket, just so she could wrap it around herself and get the courage to speak to him, to tell him everything that's going on over the phone.

"Can you come over?"

# CHAPTER TWENTY-THREE
## Sarah

IT'S WEIRD TO HAVE ALEX IN HER HOME. SHE'D never been allowed to have boys over whilst living with Uncle John, and here Alex is, standing in the doorway to her room. Gabby and Kelly stayed home, Elizabeth has a shift at the zoo all day, and Mark is doing some grading in his home office, so they're alone. She wants to go to him, to wrap herself in his arms and kiss him until she forgets about the death and danger.

"Are you sure you're alright?" he asks. She'd been worried the whole time he was driving over that he'd be mad at her, that his tone over the phone had merely *sounded* okay. Instead, he looks like he wants to come to her as much as she wants to go to him. Still, they're so far apart while she sits on the floor by the fireplace.

"I..." She doesn't want to lie to him. She takes a deep breath. "I'm terrified, honestly. There's so much happening."

He nods, then finally walks over, sitting next to her and wrapping an arm around her shoulder. She leans her head against his shoulder and closes her eyes, pretending for just a moment that this is a normal day, that they're a normal couple that does normal things like sitting by the fire on a chilly Sunday afternoon.

"Sarah," he says, his voice slow, careful.

She doesn't open her eyes, but she twists her head just enough to kiss his neck softly. "Mmm?"

"Why is there a dragon egg in your fireplace?" She freezes.

He reaches into the fireplace, and Sarah tries to warn him not to touch it. The fire doesn't hurt him, though. He lays his hand on the egg, his thumb rubbing gently against it, the same way he rubs her hand when their fingers are intertwined. A small smile falls across his face, his eyes glistening with the light of the fire.

"I can feel it moving," he says, looking up at Sarah, his face now a picture of childlike joy. During their study sessions, whenever he talks about his dog back home, he gets excited, his hands animated as he tells story after story about it. Now, he has the same expression across his face, and it causes Sarah to grin.

"What's it feel like?" she asks, standing away from the open fireplace. Her voice is meek—she's still afraid that he'll be mad at her. Instead of answering, he takes the egg in both hands and takes it out of the fireplace. After giving it a moment to cool, he holds it out to her. She's nervous about touching it—she hasn't tried since the first day she had it. After that, she's kept it at a distance, only using the tongs or the fire poker to adjust it.

The moment she takes it into her arms, energy thrums just below the surface. It's the same energy as when it was given to her, but now, she feels movement, too, like the creature inside is twisting beneath her hands. She holds it to her, embracing the egg, and it moves even more, excited by her body heat. A humming noise purrs gently in her head. The energy is the same as the mother dragon, the same as Hawthorne.

As much as she doesn't want to, she says, "We need to take it to the zoo."

IT TAKES A LOT OF CONVINCING FOR MARK TO ALlow them to leave the house—it's still under a heavy protection spell, and it's the only place they know is safe from Helen. They don't tell him about the egg.

After a lot of begging, he looks Alex up and down. "You're a pyromancer? A good one?"

Alex nods.

"Fine. But I'm putting a spell on your car, too. Don't get out anywhere without a lot of people within eyesight."

After taking another twenty minutes to put a protection spell on the car, Mark lets them go. He doesn't even ask why Sarah needs to bring a backpack to the zoo, or why it looks so full.

She texts Elizabeth on the way to let her know they're coming.

*I want to see Hawthorne. I think it would make me feel better.*

Elizabeth doesn't argue, only responding with a thumbs-up. Since it's two in the afternoon, she must be getting ready to feed the zoo's baby dragons, which have all hatched since the last time Sarah saw the eggs in the incubator.

Instead of using the free street parking and walking a mile, Alex pays the fifteen dollars to use the nearly empty lot. Sarah tries to argue that she isn't going to get attacked in broad daylight, but he still pays his hard-earned money for the spot. They have to walk through half the zoo to get to the aviary, and Sarah freezes before they get to the employee door.

"I'm probably going to be grounded for the rest of my life," she says, her eyes darting to Alex. This shouldn't be a concern. Someone is literally trying to kill her, but she's worried about getting grounded.

He wraps an arm around her shoulder and squeezes. "Legally, they can't ground you past your eighteenth birthday."

That doesn't help, but the door opens, and Elizabeth is standing right in front of them.

A smile breaks on her face, although her eyes are concerned. "How are you feeling today?" she asks, resting a hand on Sarah's shoulder.

Sarah opens her mouth to speak, then shuts it again. She pulls her backpack off and wraps it in her arms, the need to protect it suddenly immense.

"Did you bring the egg with you?" Elizabeth asks, her eyes sparkling and eager.

*The egg.*

Like she knows already.

Sarah is frozen with surprise, and she can't form a coherent sentence. "You...I...No! I mean, yes, but..."

Elizabeth tugs them both into the employee area.

"Sarah," she says, placing her hands on Sarah's shoulders to ground her. "I am a psychic. I knew about the egg three days before you found it. The only thing I don't know is how."

Sarah doesn't know how to respond to that. Elizabeth isn't angry, or even mildly upset. What is going on?

"I need to see Hawthorne. It's really important," Sarah pleads. Elizabeth nods and leads the way.

They go through the lab and into the cage area before Elizabeth lets them through the gate. Alex hesitates. "Are you sure this is safe?"

Sarah shrugs. "If not, you're fireproof anyway."

He blanches, so she leaves him behind, pulling the egg out of her backpack. "You aren't, though!" he calls. She tries to feel for Hawthorne using a mental technique from her Spiritual Magic class, but she gets absolutely nothing. Elizabeth calls for him, the same call she used before.

Within moments, a rush of wind assaults them. Now that it's truly autumn, Hawthorne's feathers have all but lost their greenness, replaced by bright reds and golds and oranges with just a few brown ones interspersed.

His presence is back in her mind, and her heart races with excitement as he immediately catches the scent of the egg.

"Hey, boy," she whispers, holding the egg out so that he can see it.

"What are you doing?" Elizabeth calls frantically. "He could destroy it! Male dragons will kill eggs that don't belong to them!"

Sarah ignores her, moving closer to Hawthorne.

"Sarah, stop!" Alex calls, presumably following Elizabeth's lead. Still, he doesn't approach the huge dragon. "He could kill you!" Surely, after telling him about her last experience, he doesn't believe that.

"I should've brought this to you a long time ago," she tells the dragon.

He doesn't move, eyeing the egg with care.

Relief floods through her, and she can smell the egg from his point of view. This connection is far more powerful than anything else she's had, and it makes her dizzy as she tries to distinguish where she is, watching herself walk toward Hawthorne through his eyes. Elizabeth and Alex are still standing by the gate, eyes wide with terror.

She sits on the ground cross-legged and sets the egg in

her lap.

"It's okay," she whispers to it. "You're home now." The surface is hot, the baby dragon rolling around with excitement just below the surface.

Hawthorne does something completely unexpected. She thought he'd take the egg in his maw and carry it with him to raise it properly, but he lays on the ground, all fifteen feet of him. His head is giant, and he rests it gently next to Sarah's body. She forgets how big he is every time she comes here, at least until she's up close with him.

She strokes his forehead and lays the egg on the ground closer to him. At that point, Alex speaks, much closer this time. "What is going on?" She turns to him, and he's only a few feet away, although he's still clearly terrified of the dragon on the ground.

She buries her fingers in Hawthorne's feathers and uses her other hand to grip his horn. The rough texture is starting to give way to autumn fuzz, which will soon disappear completely as his horns shed for the winter.

Alex and Elizabeth join Sarah on the ground as she tells the entire story, starting with the trap, with Helen collecting the fang and blood and feathers, and then the part about finding the den, the dying female giving her the egg. She will never get the dragon's death out of her head, the feeling of the connection splitting the moment she died. A tear falls slowly down her cheek.

When she's done, Elizabeth sighs and runs her fingers

through her hair, which came loose from the ponytail that a fairy dragon is now chewing on.

Hawthorne is practically purring, a low grumble coming from his throat while Sarah and Alex pet him.

For this moment, everything is perfect. She's sitting in a warm field with the boy she likes—who likes her back—and Elizabeth, taking in the artificial sunlight while dragons frolic around them. She doesn't want this moment to end.

"You can't just give him the egg," Elizabeth says, her voice gentle. "I know you want to, but you can't."

"I can't keep it. There's too much going on. And Hawthorne should take it. It's *his* egg." Her grip on Hawthorne's feathers gets just a bit too rough, and he lets out a light grumble. She immediately releases him and puts her hands back on the egg.

Elizabeth sighs. "I know it is. The problem is, forest dragons are different than most. That's why I'm studying them—there hasn't been much research in the past. Most dragons are just animals, nothing special except their ability to breathe fire or ice. Forest dragons are a little more magical than most." Her face lights up as she talks about the dragons, and her hands get more animated. Usually, she's a distant creature, but now, she's so human that Sarah doesn't feel so intimidated by her ethereal beauty. "The mother has a psychic bond with her egg. If she hadn't passed it to a psychic, then Hawthorne could, in theory, take it and form that connection. But now, he won't be able to feel anything from it, to communicate when it hatches, because it's bonded to someone else. When it hatches, it needs that parental bond to survive."

Sarah purses her lips. If she, a human, can feel the hint of the baby dragon, he should be able to. With her hand pressed on it, the pulsing heart rate of the dragon inside is obvious.

"This female must have passed on her bond when she died. To someone with psychic abilities." Elizabeth's tone is slow and careful, as if she's giving Sarah some sort of news. Treating her, once again, like a wild animal.

"Then how is this egg alive?" she asks, stroking the holographic striping along one side. "It shouldn't be possible, right? It's some sort of fluke?"

Alex puts a hand on Sarah's, his long fingers brushing over the surface of the egg. "Sarah." She turns her eyes to his, and he looks concerned. Careful. "Have you ever exhibited any sort of psychic abilities?"

*Of course not*, she thinks. She opens her mouth to speak, but she can't make the words happen. Because it isn't true. She'd seen everything from the dragon in the woods, and then Hawthorne's memories. Alex is a telepath—he couldn't have been the one to have the vision of them kissing at the party. She'd just been too naive to see it. Or in denial.

People are afraid of psychics. Not the same way they're afraid of heights or car wrecks, but in a deep, primal way. Like how they're afraid of the dark. They won't say it, not in this day and age, but it's there. It's the reason women were burned at the stake in Salem, despite half the townspeople being magic users. It's why there are neon signs that say "psychic" at carnivals, where teens like Penny will giggle nervously, hearts racing as they go in while adults give the tent a wide berth.

It's why Sarah hasn't admitted it to herself. Dragons, blood magic, the wild fae, and sirens are all things that people should be wary of, but the thought of someone else knowing the deepest, darkest parts of yourself? That's more terrible than anything that could steal you away into the night.

"It's okay," Alex says, pulling her into his arms. "You know, Cynthia was a psychic, and everyone thought she was awesome."

That should make her feel better, but she can only think of how Cynthia was viciously murdered. Being a psychic didn't save her.

Elizabeth smiles and says, "Don't forget your favorite aunt." Sarah laughs at that. With how her semester is going, "favorite" aunt is a pretty low bar. The other one is a serial killer. "Although you seem to have more of an affinity for animals than I do." As Elizabeth says this, a prairie dragon climbs into her lap, swiping at her hair with its little paws.

Sarah looks up at the sky, dragons swirling through the air in the distance. "I guess that's one perk."

# CHAPTER TWENTY-FOUR
## Sarah

SARAH HAS TO DODGE ATTENTION WHEN school starts back up again Monday. Someone found out that she's related to the murderer —a quick Google search could reveal that now that the police have released Helen's name and photo. She's grateful for the abandoned classroom and her friends treating her normally.

When she reveals to Gabby that she's a psychic, her only response is, "Oh my god can you tell me if I get a job at Sequoia National Park after college?" Sarah feels bad that she doesn't know how to do a specific reading, but Gabby just waves her off with a smile.

She doesn't recognize the name of the girl who was killed over the weekend. Gina Sanders. Sarah commits it to memory now, looking her up on social media when she gets the chance. It only takes a quick scroll to see that she'd been well-loved in her friend group, a bunch of nymphs and mermaid-related water mages. The usually loud halls are filled with whispers and stares every time Sarah is around, and even more so when she walks through the halls with her hand in Alex's.

The most recent murder has everyone on campus even more rattled than before. One murder is an anomaly. Two St. Merlin's girls killed within weeks? It's hard to be light-hearted when death feels imminent.

Studying after school on Friday is a relief. Sarah is stretched out on the couch, trying to focus on her Potions textbook, but she ends up reading the same page three times without retaining any of the information.

"Gabby, what did you get for number nine?" Alex asks, leaning forward in the computer chair while Gabby sits up on the bed, still in her uniform by six p.m. for the first time since Sarah's started hanging out with her.

Sarah looks out the little round window that shows the front yard and road, and, sure enough, a police officer is parked across the street in the same black Crown Victoria that has been following her all week. She hasn't met this officer, but she's heard that Nina Gonzalez is one of the fiercest officers St. Louis has to offer. Sarah hasn't asked, but she's fairly certain that Detective Gonzalez is following her in hopes of catching Helen before another murder.

"You alright?" Gabby asks, and it takes a moment for Sarah to realize she's talking to her.

She nods but doesn't say anything. Her eyes burn with

tears as ice begins to course through her—the attacks are more and more frequent lately, the thought of the ferocity of them immobilizing her. Alex stands up and walks to her, wrapping her into his arms. She hadn't even known she was really cold, but his skin is warm against her bare arms. She sighs into his neck, forcing herself to relax. It's easier to let the anxiety attack run its course than try to quell it.

"I'm gonna go get something to drink," Gabby says, and her feet pad away across the antique rugs that cover her floor. It makes sense that she wouldn't want to be in a room with such turbulent emotions. Sarah will never fault her for it.

For the first time since the zoo trip, Sarah and Alex are alone. If only it could be when she isn't falling apart. She clings to him, her anchor in a raging sea of emotion. He doesn't ask what's wrong, doesn't tell her to calm down. He just holds her, keeping her from being swept away as she shakes and gasps.

Eventually, it subsides. Just like it always does. She shudders out a big breath and pulls away from Alex. His eyebrows are upturned with sadness or concern or both. This isn't the first anxiety attack he's helped her through, and she's sure it won't be the last.

He leans forward and presses his lips against her forehead. When he starts to pull away again, she leans up and kisses him. It's gentle, just like their kiss under the waterfall. He doesn't push her for more.

When Gabby returns, they're sitting together on the couch, and she passes out sodas.

Instead of going back to his textbook, Alex is scrolling through his phone. Sarah and Gabby chat amiably about their Literature midterm when he gasps.

"I think I figured it out," he says, his voice quiet and serious. Before they have a chance to ask, he continues. "I remember from the ritual I did that Helen was using certain people. Certain types. I couldn't remember it at the time because it was through Cynthia's memories, which were fuzzy at best."

He points his phone at Sarah, and the same symbols she can't seem to escape are staring right at her. Her jaw clenches at the sight.

"These seemed really random, like she chose them out of an encyclopedia. But look here." He scrolls down, and there's a scan of a piece of paper, words scrawled in an elegant hand. Like part of a recipe. She squints and then takes his phone to read it over. The page is ripped, so there are only three things written down, but next to them are those same symbols.

*Blood of a dragon*
*Flesh of a seer*
*Hair of a mermaid*

The flash of memory comes back, blood slowly dripping from the steel wires strung through the forest. Sarah's neck stings for just a moment, and she presses her fingers carefully against her throat.

"Cynthia was a psychic, right?" she asks, looking to Gabby for confirmation. She simply nods. "And Gina. She was definitely a mermaid. At least partially." Why did Helen have to kill her, though? None of these things seem worth killing over.

"Is this stuff that she needs in order to do whatever she's planning? To summon demons or whatever?" Gabby asks when she's handed the phone.

"It said on the first page, if you click back to it," Alex gestures to demonstrate a swiping motion, "that it's not to start the ritual. It's to reanimate an old ritual. Or something. It says there are five ingredients, but the person who wrote this article couldn't find anything listing the other two."

Gabby bites her lip, and Sarah has to fight to keep from doing the same.

"What type of old ritual could she be—" Gabby is interrupted by a car horn, Elizabeth's SUV that Sarah rarely rides in, although she'd insisted on picking Sarah up today. She jumps up and grabs her bag, shoving all her books in it.

"I'll see you guys tomorrow," she says, her heart racing as more panic worms its way into the depths of her mind. This would be the closest sequential attack yet. Not even half an hour.

Alex stands, too, and his bag is already put together. It doesn't take him more than a moment to meet Sarah on the landing.

He tilts his head. "Are you alright? You seem really freaked out."

She wants to tell him so badly, but the words get garbled before they can even make it to her throat. *It's fine, but I think it's my fault all this is happening.* Instead, she takes his hand and tugs him down the staircase that leads to the first floor. The descent through the house is quiet—Sarah has become accustomed to the comfortable silence that she and Alex often share, and he traces his thumb along her palm as they walk. When they make it to the last set of stairs, she stops, pressing a hand against his chest.

"What's wrong?" he asks, looking around. The stairway isn't well lit, the only light source coming in from an upstairs window. Stark shadows cross his face, sharpening his features and making him appear more formidable than he really is. If she didn't know him, he might be frightening, a stranger in a dark corner. Her heart races, and her eyes trace over his face—his always mussed black hair, his deep, almost black eyes, and his full lips, which are parted with concern.

She takes him by his St. Merlin's tie, which is loosened around his collar, and pulls him down to press her lips against his.

His tension dissipates as his mouth forms a smile against hers. All the fear floods out of her when he wraps an arm around her waist and pulls her up against him. Heat rushes through her, so she threads her fingers through his soft hair, and pulls gently. It's surprisingly soft for how messy it looks.

A quiet moan escapes him, and she throws her arms around his neck, pressing her lips tighter. There's nothing else but this, their moment stolen in the stairwell. His lips on hers, his breath hot on her face.

She gently bites his bottom lip, and he runs his hands through her hair. They stay tangled together, pushing and pulling their energy—she can practically feel his thoughts, his emotions, his memories, just tangible enough for her to glimpse but not solid enough to grasp. He can surely hear her thoughts as well, although they're all a jumble. For this moment, nothing is wrong. Right now, nothing bad can touch her.

When the car horn lets out another short honk, she pulls away, her face flushed with the warmth that's coursing through her.

"Well," Alex says, his voice rough. "I guess I'll see you Monday." He leans down and kisses her once more, gently this time, and she wants to press him against the wall and kiss him until the sun comes back up, but he pulls away with a smile. "Tomorrow," he relents, giving her a peck on the nose. "I'll come over."

Instead of leaving him in the stairwell alone, she takes his hand, and they walk out together.

# CHAPTER TWENTY-FIVE
## Alex

INSTEAD OF WASTING HIS SATURDAY MORNING lying in bed and thinking of Sarah, Alex puts his energy to good use. He knocks on Phillips door at nine in the morning, which is met in kind with cursing, both in English and Belgian. He hears banging through the apartment, followed by more cursing. That's not a great sign.

When Phillip finally makes it to the door, he's still in his flannel pajamas.

"Do you have any idea what time it is?" he growls.

Alex looks at his wrist as if he's wearing a watch. "Looks like a logical time to be awake to me, sir," he says, leaning against the doorframe.

Phillip glares at him under his heavily lidded eyes. "I don't pay you to be a smartass, Locklear."

Alex shrugs. "You don't pay me. Up for some drills?"

Phillip glares at him for a moment longer, then closes

the door. Alex waits, and it only takes a couple minutes for Phillip to emerge in a pair of jeans and a polo shirt. "Coffee first," he says, only slightly less grouchy. Alex had been expecting this—Phillip is always grouchy in the morning. It's why he only teaches one class in the afternoon and is a dorm attendant the rest of the day.

They take Phillip's car, a newer model Prius that barely fits the two of them.

"My treat," Phillip says. He spends his money on students a lot. When Alex asked him about it last year, he replied, "What else am I supposed to spend it on? More collectibles?" Alex hadn't pointed out that his "collectibles" looked more like junk.

The car is more cozy than Alex is accustomed to, so he can't escape Phillip's glances. Or his questions.

"Any more partying lately?" Although Phillip mostly trusts the pyromancy students, Alex has had two random drug tests since the party, both coming up negative. The love potion had been successfully flushed out of his system.

"Definitely not." Alex keeps his expression open and plain. If Phillip finds out that he's been trying to solve the recent murders, he would be angry, and he probably wouldn't agree to give Alex the extra training today. Good students keep their heads down and don't attract the attention of murderers.

They spend the rest of the ride talking about the midterm, which is always just an evaluation of where each pyromancer is in their training. As long as they aren't somehow worse than they were at the beginning of the semester, they pass with flying colors. Phillip doesn't believe in standardized testing. "The real test is life," he tells Alex for what must be the hundredth time. It's either a hipster sentiment or a remaining military mindset.

They're only out for twenty minutes, and Alex is glad for the extra shot of courage Phillip had ordered in his drink. He sends a selfie to Sarah with his Starbucks cup with the caption, *Ready for Fall! #blessed #NoFilter*. When they get to the courtyard, he puts his phone away and helps Phillip set up the four practice cones so they don't burn down the lawn. Phillip keeps nudging the cones further out until they have a forty foot circle.

"Lots of space," Alex notes, taking another sip of his mocha latte.

"You wanted to do drills. You're going to do some real drills," Phillip says, shaking his hands and letting sparks fly out of his fingertips.

He runs Alex through the normal warm up, and then his usual drills. Alex expects for him to teach him some new maneuvers, but he doesn't. It only takes half an hour for him to get through his normal set. It's all a bit underwhelming, and he's still jumpy and filled with energy.

"That's it?" Alex asks, not sure if he should leave. His fire isn't even close to being done, begging to pour out of him.

Phillip, now that Alex is done with his drills, begins to

stretch. "No," he says. "No, that's not it. Today, we are going to spar."

Alex's throat tightens. He's never sparred before. Once, when he was younger, he got in a fight with a boy from his neighborhood, and he'd accidentally burned the boy's arm. It wasn't a bad injury—the boy didn't even need a bandage—but Alex has avoided using his fire violently, recognizing the consequences to such a chaos-fuelled magic.

Two girls are dead, though. His lack of training could get Sarah killed as well.

Instead of arguing, he nods.

"It's getting dangerous around here," Phillip says. "Just knowing how to create fire isn't going to help you. You need to know how to use it." Of course, this is what Alex had hoped for. If he'd asked Phillip directly, he probably would've been denied. Now that he's being given what he wants, though, he isn't sure what to do. Weeks ago, he would've fought this type of training. He would've laughed at the idea of needing to use his fire for violence rather than showmanship. Now, he's not so naive.

He expects for Phillip to indicate the start of the match, perhaps with a countdown, but he just runs at Alex, and when Alex tries to dodge, he throws a burst of flame forward. Alex knows that he has nothing to fear when it comes to fire—it can't hurt him. However, Phillip feigns left before throwing the flame, so Alex dodges to the right, where Phillip's palm connects with his chest and knocks him to the ground. The wind is knocked out of him when he crashes down, and it takes a moment to regain his breath.

So it's that kind of sparring.

Phillip holds out his hand, and Alex takes it.

"Again."

They go like this for hours, and still, Alex makes no progress. Because Phillip is a gentle-hearted teacher, Alex has let himself ignore that he spent four years in the military as a Pyromancer, so he's quite skilled in combat. Every thirty seconds or so, Alex finds himself flat on his back, the air forced out of his lungs from the impact. Even when he's gasping for breath, Phillip doesn't let up.

Again and again he falls, getting angrier and angrier. Attack. Dodge. Fall. Attack. Dodge. Attack. Fall.

What if Helen shows up again? What if she tries to kill one of his friends? His mind races to Sarah, who is in more and more danger the longer it takes the police to find her aunt.

He dodges and blocks the attacks he can, but he can't regain his balance enough to be on the offensive. He knows the moves Phillip is using—they're all just more aggressive versions of his drills, and Alex should be able to replicate them, but he keeps getting beaten down.

His chest hurts, and there must be bruises developing on the back of his ribcage, but he doesn't back down. He's wearing thick fireproof clothes, but the padding doesn't keep him from hurting every time he slams into the dirt.

When he can't see straight from his burning anger, Phillip holds his hand out. Alex takes it; he's ready to win this time. For real. He will not get knocked to the ground again. They've gained an audience, which includes David and a few of the other dormitory students. He stands up, and Phillip says, "We're done for the day."

The students standing around the cones groan and amble away. Once he's caught his breath, Alex drinks an entire bottle of water and checks his phone to find dozens of notifications. He checks his text messages first, to which he finds two messages from Sarah.

*Looks yummy*, she replies to the Starbucks message.

*Have fun getting your ass beat.* And the kissy face emoji. That stalls him for a moment. He checks his social media, and there, at the top of his feed, is the reason that he has so many notifications.

David posted a live video of the sparring session, and it has over five hundred views. Hundreds of comments thread the post, suggesting movements for Alex to try in order to stay on his feet longer. Of course, none of them are helpful today, as he was too busy getting the shit beat out of him to check the comments of a video he didn't know was being made.

He sits, his muscles trembling too much to keep him on his feet. The hours of strain are out of character, so he'll definitely be in pain tomorrow. He could go for a shower and a long nap in his dorm.

He texts Sarah instead.

*Lunch? My treat.*

Maybe he can fall asleep on her couch.

# CHAPTER TWENTY-SIX
## Sarah

AFTER SPENDING YESTERDAY WITH ALEX, PLAY-ing video games and binging TV shows with Mark and Elizabeth, Sarah is on campus at nine in the morning to watch him train again. Elizabeth drops her off, along with lawn chairs out of the garage and a special charmed heating pouch for the dragon egg. Now that it's no longer a secret, she takes it everywhere with her except school and Gabby's house. It turns out that Elizabeth has had a permit as long as Sarah's had the egg. Maybe being a psychic will come in handy when she actually learns to use her power.

She keeps her eyes on Alex, entranced by the graceful way he handles fire, his body moving fluidly from one position to another. She wants to join him in this dance, her body flush with his as he moves fire around her. She shakes the thought away, running her fingers along one of the shining pink veins in the opal.

She now understands that the energy running through her when she touches it is the dragon, and the humming is its mind excitedly connecting with hers every time she makes contact with the shell. Elizabeth had done a few spells, and she told Sarah that it was around forty-six weeks along, so it could hatch at any time within the next month.

Alex falls to the ground once again, but he had actually gotten an attack in this time, flame shooting across Phillip's shoulder. Because they're both pyromancers, though, this didn't faze him. Alex is on his back for the third time this morning.

Sarah wraps her arms around herself, the October breeze cutting into her light sweater. She'd checked the weather before leaving the house this morning, but it's much colder than it had claimed, so she's stuck freezing in her thin clothes until Alex and Phillip finish their training.

"Nice to see you again, Sarah," a voice says. She twists around, and David is standing over her. He shakes out a lawn chair and puts it next to the one she'd brought with her, and they watch the match together. He tosses a Star Wars blanket over her, and she thanks him quietly. David's fingers twitch as he watches the match, and he flinches just slightly every time Alex is knocked around.

"Are you up next?" Sarah asks.

David laughs. "Nah, I'd rather not get my ass handed to me today. Phillip is using some really advanced moves, so I'm surprised that Alex is still standing."

She looks back to the match and nods. She doesn't know anything about pyromancy, so she doesn't know what to watch for, but it's clear that Phillip is far more skilled than Alex. Still, Alex is getting better. She'd had the livestream from yesterday playing on her phone, and he hadn't come anywhere near an offensive position, and today, he's occasionally getting an attack in. During their late-night texts since they started hanging out, he's told her about his concerns about being a pyromancer. He's afraid that he isn't good enough, but all she can see is how quickly he's learning. A few more months of this, and he may even outshine his professor.

David takes video of their performance, but, unlike yesterday, he doesn't post it online.

"How's Kendall?" she asks. She hasn't spent any time with David or Kendall this week, so she's really asking if their relationship lasted more than the one night. Alex has been too distracted to bring it up.

He shrugs, but a smile finds its way to his lips. "She's alright." He looks at her. "We're doing great."

Sarah nods, satisfied. They sit in a amiable silence, watching the match. She notices that Phillip tends to come at Alex on the right, so she makes a mental note to tell Alex that later. Moments later, though, Alex clearly notices the same pattern, and. During the next match, he's able to dodge more of Phillip's attacks. He sweeps his leg, a burst of flame shooting forward and causing Phillip to stumble.

Phillip smiles, and Alex is back on the ground an instant later.

"Good job today," Phillip says, helping Alex to his feet. "Much better than yesterday." He looks over to where Sarah and David are sitting and calls, "David, would you like to try? I can be ready if you give me ten minutes."

David throws up his hands and laughs. "I'm good. Not really in the mood to lose a fight."

Alex jogs over, glistening with sweat. "Either of you want a go?" He winks at Sarah and then turns his attention to David. "You could bring Kendall down and spar with her."

Sarah hands him an icy water bottle, and he drinks the entire thing in seconds.

"I'm good. Maybe next week," David says with a shrug. "I'm headed to grab some lunch with Kendall right now. Do you guys wanna come?"

Alex shakes his head and replies, "I need a shower so bad. Some other time, though!" He takes Sarah's hand and steers her toward the dormitories, which she's never been inside. She'll get to see his room. The thought sends a little thrill of nerves through her, although, from her experience, boys' rooms are never anything special.

When he opens the door, she laughs at the matching Star Wars bedspreads. It's clear from the split of the room which bed her borrowed Empire blanket is from. The other bed even has a little Ewok plushie that looks well-loved. "I love it," she says, then looks at him, trying to make her face serious. "Rebels or Empire?" She holds the egg closer to her body, the heat from inside the pouch warming her just a little.

Alex smiles. "Empire of course. I was born to be a Sith."

"You're a little short to be a stormtrooper," she jokes. She climbs into his bed and wraps herself in the throw blanket that David gave her, and he goes into the bathroom after kissing the top of her head. The shower starts up a moment later, so she plays a card game on her phone.

When the shower stops, she freezes. She is suddenly very aware of his presence just on the other side of the door, so she wraps the blanket tighter around herself. Her cheeks and ears heat up with embarrassment as she can't help but picture what he might look like naked. The only naked guys she's seen were from her one night of exploration into porn when she was fourteen, although she's sure he doesn't look anything like *that*.

She waits for a few moments before the door opens. Alex pads into the room, a shiver rippling through him when the cooler air of the bedroom hits him. The only thing he's wearing is a pair of slim-cut jeans. She feels a stirring deep in her stomach at the sight of his lean muscles, which are tight after the morning of training.

She sets the egg on the nightstand, stands up, and strides over to him while he digs through his closet. Timidly, she runs her fingers over the hot, damp skin of his back, and his arms break out in goosebumps. She kisses the back of his neck gently, wrapping her arms around him, her hands splayed over his chest. She's glad that she isn't much shorter than him, as their heights make it so easy to kiss.

He twists around in her arms, and their bodies are flush against each other. He rests his hand on her face, brushing the hair behind her ear before gently lifting her jaw so that he can kiss her.

Her eyes flutter shut, and she lets herself be kissed, moving her lips against his. She runs her hands down his chest, resting them on his hips, fingers splayed so that her little finger is just below the waistband on his jeans. He moans involuntarily, and she bites his bottom lip gently.

He wraps his hand in her hair, his lips pressing harder against hers. She stumbles backwards, pulling him along by his hips. When the backs of her knees hit the bed, she turns them both so she can push Alex toward the bed. He breaks from her, lowering himself onto it before she lies on him, straddling his narrow hips and kissing him once again. He grabs her by the waist, his hands moving just a bit under the hem of her shirt.

His hands are hot with flame, but it doesn't hurt. The warmth spreads throughout her, and she runs her hands over his body. *Oh my god, am I going to lose my virginity?*

When a knock sounds at the door, it's like an electric shock. Sarah jumps off him, falling to the floor before standing up as quickly as she can. She brushes her hair out with shaking fingers, but she can't do anything about the waves of heat pouring into her face. Even her ears are hot with embarrassment.

The door opens, and even more heat rushes up her face. She may not be straddling him anymore, but Alex is still lying in bed, shirtless, when David pokes his head in. "We just got back from lunch. You guys want to watch a movie? Netflix just added the new Star Wars."

How kind of him to not mention the elephant in the room. "We'll meet you in the lounge in a minute," Alex says.

David winks, and, the moment the door is closed, a laugh bursts out of Sarah.

Moments ago, she thought she might be having sex. Instead, Alex finishes getting dressed and they curl up under his comforter on one of the loveseats in the student lounge, the dragon egg safe in her lap. David and Kendall are snuggling on the other, and Sarah politely ignores the tears streaming down David's face when Carrie Fisher comes on screen for the last time.

In Alex's arms, watching a movie with friends, Sarah can't help but smile. Despite everything going on, she can't help but be optimistic.

# CHAPTER TWENTY-SEVEN
## Gabby

GABBY HATES VISITING HER BROTHER IN CHICA-go.

Every couple months, her parents make her go with them to visit Rudy in the mental health rehabilitation center. She always ends up stuck in the hotel, waiting for them to go home. She's never allowed to see him. She hasn't seen him since they went to the hospital after his breakdown this spring. "He's too sick today," Mom will say sadly. "Maybe next time." Even when Kelly comes over, there's not much to do since Gabby can't leave the hotel. This time around, Kelly's family is out of town, so the weekend is unbearable.

Saturday ticks slowly on, and Gabby spends most of it scrolling through Tumblr instead of doing homework or researching the Helen issue.

As children, Gabby and Rudy were close. He would design treasure maps, and they'd go exploring their neighborhood in search of the X. Most days, their parents were either working or in school. Dad was working his way through medical school, always promising that things would get better.

"When I'm a doctor," he would say, "We will have dinner every night in our mansion, and you will go to the best schools and we will see the best places."

Now that Dad is a doctor, Gabby sees her parents even less. When he isn't working, they're out at some event, some dinner with his coworkers, or off on a trip together, usually visiting Jasmine on the coast or dealing with Rudy. Gabby spends a lot of time in her room, which is why she lives in the attic. It's easier to stay in hiding when she's out of the way.

This semester, though, it hasn't been quite so lonely. As she sits in the waiting room at the rehabilitation center on Sunday, she misses Sarah and Alex's familiar presence, which somehow keep her mind calm instead of their tumultuous emotions welling up inside her, threatening to explode. It's the same way she feels when she's with Kelly.

Sarah has been texting her throughout the weekend, occasionally sending her pictures of what she's doing. Saturday morning, it was a selfie with Mark, their faces blurry in their living room, a video game she doesn't recognize on the TV screen behind them. Later that day, she sends a video of Alex being terrible at Mario Kart. Sunday morning, there's a video of Alex being thrown to the ground during training, and Sarah's laughter can be heard in the background. The constant updates keep Gabby's spirits up.

After receiving a photo from the latest Star Wars movie comes though, the doors open to the sickly green waiting area. Gabby's parents aren't alone.

Rudy has always been a stocky, muscular boy, and he grew to six feet tall by the time he started high school. When he graduated, he was six-foot-five, and one of the widest boys on the school's football team. He was given a scholarship to play for the University of Missouri, but then he got sick.

Mom didn't use to believe in mental illness, and Dad didn't notice it in his son until it got really bad. His first semester in college, Rudy got all A's, and his professors used words like "genius" to describe him.

Over winter break, Gabby couldn't help but notice how tired he seemed. When he wasn't helping move boxes into the new house, he was asleep. Once, she found him curled up at the base of one of the staircases on her way up to her room. Mom said it was because of all his studying, but Gabby also caught him crying, and she'd never seen her big brother cry before. It had rattled her.

Before the end of the semester, he had to drop out because he was failing all his classes.

When she sees him for the first time in months, Gabby's heart shatters. Rudy, still tall, is now thin as a rail. His cheeks are hollow, and his eyes don't quite connect to the weak smile that plays across his lips. Everything about him sags, like his whole body is just too tired to stay up. Her stomach flops.

"How's it going, sis?" he asks, that weary smile stuck to his face.

She stands up and hugs him, not squeezing too tight lest she break him. He's always been the one to look out for her, her partner in crime, and it has definitely taken its toll.

"I missed you," she says, her voice thick with tears.

"I know," he says, squeezing her before letting go. She can feel everything he feels, of course. The nausea, the sadness, and, behind it all, the overwhelming emptiness. Still, it's better than the absolute dread and hopelessness from this spring. Even a slight improvement is an accomplishment.

Mom suggests pasta, and Gabby knows that it's because of the carbs, and because it's always been Rudy's favorite. The car ride is long due to downtown traffic, and, to distract her from his ever-present emotions, Rudy tells Gabby a story, designing a treasure map on the back of a receipt. He pretends that they can go out in search of the imaginary treasure. She pretends that there's a treasure to find—that, maybe, if they go to the end of this map, they can make him better.

Being in such close proximity with him is horrible, yet she never wants to leave him. She should've called him more at school. She should've made him stay after winter break. She should've gone with him—surely there was a private school she could've gone to in Columbia while he was at Mizzou?

His hand pats her on her head. "Stop thinking so much. It's giving me a headache," he jokes.

Rudy, like Gabby, has powerful spiritual magic. Unlike her, though, instead of knowing the feelings of everyone around him, he knows their thoughts. Like Alex, he's a telepath. However, Rudy can only hear the loudest thoughts in someone's head, and, even then, only when he's touching them. Right now, he must hear Gabby despairing over how much she couldn't do for him.

The restaurant they choose is packed, but Dad must have called ahead with a reservation, because as soon as they're through the door, they're seated. Despite their parents' disappointment at Rudy's life over the past year, lunch is amiable, like they do this all the time. Like they're visiting Rudy at college instead of a facility. Dad talks about weird cases he's seen at the hospital, and Mom talks about the weird people she meets at Dad's dinners.

When they're almost finished with their meals, Rudy says, "I was thinking about becoming a psychiatrist."

Mom drops her fork. "You want to go back to school?"

Rudy elaborates, his voice gaining traction the way it does when he's excited. "I was looking into online programs. That way I can....fix myself. And then maybe look into getting my doctorate. Like Dad." He adds the final part to gain Dad's favor. Dad has always wanted his children to go into elite fields—that's why he's so proud of Jasmine, and so disappointed by Gabby. "There's a great program in St. Louis, so if I wanted to try on-campus classes again, I could do that."

Dad's chest puffs out with pride. "That sounds like a great idea. I'll see what I can do." Of course Dad, neurosurgeon extraordinaire, would have connections to all the best programs in the city.

The rest of the meal is electric. Dad's eyes glisten with excitement while he plans out loud, and Rudy seems less tired than before. The meal has him less grey, a bit of color coming to his face. Gabby laughs at a joke Mom makes about all the men in this family being the same, and the trip back to the mental health center is charged with happy energy. Maybe, finally, things are going back to normal.

# CHAPTER TWENTY-EIGHT
## Sarah

GABBY AND ALEX BOTH HAVE STUFF GOING ON after school, so Sarah takes an Uber home on Wednesday, using the account that Elizabeth set up for her. She would've taken a cheaper Lyft, but Ubers have more protection spells built in to the app for riders and drivers. Her driver's name is Todd, a burly, stoic man that reminds her a bit of a bulldog.

"So what do you do in your free time?" Sarah asks. "I mean, when you're not driving."

She isn't sure if it's customary to talk to your Uber driver, but his profile does say that he's known for his conversation skills.

From the rear passenger seat, she can see a thin smile come across his face. "Crochet."

That surprises her. He looks more like he beats people up in dark alleys or does mixed martial arts. Maybe avenge his murdered family and/or dog.

"My boyfriend says I'm terrible at it, though," he elaborates.

She laughs and says, "I'm sure that's not true. I'll bet you're the best crocheter in the Midwest. Are there competitions for that? If there are, you should enter."

He barks out a laugh, which does nothing to ease the bulldog appearance. "Probably. But I won't quit my day job just yet."

"Which is driving?"

He shakes his head. "I'm actually a defense attorney, but I got this gig to save up for a vacation to Tokyo. Public attorneys don't get the best pay. I'm gonna propose to my boyfriend while we're there."

"That's so exciting!" Sarah says as they pull into the driveway. She hops out and hands him her last five dollar bill, noting that she should probably get a job over winter break.

"Have a good day!" he says with a smile, going around the circle drive and pulling out.

Sarah hasn't been completely alone in a long time. A sense of calm surrounds her, seeps into her. It's a perfect afternoon—the leaves are just the right mix of gold, orange, and red, and the air is warm but with a slight breeze. She breathes in the scent of fall and starts walking. Everything feels so normal today, like nothing could go wrong.

She hasn't walked through these woods since she found

the dragon egg, but the moment she steps over the line and into the copse of trees, a sigh tumbles out of her. The egg is tucked safely in her fireplace, incubating like any other school day, so a short walk can't be that terrible of an idea.

The days are getting shorter and shorter, so the light is already beginning to wane golden through the leaves. She listens for the stream, and, when the faint bubbling catches her ears, she starts walking. When she finds it, she removes her shoes, rolling her slacks up past her knees. She abandons her bag and shoes by a tree and treads lightly into the icy water, sucking in a breath as the cold stabs up her legs. Another moment after adjusting, though, the movement of water over her feet and between her toes is calming. She used to do this as a kid, explore her parents' property and play in the creek that cut through the middle.

She listens to the stream and watches for creatures—on her walks throughout the summer, she would often see deer and birds, and, on special occasions, she might see a griffon or a wood sprite. Today doesn't disappoint—far downstream, she spots a shining white creature, pale as the moon and just as bright.

She approaches slowly, careful to not make any noise as she wades through the soft mud of the creek bed. When she gets closer, the form is more clear to her. Not thirty feet from her, a unicorn drinks from the stream.

She slips on a stone slick with algae, making the tiniest of splashes when she catches herself, her button-up shirt soaked to the elbow, and she cringes. The unicorn lifts its head slowly, its ears pricked forward in calm curiosity. It's unlike any wild animal she's ever seen. Instead of bolting at her presence, it watches her. At its stare, she crumples to her knees, her uniform soaked through with frigid water as she's thrown into a memory.

*THERE WAS SO MUCH BLOOD.*

*Helen led the unicorn out of the stable, onto the grass near where Sarah was standing. At that point, it stumbled and fell backward in an attempt to rear away from Helen. The ground beneath its body was churned up as it kicked and squirmed, but it couldn't stand back up. Sarah reached for it, her hand shaking as she thought of ways to help. What in the world had happened? Had Helen heard the screaming too?*

*"Get the fuck out of here," Helen shrieked, her eyes wild. She was looking at Sarah, but her face was wrong. Her hair was out of its usual braid, whipping wildly around her. There was something wrong with her eyes, but Sarah couldn't place it in the shadows.*

*Sarah looked at the unicorn. "What's wrong with it?" she begged, her eyes filling with tears. Its head lolled toward her, the horn digging into the winter-hardened ground. Its eyes were so wide that the whites were showing, and a high-pitched whine escaped through its throat.*

*"Get away from it!" Helen screamed, pulling a knife out. Instead of forcing Sarah away, she began to carve a symbol into the unicorn's neck.*

*No. Not Helen. However, through the blood, there are more markings, symbols that shouldn't be there.*

*Sarah wanted to throw up, to run away, but the unicorn was screaming again, and the horses in the barn were calling and kicking at its pain. She stroked its face, sobs bursting out of her. "Stop it!" she screamed, not making any move toward Helen. Instead, she just kept petting the unicorn's baby-soft fur. "You're hurting it!"*

*Helen ignored her and started another symbol. There were now five down the entire right side of the unicorn's body. They were carved deep, and even in the dark, Sarah could see the muscles moving separately underneath the skin. She wanted to throw up.*

*At that point, Dad came running out of the house. Helen twisted toward him, knife in hand, but he thrust his hand out, and a blue spell threw her to the ground, binding her in place. He threw the knife away from her, toward the porch. Mom ran outside then, and, as Dad dragged Helen away from Sarah and the unicorn, Mom collected Sarah in her arms and took her to the truck.*

*After disappearing into the house with Helen for a moment, Dad came back out, his shoulders shaking. He took the unicorn by the lead and coaxed it up, helping it shamble toward the trailer. When it was loaded, he got into the driver's seat and sped out of Helen's farm as quickly as possible.*

SARAH GASPS WHEN THE MEMORY RELEASES HER. The unicorn is still watching her, so she stands on shaky legs and walks toward it, her feet splashing through the shallow creek. Toward the middle, it drops, and she sucks in a breath at the cold that is suddenly up to her thighs, but she continues across. The unicorn does not move.

When she reaches it, the unicorn tosses its head, letting out a gentle nicker. She reaches a hand out, now standing in ankle-deep water and shivering. If she moves one more step, she'll be able to reach the creature, but she's also wary of the two-foot spiral horn protruding from the center of its forehead.

"Hello," she whispers. The unicorn stretches its head out to sniff her fingers, and it tosses its head, lifting its lip in the air, a very horse-like motion for such a mystical creature. "It's okay," she says, keeping her voice low. "I won't hurt you."

The unicorn prances back as she continues to move forward, tossing its head once again, this time a bit too close to her outstretched arm for comfort. She drops her hand. It trots in a circle around her, its head leaning slightly toward her. The icy water splashes her when it trots through the creek, but she doesn't move as it regards her. After a moment of circling, it turns on its heel to trot around her the other way, and she sucks in a sharp breath.

All along its right side are scars. Not scars from living in the wild, though. Unicorns are hardy creatures, and nothing but a traumatic injury could leave a permanent mark. These scars are familiar, five symbols carved into the side years ago by a demented woman.

It survived? The unicorn was never found after the wreck—the aluminum trailer had been wrapped around a pole, and the main door had been ripped off from the impact. She'd assumed that it had stumbled off and died.

"It's you," she whispers.

The unicorn stops its parade and drops its head, closing its eyes. This, unlike the tasting of the air moments ago, is not the behavior of a horse, let alone one that's lived in the wild for nearly seven years. She walks over to it, her body shaking, either from the creek water seeping into her bones or the revelation of the unicorn standing in front of her.

Her mind replaces "revelation" with "miracle." She reaches out and traces the scars on the unicorn's hide, and it shivers at the touch but doesn't run.

"What happened to you?" she asks. She pictures Helen carving the symbols into its thick skin, but she has no idea what made that happen. Until that point, Helen had been a kind, compassionate woman who cared about nothing as much as she cared about her horses. That night, her eyes had been obscured in shadow.

No, not obscured.

Blackened. As the walls are torn down, the black eyes are visible, clearer than they'd been that night.

*Demon*, a voice whispers in her mind, the word sharp and glistening like a diamond. Sarah gasps and steps away. The unicorn turns its head toward her, placing its soft nose in her palm. Its nostrils flare, and the word is there again. *De-*

*mon.*

She looks into its eyes, but they don't betray any other information. She asks, "She's a demon? Is that what you're saying? That Helen—"

The unicorn tosses its head, narrowly missing Sarah's throat with its horn. She dodges back and nearly falls back into the water. It keens loudly, the whites of its eyes visible as it cranes away and then runs, disappearing into the fall forest.

It's only then that the silence reaches her. The same absolute silence from the last time she was here, that unnatural emptiness that heightens her senses. She turns slowly, searching through the brush to find the culprit.

Here eyes skim over gold and yellow and red and brown, but there isn't anything out of place. The only thing off about this moment is the absolute stillness of it. She walks away slowly, treading gently through the stream to avoid making a sound, all the while keeping watch over her surroundings. It's not like her stuff is that far: her black satchel and shoes are obvious amongst all the warm hues.

It isn't until she's too close that the extra shape becomes evident. A figure in black clothes, crouched on the ground to inspect her things. The red hair blends almost seamlessly into the foliage, but when Helen turns toward Sarah, those black eyes are never ending pits, not unlike how she remembers her parents' graves. Endless and enticing. She could dive into them and drown.

Air doesn't come to her. Her lungs don't work. An invasive calm tries to overtake her, but she doesn't give in to it. Now that she's waiting for something, the deceptive calm that had convinced her to come to the woods in the first place is obvious. This is something dangerous, burrs that dig into her clothes so that she can't dig them out. If she gets any closer, Helen will have her.

She doesn't wait for Helen to react before turning and running, abandoning her things.

As soon as the silence breaks, so does the spell, just enough that Sarah can breathe again. She hurries out of the stream and runs as quickly as she can. The walk hadn't felt long, but the sun is already setting past the rolling hills, a blue hue coming over the forest. Her eyes won't adjust enough for her to avoid all the thorns and branches trying to keep her there.

She weaves through the woods, running as fast as she can and ignoring the aching and stabbing pains in her feet as she sprints over brambles and rocks and whatever else is all over the ground.

One of her old blue ribbons catches her eyes, faded and subtle as it flaps in the breeze, but definitely there. She keeps running and searches for another, and then another until she can see the house ahead of her.

"It isn't that easy," a voice calls, too close behind her. She stumbles but doesn't fall, picking up her pace even though her feet are killing her and her lungs are burning.

Electricity envelopes her, like the static before a storm. She made it. She's home. Her feet slow.

Elizabeth is standing on the porch, phone in hand and eyes wild with worry.

"Elizabeth," Sarah gasps. She tries to stumble toward her, but her feet just won't carry her any further. She stumbles and falls, and when she tries standing again, she sees tiny streams of blood trickling down her calves. When she puts weight on her left leg, she crumples to the ground again, crying out. Whatever happened, it's a miracle she was able to stay on her feet long enough to get past the barrier.

Elizabeth rushes over, putting her hands on Sarah's face and swiping away her tears. "Let's get you inside," she whispers, her gaze hard over Sarah's shoulder. Sarah turns her head to look, but Elizabeth's hold is firm. "Don't turn around. Just get in the house."

Sarah limps over, careful to not put too much weight on her damaged leg. Elizabeth walks behind her, so she isn't tempted to turn and see Helen watching, waiting. She must be standing there. The hairs on the back of Sarah's neck raise, a warning.

Elizabeth helps Sarah to her bed, and the crackling fire grounds her back to reality. She's safe. She's safe she's safe she's—

"Stay in here. Don't open the door, don't look out the window," Elizabeth says, her voice hard. Her green eyes burn into Sarah's, so all she can do is nod. After casting a spell that turns the window black, Elizabeth runs out of the room, locking the door behind her.

The minutes tick by like hours as Sarah waits. Her phone is in her bag in the woods, so she has no way to know what's going on, or how long it's been happening. She keeps herself in her armchair, silent as the time sweeps forward with no sound from outside, so she only has her breath and her racing heart for reference. She should get a towel or something to staunch the blood coming out of her leg, but it's already slowing. It will probably be a simple spell for Mark or Elizabeth to fix it.

The flames turn into embers, and, staring away from the fireplace, she loses track of whether her eyes are open, or if she's breathing, or if her heart is beating. Her mind goes absolutely blank, her body numb to her surroundings, numb to her pain. A light starts to shift on the floor, separate from the dull red of the fireplace, but the movement barely registers. Before long, a gentle figure appears, lying on her back. Distantly, Sarah should recognize her, or maybe she should be concerned, but she doesn't move. She just keeps watching as the light shifts and wavers.

The girl is gasping for breath, her hair covering her face. Something is very wrong, and everything sharpens, like the focus adjusting on a camera. The girl is wearing a St. Merlin's uniform, chest heaving. Sarah moves her legs to go to her—at least, she tries, but her muscles won't cooperate.

There's no sound as the girl drags in breath after breath,

her limbs splayed out in all directions. A mark begins to make its way on one of her wrists, and her body starts to shake as she struggles against it. When she tosses her head, she looks directly at Sarah, her eyes pleading.

It's Kendall.

# CHAPTER TWENTY-NINE
## Sarah

THE WOODS ARE A LIVELY PLACE AT NIGHT. EVEN with the plethora of spells protecting the estate, the lights of faeries and creatures play through the trees, calling to those who aren't looking for them. It's cold now, but still, they dance. She can't help but picture Kendall, whose body was twisted and carved into as though she'd been made of clay, her form desaturated in the dimness of Sarah's room.

Sarah mentioned the vision to the police the moment they arrived, of course, and they found Kendall studying in her apartment with her older sister. She was fine. Safe, at least for now. And Helen has disappeared yet again. Elizabeth hadn't found a trace of her when returning to the woods.

Sarah falls asleep in the armchair, which is pointed at the window so she can watch the magical lights of the evening—or is she looking for a sign of Helen? At least from here she'll be able to see her coming. The fire crackles and lulls her into a restless sleep.

*S*HE'S *BACK IN THE FOREST. THE ICY WATER SEEPS into her clothes, and her pace will make it hours before she reaches the unicorn just on the other side. Every time she gets close, she trips, the water dragging her down, down, down into impossible depths.*

*A strong grip pulls her out of the water, to which she's thankful. When she reaches the surface, her eyes are met by the dull, gray eyes of Cynthia, a girl she's only seen a few times before. Her arms are bleeding from the familiar marks carved into them—the same ones Sarah saw on the unicorn.*

*"Don't kill me," Cynthia begs, but she's already far past dead. A maggot crawls out of her mouth, and Sarah pulls away, spinning around to run, when the unicorn enters her line of sight again.*

*Her hand is reaching out to touch it, but this time, when she strokes the silky fur, its skin peels off in her hand. It turns its head calmly to her, its right eye rotting out of its skull. When she looks down, she sees that she's been run through by the unicorn's horn, and her arms burn as Helen carves the markings deep into her skin.*

*I*T ISN'T THE NIGHTMARE THAT WAKES HER, BUT a knock at her door. She startles up, her neck cramping from the position in the armchair when she turns her head. Her throat is thick, and her eyes are still heavy, but she says,

"Come in."

Alex opens the door but doesn't enter. He's in his charmed pyromancy clothes, a pair of black leggings and a skin-tight athletic tee, hands shoved in the pockets of his overcoat. "Mark sent me a message. So did Kendall." He doesn't continue, and his eyes don't focus on her. His voice is quiet and shaky.

"You didn't have to come all the way out here," she replies, standing, careful on her now healed leg. The cut had been deceptively small, but it ran all the way to the bone. While Mark healed it, she bit the leather strap of the watch he gave her to keep from screaming. "It's late," she points out, although she doesn't actually know what time it is. It must have been hours, though.

He takes a step toward her, closing the gap between them and wrapping her in his arms. "Do you want me to leave?" he asks, his voice gravelly and muffled by her hair.

She doesn't answer. They still have school in the morning, so she should tell him to go back to campus and get some sleep, but she Helen's dream knife is still making its way into her skin, taking everything it can from her.

"How'd you get past the curfew?" she asks in lieu of a response—the gates shouldn't have allowed him to leave the school so late. In fact, he should be in huge trouble for not being in his room by now.

"Phillip," he says. Of course. Only Phillip, softer than he looks, would've been able to get Alex off campus without sounding any alarms. "He let David leave to stay at Kendall's apartment, too."

Elizabeth appears in the hallway, her eyebrows tilted up in concern.

"Are you planning on staying?" she asks him apprehensively. There's no sign of her earlier immovability. She's just Sarah's vaguely aloof guardian once again. In her hands is a teen parenting book. It's so normal that it throws Sarah, and she has to suppress a laugh.

Alex pulls away from the embrace and looks at Sarah questioningly.

"If that's okay," Sarah whispers, burying her face back into his chest, unembarrassed by the show of affection in front of Elizabeth.

Elizabeth looks between them, then sighs. "You can stay, but you have to sleep on the couch. I don't want any...permanent consequences." For the first time ever, Elizabeth's face is turning pink with embarrassment.

Sarah suppresses another laugh, and Alex tries to pull away, but she grabs his shirt with desperate fingers to keep him from moving. "Get some sleep. School tomorrow," she says before walking away, leaving the door wide open behind her. A set of linens appear with a *whoosh* on the couch in the sitting room, along with a couple pillows and a comforter.

Sarah does not want to think about school, about facing Kendall after her vision. She shakes her head at the image, and Alex wraps her inside the black peacoat he's wearing. She's seen it a few times, and she's sure she'll see it more as the season wears on. For now, though, it smells musty, like it was only recently taken out of storage.

"You need to wash this coat," she says, holding him tight for another moment before letting go. They stand like that for a moment, a foot apart. It feels like a mile. "I'd better change into my pajamas."

Her pajamas are still bunched up on the floor of the bathroom, and she wonders how so much could've changed since this morning. She washes her face and brushes her teeth quickly after changing—she's anxious to get back to Alex, so she doesn't consider the fact that she sleeps in a dragon kigurumi—basically a baggy onesie that Elizabeth bought her—until she's standing in the doorway, and Alex is making the bed, wearing just a pair of Mark's flannel pajama pants.

She feels herself flush when Alex turns around, and a grin breaks out across his face.

"You look adorable," he says, opening his arms for her to walk into. It takes a moment for her to tear her eyes away from his narrow, chiseled body. Is he always this hot, or does she always just happen to catch him at a good time?

She folds herself in between his arms, nuzzling his neck once again, but his bare skin is hot against her face, and she rests her hands on his chest.

"You don't look so bad yourself," she mumbles, tilting

her head so that her lips are pressed against his scruffy jaw-line, the beginnings of a beard rough against her lips.

His breath hitches at her movement, and his arms tighten around her.

"We should really get some sleep," he whispers, his conviction surprisingly strong given the situation. Probably the pink dragon kigurumi. It's not exactly sexy. Her mind moves back to Sunday afternoon, when they'd been behaving much worse without complaint.

She sighs and pulls away from him. She looks into his eyes, the irises black in the dark of night. Somehow, they don't scare her like Helen's pitch-black eyes. He leans just enough to brush his lips against hers, and she runs her tongue along his bottom lip gently, teasing him.

He lets out a sigh and puts his hands on her shoulders, using the leverage to distance himself. She plants an exaggerated pout on her face, but he isn't swayed.

"I'll be right here all night," he says. She gives him a quick peck on the lips and then crawls into her bed, and he lays under the blankets on the couch. She can barely see him across the room and past the doorway, but knowing he's there is comforting.

"Good night," she sighs, her eyes fluttering closed as soon as she's caressed in her warm bed.

"Good night, beautiful." Her lips turn up at the word beautiful, and she falls asleep with a smile.

WHEN SHE BOLTS OUT OF BED FROM YET AN-other nightmare, it's early in the morning. In a couple hours, everyone will be awake. Her right hand is wrapped tightly against her left arm, and when she lets go, she expects for it to be sticky with the hot red blood that had just been pumping out of her, but there's nothing there. *Just a dream. It was just a dream.*

She tries to steady herself to the pace of Alex's breathing in the other room, but the cold air presses against the window and slips under her covers. She shivers. She runs her fingers through her hair, eyes darting between Alex, asleep on the couch, and the house's front door, clear as day even from here.

Another shiver rips through her, and she's not sure if it's from the chill in the air or the fear from the nightmare, so she wraps herself in her comforter and walks over to the couch. A draft makes her even colder, and she looks around, expecting to see Cynthia or Gina's ghost. This time, they'd both been holding her down while Helen cut into her, Cynthia bleeding while chunks of scalp slid off of Gina's head.

"Alex," she whispers, and he startles awake. Her stomach roils at the sight of the front door and the thin glass of the windows—so flimsy.

It takes him a moment to get his bearings, but when is eyes trace her shivering form, he opens his arms. "C'mere," he mumbles, and she doesn't need any convincing. She lies on the couch—or, more technically, on him—and stretches out, absorbing his heat as well as she can. He wraps his arms around her and kisses her on top of her head, and she finally falls into a dreamless sleep.

# CHAPTER THIRTY
## Alex

WHEN ALEX AWAKENS, HIS WHOLE BODY IS stiff. Twisting his neck is agony, but it's worth it to have Sarah's weight on him, her warmth blending with his own. Her hair tickles his nose, but he can't get away no matter how much twisting and turning he does. For a girl with short hair, she sure has a lot of it. The scent of pomegranate wafts up to him.

"Good morning," he says, his voice quiet and gravelly with sleep.

She stirs gently, curling into him and letting out a sigh. "Morning." She buries her face in his neck, her breath tickling him. After another moment, she says, "Your face is stabby." He hasn't shaved since Tuesday, so it makes sense that he's getting a little scruffy.

He chuckles. "We have to get up." Instead of letting her go, though, he traces his fingers in random patterns on her back. She mumbles something that he doesn't catch, but he doesn't ask her to clarify.

They lay there in silence for a few minutes as the pale blue light begins its waking shift into gold. The crackling of the fire in Sarah's room is the perfect white noise to keep them grounded here, in this moment. Together.

"How do you keep the fire going in your fireplace constantly?" he asks. There's probably a spell or a potion that does it, but he can't think of one off the top of his head. Maybe Elizabeth gave her something that the zoo uses.

Sarah sits up, her eyes boring into his. "I don't. I usually just add more wood to the embers in the morning and after school."

The fireplace is still crackling, though. The sound is unmistakable—fire has a very distinctive sound, one he is intimately familiar with.

Sarah looks to her room and then back at Alex before climbing off of him. She walks into her room, and, just as Alex's eyes are about to drift closed once again, he hears a scream.

"Elizabeth!" she yells, and Alex jumps off the couch and runs in to see what's going on, but not before banging his shin against the coffee table. He hops toward the bedroom, ready to light something on fire if there's any danger.

Sarah is crouched on the ground by her fireplace, eyes glittering with excitement, hands braced on the stone hearth.

"What is it?" Elizabeth asks, sweeping in behind Alex in

a floor-length silk robe.

Sarah looks toward them, a grin like Alex has never seen spread across her face. "It's hatching."

After a pause, Alex and Elizabeth move at the same time. Elizabeth goes to the dresser, grabbing the heated pouch, and Alex picks the egg out of the fireplace. Within moments, Sarah is sitting cross-legged on the ground, the egg nestled in her lap.

Another crack, and a dime-sized chunk falls off the top of the opal shell. It's always looked thick and endless, a precious stone. Now, though, it's clear how paper-thin it really is. A tiny white beak pokes out, digging aggressively at the shell. More of it breaks away, and this time, a full snout pokes out, pink and featherless as the nostrils flare with its first breath of air. Sarah puts a hand over her mouth, tears flooding her eyes.

"It's actually happening," she chokes out. Alex moves toward her, but Elizabeth stops him.

"She has to be the first person it sees," Elizabeth says. He looks to her, and her eyes are alight.

"Have you ever seen a dragon hatch?"

She looks at him, a smile spreading on her face. "Not a forest dragon."

They don't move, watching the dragon slowly destroy the opalescent shell. It isn't until another knock at the door that Alex remembers that they're supposed to be getting ready for school.

"You two will be late if you don't leave soon," Mark says, bringing the smell of breakfast with him. He must not have heard Sarah yell for Elizabeth. "Oh my god." Mark trots over and leans against the dresser, and they all watch the spectacle of the egg hatching. It's only a little weird for Alex to be in his calculus professor's home—he has to keep himself from straightening up and calling him Mr. Halacourt.

He hasn't finished his homework from yesterday.

Another hole forms, and a crack forms between the two. The tiny snout shakes violently, and the hole is suddenly big enough for the entire head to poke through. Alex should probably tell Sarah how cute the creature staring at her is, but he'd be lying. It's a nearly naked pink creature, only a sprinkling of off-white feathers covering its body, similar to the chicks that he once hatched when his parents decided to raise chickens. It's skinny, its bone structure obvious under its hollow cheeks. Unlike the chicks, though, its eyes are open and watchful as it stares directly at Sarah. It sucks in air for a few moments as it rests its head along the edge of the shell, preparing itself to thrash around some more, tiny claws tearing away slivers of opal.

"He's beautiful," Elizabeth sighs. The dragon ignores her, destroying as much of the shell around it as possible, desperate to get to Sarah.

When the shell has been demolished, a creature the size of a small cat is lying on the blanket, its breathing rapid and strained from the effort of hatching. Sarah doesn't look away from it, and she runs a careful finger along its spine. The dragon squeaks and jerks its head to the side to get a better look at her. The entire process took less than fifteen minutes.

"I'll tell your teachers you won't be at school today," Mark says to Sarah. Then, he looks at Alex. "Unfortunately, I can't get you out of classes. We're already late."

Disappointment floods through Alex, but he supposes that it's for the best. Sarah deserves the day to bond with her new pet. He goes to the bathroom and hurriedly changes into his only clothes—the new training outfit Phillip gave him yesterday—and rides with Mark to school. He can pick up his car later, as Mark's is much faster.

# CHAPTER THIRTY-ONE
## Gabby

G ABBY HAS TO SIT ALONE IN LITERATURE CLASS. She got a text from Elizabeth yesterday about the Helen situation, and Sarah texted her from Elizabeth's phone this morning about the egg hatching. Her fingers twitch, aching to pull her phone out. Not to text anyone, but to scroll through Instagram. Instead, she tries a new breathing technique that Rudy taught her when she visited him last. She can't concentrate on anything the teacher is saying, although it's probably important information for the midterm.

Come third hour, Alex slides into the seat next to hers. There aren't assigned seats in this class, but everyone pretty much picked their permanent seats at the beginning of the semester, so a few students gawk when Alex changes the order of things by sitting next to Gabby. "This morning has been wild."

She smiles. "For Sarah, yeah. I guess she texted you about the dragon egg, too?" His face goes red, and her eyebrows shoot up. "What?"

It's his turn to seem anxious—she takes note of his fingers tapping out a song on his desk, and the added emotions rush into her. "I sort of…" He looks at the board, and then out the window. "I stayed the night at her house." She can feel his heart racing, the nerves bundled up in his throat.

"You slept at Sarah's house last night?" Her voice is controlled, careful. She keeps all emotions—his and hers—from reaching her words and taking control. She has no logical reason to be upset, but still, the betrayal is there. Her best friend had two vastly different yet equally important things happen, yet Gabby hadn't been invited.

He looks down at his notebook, almost like he's reading something, but the page he has open is blank. She can still feel his embarrassment, but she's also absorbing Paul-from-two-seats-up's fear over passing the exam, and the fact that Wendy Thomas, at the back corner, is desperately sad. "I slept on the couch," Alex says slowly.

She tries to smile, to make a joke of it. "Alone?" His face flushes and he looks away. Before she can say anything else, the teacher comes in and starts the lesson, confused momentarily by Alex's move when he goes over the roll-call sheet.

Their teacher's voice and Alex's embarrassment and everyone else's *everything* is just too much right now, so right as the teacher starts speaking, Gabby stands up and runs.

She locks herself in a bathroom stall and buries her face in her hands, sobs wracking her body.

Gabby doesn't know why she's jealous. They've always spent time with her, hanging out at her house after school, eating lunch with her during the day. Hell, they went to the dance with her. Now, though, she can't help but think that they don't need her anymore, that Sarah only needs Alex. It's just like the fact that her parents don't need her, don't pay any attention to her. Maybe she'll just disappear when everyone forgets her, like Tinkerbell from Peter Pan.

BY THE TIME LUNCH COMES AROUND, SHE'S DE-bating whether or not to actually go to their usual abandoned classroom. Usually, Sarah is there, a sort of buffer between Gabby and Alex. Gabby doesn't know what it would look like for her and Alex to be friends without Sarah.

She decides to go, if only for the fact that it'll be a safer than trying to eat in the cafeteria while she already has such a tenuous grip on her current stability. She will not end up like Rudy. She won't let herself hurt that bad. It would only make him feel that much worse. And her parents would be so disappointed in her.

When she walks into the classroom, Alex is already there with his food. She could turn around and walk out. Wait until he forgets about her running from him this morning. Would a month be long enough? Surely, after a month of avoiding him, they could pretend her outburst never happened.

"I'm sorry," he says, his eyes on hers.

She freezes, her mind going still. "What?" Her voice cracks under the stress. She doesn't try again.

He repeats, "I'm sorry. I should've texted you or something. To let you know I was going to Sarah's. I wasn't actually invited, but when I heard what happened..." She isn't sure what to say, but after a moment without a response, he continues. "I know it's hard for you. Being left out of stuff. And with everything going on...I should've gotten ahold of you."

Well now she just feels like a brat, although his face is nothing but earnest. She sighs. "Sorry I ran out earlier. There were just so many...feelings. You know what I mean?" She sinks down onto the teacher's desk where she usually sits, leaning her head on his shoulder.

He lets out a humorless laugh. "Yeah, I get what you mean. Not as bad since I only sometimes hear thoughts, but still. Being around other people is the worst."

Her heart slows in time with his, and they eat their lunch in silence. Just before the bell rings, Alex says, "Hey, you should come with after school and meet the dragon. He's really..." She waits for him to continue, but it seems that he can't find the right word.

"Sarah sent me a picture fourth hour. He's hideous." At the same time, they laugh, collecting their stuff to get to fifth hour. "Meet me at the parking lot. I'll give you a ride there," she says.

He waves as they part ways. Her heart is back to normal again, and she smiles as she goes to her next class. She can't wait to go to Sarah's house.

After school is out, she goes to her car. It's almost like any other day, except instead of going to her house, she goes west on a different interstate instead of going south. Alex is sitting in the passenger seat, holding on for dear life. She's so excited to meet the dragon that she ignores the emotions flying through traffic and jumping in and out of her like lightning.

# CHAPTER THIRTY-TWO
## Sarah

WITH MIDTERMS THIS WEEK, IT'S HARD TO PUT as much effort into finding Helen as usual. Despite the imminent threat, Sarah is concerned about failing her Practical Magic course. If she fails any of her classes, she'll get kicked out of St. Merlin's, even if her legal guardian is one of the teachers.

Gabby's parents don't want a dragon in their house, so they've spent the weekend studying in the living room at Sarah's house. A snack bar is set up on the vintage table behind the couch, and textbooks overlap on the too-small coffee table. Mark had forbidden Sarah from attempting an expansion charm on it. "I've seen your Practical Magic grades. We love you, but we don't want our table to be bigger than the room." So they make it work.

"Ingredients needed for a Sleeping Draught," Alex says from the armchair across from her.

"Valerian root, lavender, and....something...scales?" Sarah replies. Both Alex and Gabby boo her, tossing bits of popcorn in her direction. Gabby hits their buzzer, a cheap dollar store button she found that makes an annoying noise. They press it anytime someone gets an answer wrong. "Arthur, no!"

She scrambles up as her dragon—named after King Arthur—clambers out of his heating pouch to chase after the bits of popcorn all over the table. His little claws scrape at the pages; it's a good thing Alex put a spell on their textbooks to make them indestructible for a few hours. Arthur's baby feathers have come in since he hatched the other day, so he's now a fluffy gray thing with white speckles.

He's already gained five pounds in the few days since he hatched, and he's as clumsy as a puppy. His wings are tucked against his body, but he waves them around when he trips over a bowl of salsa and falls to the floor. A dull blue color seeps into Sarah's brain, the feeling she gets every time he's nervous. Much like with Hawthorne, she can feel Arthur's emotions and memories, although most of his are in the form of colors and scents since he's a baby.

She rolls her eyes and scoops him up, putting him securely back in his pouch, which promptly begins smoking. He tends to tantrum when she puts him up, but he got salsa all over their books.

"I'll take him," Alex says. He's the only one who's fireproof, so he holds him whenever he tries to set stuff on fire.

Sarah passes the pouch across the table, careful to not knock down any of their drinks.

"Okay, my turn," Gabby says, eyeing them. Sarah crosses her fingers that she isn't asked a question again. "Alex!"

They go on like this, throwing rapid-fire questions at each other. It's not the most effective study method, but it's definitely fun. Mark and Elizabeth are in the proper living room in the newer part of the house, probably trying to stay as far away from the three sugared-up teenagers as possible.

None of them talk about her vision. They don't mention how different everyone is treating her at school, and Sarah is relieved at that. She doesn't want to talk about it. The knowledge of her vision spread like wildfire—most psychics don't have to deal with life-threatening situations, especially not dark rituals that have already taken the lives of two classmates. Some of her less polite classmates have found a different word for her—witch. A psychic, though? A psychic could ruin you.

Gabby and Alex treat her no differently, and Kendall and David were kind to her yesterday, but she can sense their apprehension. She should've expected nothing else—Gabby is a Spiritual Mage, but empaths aren't considered to be much of a threat.

Because of the vision, though, Kendall is safe, protected at all times by a security guard her parents hired. David and Alex are also keeping watch at school. It's fine. Sarah just has to learn to control her newfound abilities, although the vision seemed to spark something primal in her, something she never knew existed. Every time someone bumps into her in the hallway or brushes their fingers against hers, she gets little flashes, like she got with Hawthorne and the female dragon. Instead of glimpses into the past, though, these are tiny snippets of the future. Yesterday, when Alex took her hand, she saw him tripping. Hours later, he came into their lunch room with a slight hitch in his gate—he'd fallen while coming up the stairs.

"Sarah," Gabby says, resting a hand on her shoulder. A flash of Gabby lying in bed crying comes to her. She shakes it off. "It's your turn."

She blanches, hurriedly flipping through her notecards. "Gabby," she says. "This is a graphing question. No calculator. What's the difference," she shows Gabby the graph on the back of the page, "between this graph, and…" she reads off the equation for Gabby to write down.

"I know that one!" Mark says, his voice floating in from the kitchen. The scent of fajitas floats in, and Sarah's stomach grumbles despite their snacks.

"No cheating!" Alex calls back.

At the same time, Gabby shouts, "You should just give me a copy of the test! Show some favoritism!"

A laugh trickles in, and Mark sets a giant platter of chicken fajitas on the couch, as they're all sitting on the floor. Arthur scrambles out of the pouch and chirps, tripping over to the plate. Sarah grabs him before he can steal their dinner, but she feeds him little bits of spicy chicken when nobody is looking.

Both Gabby and Alex stay over the whole weekend— Gabby sleeps in Sarah's bed with her, and Alex is relegated to the couch once again.

It's going to be alright. The police are catching up to Helen. Even Detective Gonzales is optimistic. This will all be over soon enough, and days like this won't be undercut by a layer of tension.

# CHAPTER THIRTY-THREE
## Alex

IN PREPARATION FOR FALL BREAK, ALEX IS CLEARing out his locker over lunch when he hears the girl's scream. It reverberates throughout the hallways, stopping students in their paths as they turn to figure out where it's coming from. Alex is absolutely paralyzed as the scream goes silent for an instant, his adrenaline burning through him and bursting out of his fingertips in flames.

Another scream rings out, somewhere toward the stairwells at his end of the building. *Sarah.*

He runs. The hallways are crowded—most of the other students have finished the remainder of their finals, so they're making their way to the parking lot to leave for the next week and a half. If he hadn't had his pyromancy test after lunch, Alex would already be back in his dorm, packing to go back to Kansas. Instead, he's desperately pushing through the crowd of people, struggling against the tide as it washes out in the wrong direction. He stumbles on one step when an image flashes in front of his eyes—red. Pools of red. He runs up and through the second-story hallway toward the abandoned classroom, where the screams are radiating from. His head is throbbing just behind his eyes, but he can't stop until he makes sure Sarah is safe.

Of course she isn't, though. Why else would she be sending him nothing but red. He didn't even know she could do that.

She's still screaming when Alex arrives, and he watches Mark drag her out of the room. She's trying to get away from him, to get back in the room. She claws at him, her arms coated in that same slick red. Alex wants to go to her, to staunch the bleeding, but when her eyes lock on his, tears streaming down her face, there is no pain. Only fear. When she goes slack, Mark is able to get her out. A dozen people are standing around, staring either at Sarah or at whatever is in the room.

Instead of stopping to ask what's going on, Alex goes into the classroom.

Something must be wrong with his eyes. It's not possible for there to be this much red. The images Sarah had projected toward him hadn't just been her fear leaching into her thoughts. No, her fear had been *because* of the images. People are not supposed to bleed this much.

A girl is lying on the floor, her white shirt drenched with blood. Her blue eyes are vacant as she faces the ceiling, her arms stretched out to her sides like an angel, but for the symbols carved into her skin.

His fire goes out immediately, and he freezes. When Cynthia was murdered, he had something to go after. Helen had been right there, ready for his attack. He shouldn't have hesitated. He should have killed her right there. Now, Kendall is lying in the blood that seems to be everywhere except inside her.

Someone else is yelling behind him, but nobody breaches the doorway. Why isn't anyone else helping her? He finally moves toward her. He falls to his knees, the blood immediately soaking into his clothes, his skin sticky. He timidly reaches for her, moving his hand to close her eyes, but when his fingers brush her cheek, she drags a breath in. The movement jolts him into action.

"Call an ambulance!" he shouts, hoping someone hears him. He puts his hands on her cheeks. "Kendall, stay with me. You have to stay awake." His eyes dart down to her bare arms, and he has to find a way to staunch the bleeding. She's barely alive as it is, and if she keeps bleeding, the paramedics will arrive to a dead girl. Even if he's successful, she still might die. She drags another breath in, far too long after the first.

There's only one immediate method he knows will stop. *It won't hurt her. She's a pyromancer, too.* The thoughts aren't quite convincing enough, but he lays his hands on her arms. Bright blue flames come to life on his palms, and he gags when he smells the burning flesh. Kendall doesn't react. She just keeps staring at the ceiling, tears creating pale streaks through the blood on her cheeks.

He sits her up so she's not lying in blood, but her hair has been dyed red by it. Her skin is slippery against his, but he holds tight.

When her eyes flutter shut, he begs, "You have to stay awake. Just a little longer. Open your eyes." Sirens are clear in the distance, getting closer every moment. Every beat of his heart pounds through Alex, and he has to breathe through his mouth to keep out the scent of copper and burning. It's the longest five minutes of his life. Longer than when he found Cynthia.

He doesn't leave her, not when the paramedics put her on a stretcher, not when they've got her in the ambulance, and not when they arrive at the hospital. He keeps her hand in his, and he can't stop talking to her. "Remember how David looked when he saw you at the dance? Wasn't it funny that we saw you at Imo's the first day of school? Hey do you remember the first time we met? You came into class last year and looked terrified, but David just started talking and probably hasn't stopped since."

Her eyes stay distant, but he's afraid that if he stops, she'll stop breathing altogether. It isn't until a nurse pulls him away at the hospital that he loses sight of her. The nurse leads him to an employee restroom and gives him a change of clothes—mint green scrubs—and it's only then that he remembers he's covered in blood.

"Take your time," the RN says gently.

He changes quickly, tossing his ruined uniform in the garbage. He'll find a way to afford a new one. Maybe he can pick up work at the diner over break. Right now, though, he just needs it to go away. He won't be able to touch it without feeling the remnants of today.

He sends Gabby a text after wiping his phone down with a baby wipe. She finished her last final yesterday, so she wasn't at school this morning. He explains the whole situation, leaving out the blood.

*It was bad. Sarah needs someone to be there*, he says instead of gory details.

*On my way!* She replies almost instantly.

"You did a good job," the nurse says when he comes back out. "Not many kids your age would've been able to do what you did for your friend. Or most adults, for that matter."

She takes him to a small waiting room, and he waits. Hospitals always make him uncomfortable. The waiting room smells overly sterile, and he keeps picking at a chip in the fake wooden arm of his chair.

Another text from Gabby comes in. *Just got here. LOTS of cops. Total chaos. Some guy in a suit is pissed. Has no idea how this happened, etc etc.*

Alex responds. *Take care of Sarah. You know how bad she can get.* He keeps seeing her clawing at Mark, arms dripping with Kendall's blood. She'd been a wild animal, uncontrollable. She needs someone who's good with emotions right now.

When a tall, blonde woman not much older than Alex runs into the waiting room and collapses into a seat across from him, he recognizes her immediately as Kendall's older sister. Her makeup is smeared, and her hair is a mess, but it's definitely her.

He stands up and goes to her, his heart racing.

"Heather?" he asks.

The girl looks up slowly.

"Are you a nurse?" she asks, her eyebrows bunched in confusion. Alex is definitely too young to work here, and it's obvious to anyone who looks past the scrubs at his face. She isn't really looking at him, though. Her eyes look straight through him, her face puffy and red. His phone buzzes with another text, but he ignores it for now, although his hand tightens around it.

"I'm a friend of Kendall's," he replies, ending the sentence with a question mark. He shoves his hands in the teal pockets of his borrowed outfit. It makes sense that Heather doesn't remember him—he's only ever seen her from a distance. It's not like they ever hang out at Kendall's apartment.

Heather just nods, but she doesn't move from her seat. Alex looks around at the empty waiting room before sitting next to her.

This text is from Elizabeth. *Thanks for sending Gabby. We didn't know what to do.*

*Is Sarah okay?* he replies.

Three dots pop up to indicate that Elizabeth is writing a text, but then they go away for a full minute before returning. This happens three times before the next message comes in.

*She will be. We think.*

After what must be hours, a dark-skinned man with black hair braided down just past his shoulders walks in, knocking on the wall. He's wearing the same scrubs as Alex, but with a white coat. "Kendall's family?" He asks, looking at his chart.

Heather and Alex stand at the same time.

"She's going to be fine," the doctor says. "We were able to suspend her in a time spell long enough to do a blood transfusion."

Heather lets out a sob and wraps her arms around the doctor. "Thank you so much," she says, her voice shaking.

"You should be thanking this young man. If he hadn't cauterized the wounds, I'm not sure there's much we could've done." Heather looks at Alex again, this time taking him in. After assuring Heather that she'll get to see her sister soon, the doctor leaves and she collapses back in her chair.

"Mom and Dad aren't even coming," she whispers, her breath hitching. He can't think of a single thing to say, so he just pats her on the back. "They can't get out of the Virgin

Islands because of a tropical storm."

He sits next to her. "What's important," he says slowly, carefully, "is that you're here for her. And she's gonna be okay."

She puts a hand on his cheek. He mascara is making black streaks down her face, and her eyes are still red. "What's important is that you saved her life."

After another half hour, a nurse leads Heather back to see Kendall.

Alex checks his phone, and, just as he unlocks it, a new text comes through from Gabby.

*Get here ASAP.*

Phillip picks him up and takes him to his car, and Alex thanks him before speeding the whole way to the Halacourts' house.

# CHAPTER THIRTY-FOUR
## Sarah

SARAH HIDES UNDER HER BLANKETS TO KEEP out the flashing blue and red police lights. Arthur is absolutely huge—after only a week, he's grown to nearly the size of a golden retriever. She strokes his soft, fluffy white baby feathers that have begun to give way to rigid pine green ones, and his wings are beginning to grow their golden flight feathers.

Gabby did something to her earlier, tracing her hands over her back and pulling away her fear and anxiety over the afternoon.

This wasn't supposed to happen. There are so many measures in place to protect everyone, to keep intruders away from St. Merlin's. According to Gabby, Kendall is going to make it. That doesn't mean she's going to be okay. Nothing will be the same after today. How naive could she be to think this would all blow over? She's spent her time going to dances and kissing a boy while girls are *dying*.

She should've done more. She should have found a way to keep Kendall safe. Maybe made her stay away from St. Merlin's for a while, or ensured there were police watching out for her. Instead, she'd brushed off the vision as soon as it was clear that, in the moment, Kendall was okay.

She was so wrong. She should've done something. Worked harder to find Helen. Faced her stupid fears. Her heart rate begins to rise again. Her stomach churns, but she doesn't move. If she doesn't move, she won't puke. Maybe.

There are voices outside her room, all hushed tones. About her. About the murders. About how she's probably going to die because if St. Merlin's isn't safe then nowhere is. They swirl around her, penetrating her mind. Not the voices of her friends and family, but the voices she heard before. Back when Gina was murdered. They're telling her things, horrible things.

*She's gonna take you home and slice you up*, they say.

*Too late to run, nowhere to hide.*

*Tell everyone goodbye.*

The air is sticky with darkness, pushing and pulling, looking for holes in the blanket to seep through. Invisible fingers prod at the too-thin fabric. She holds her breath and does her best not to move. Arthur growls, his feathers raising as he bares his small yet sharp teeth. She counts to ten, but the voices don't stop. The darkness doesn't stop.

A shudder runs through her despite Arthur's body heat.

At least, it starts as a shudder, but the shaking doesn't stop, and now she can't breathe, and she knows that maybe if she moves out from under the covers to let the cool air hit her that it'll be better, but of course she can't do that because then that horrible darkness will get to her, will take her away.

The shaking intensifies, and she should be crying, but no tears are escaping her body.

Within moments, her door opens, and she clenches her fingers in Arthur's feathers. The voices are gone, and so is the darkness. Just like that. Her loneliness and fear must be affecting her. The image of Kendall on the floor dying floods her mind once again.

"Hey, it's okay," Gabby whispers, placing a gentle hand on her shoulder through the blanket. Another weight shifts the bed behind her, a familiar campfire smell reaching her senses, and she can feel Alex's body heat through the comforter. He burrows in with her and wraps her in his arms, resting his chin on top of her head.

"I don't wanna die," she whispers, and her breath snags at the back of her throat. Tears finally begin to fall from her eyes. She burns with shame at her fear, but she can't stop herself from letting out loud sobs that wrack her whole body.

His arms tighten around her, and Gabby runs her fingers through her hair to whisper a calming spell. Sarah knows that this is just a way for Gabby to not just feel her emotions, but to take them into herself. It must be agony, but she can't bring herself to stop her. Sarah has never been good with her emotions, and she can cry for hours once she gets started, but Gabby has a way of turning this pain into tiny little freckles instead—one freckle for every piece of pain that she's absorbed for someone else. It's the purest, saddest kind of magic.

She has a lot of freckles.

Sarah can't even imagine having to carry all that around.

From there, it only takes a moment or two for the tremors to slow, and she only shakes a little every few seconds. Cool air rushes in, and the antiseptic hospital smell that Alex carried in with him penetrates her senses. There are worse things to worry about, but her nose crinkles at the scent.

"You smell weird," she whispers, her voice barely making it out. He still hears her, and he laughs quietly. There's nothing funny about today, but the release is something they all need right now.

"I look weirder," he says. She lets go of Arthur's feathers so that she can turn over. This earns her an angry squawk, and he clambers out of the bed to go lie in the fireplace, which is now covered in the flowers he collects from the magical garden out front. She buries her face in Alex's chest, but instead of wearing his St. Merlin's uniform or a t-shirt, he's clad in the ugliest shade of green scrubs that she's ever seen.

"You look *and* smell weird," she agrees. Her eyelids are

heavy from all the crying, but at least she can breathe again.

With her emotions dulled, Sarah is thankful for this moment. Lying in bed with the two people who care about her the most is more than she could've ever hoped for when she first moved here. Penny hadn't even checked up on her, although the murders have made national news at this point. She must know that Sarah is involved in this, yet she doesn't care.

Here, in this moment, Sarah is okay. She's not going to die tonight. Kendall is going to survive. With the world crashing down outside, this room, a little utopia, feels like the perfect end. Gabby and Alex stay with her until she falls asleep, and she doesn't dream.

# CHAPTER THIRTY-FIVE
## Alex

ALEX STAYS WITH HER, TEXTING HIS PARENTS AS soon as Sarah is asleep.

*I'm not gonna make it home this week. Sort of an emergency. See you over winter break. Love you guys!*

They know about the murders, of course, but they aren't aware of his involvement. If they were, they'd probably force him to come home. He has to be here, though. He'll do everything in his power to protect his friends. Gabby's parents are taking her to Chicago for the weekend to visit Rudy, so he can't possibly go home and leave Sarah alone, not until he knows Gabby will be here for her.

Saturday morning, when she finally wakes up, Sarah is catatonic. He tries to coax her into eating some scrambled eggs, but she just rolls over and buries herself in blankets. Gabby left late last night, so he has no way to comfort her. Not in the magical sense, at least. Her thoughts are so faint that he can't hear even a whisper of her mind.

Police are still swarming the property, combing through the woods, placing trackers, setting spells. It seems like they don't really know what they're doing. The lead detective, who has a base set up in the living area on the newer side of the house, keeps running her hands through her hair in frustration every time someone says something over the two-way radio hanging from her neck. She glares at Alex when he brings the plate back into the kitchen.

"Um," he says eloquently. "Do you want some eggs? They buy them farm fresh."

She rolls her eyes and turns around, listening to something else on the radio. Rinse and repeat. Alex digs through the cabinets. He'd tried making Sarah something healthy, but now he's just concerned about whether or not he can get her to eat at all.

He grabs an unopened pack of Oreos and pours her a glass of chocolate milk—they'd gotten into an argument on the way to Gabby's house about this very subject a few weeks ago, and she was aggressively in favor of chocolate milk instead of two percent for dipping her Oreos.

When he goes back to her room, she's gravitated to an almost-sitting position, petting Arthur as he licks her face. Tears shine on her cheeks, but she holds no expression.

"I got you snacks," he says, holding up the glass of milk. A small smile finds its way to her lips, but not her eyes. "I thought we might watch cartoons. Netflix has Avatar."

"That sounds nice," she whispers, her voice rough. Alex gets his tablet out of his backpack and loads up the show. They only take one break for lunch, and Sarah actually eats some mac and cheese, but otherwise finish just over a season in one day. Sarah lies on Alex's chest, and he has to hold the tablet at a weird angle, but it's nice to have this day, even though the circumstances that led them here are far less than ideal.

Arthur has taken to jumping off the high bed, holding his wings out to glide to the ground with significantly less grace than a calf learning to stand for the first time. With every crash, though, he scrambles back on the bed and tries again. Just once, he lands on the armchair and squawks, lifting his head high and proud, his developing red feathers pricking up past the back of his head. His flight feathers are new and flimsy, but effective.

"Good job, bud," Sarah croaks, tossing him an Oreo.

"What color?" Alex asks her, running his fingers through her hair, softly brushing out a few tangles.

"Orange. Really bright orange." She'd explained the color system for Arthur's emotions, but no matter how hard he tries, Alex's telepathic powers just don't work on the dragon.

"He's gonna be the size of a horse by winter break," Alex says, scratching him on his chin when he clambers back up the bed. "I think he has more feathers today than he did yesterday.

"Probably," Sarah replies.

When the sun is streaming orange through the blinds, Arthur's feathers raise along his back—one of the squad cars' sirens begins blaring an instant later, and Alex goes to the window to investigate. Arthur starts howling at the sound. There are uniformed officers running to the three cars out front, and Detective Harris is talking into her radio.

"What's going on?" Sarah asks, her voice louder than it's been all day. "Arthur, hush." At the command, Arthur closes his mouth and lies on the bed, but his feathers are still pricked.

"I'm not sure." He looks to her, and she's already curling up under the blankets. "I'll find out."

The front is absolute chaos—the first car peels out of the driveway, spraying gravel everywhere. It's a miracle that no windows are broken in the fray. Police are shouting over each other, and a man in an official-looking uniform is standing on the porch with Detective Gonzales, barking orders to the uniformed officers. Elizabeth and Mark are talking to Gonzales, so Alex approaches what must be the captain.

"What's going on?" Alex asks, standing up straighter to seem less nervous.

The man looks him up and down and then says, "Helen Jackson has been spotted on the other side of the city. The FBI has her."

Alex's relief is palpable. It's over. She's caught. Every

ounce of tension rushes out of him in one breath. He looks to Elizabeth and Mark, who look just as happy as he feels. Tears are swimming in Mark's eyes.

Alex runs back in and tells Sarah the news, and she jumps up and throws her arms around his neck to kiss him. He melts into her, wrapping his arms around her and holding her tight.

*It's over it's over it's over.* Her thoughts are loud and joyous, louder than he's ever felt. Mark comes in, and they pull apart. He's bouncing like a little kid, which is an odd sight for a thirty-something math professor.

"We're going out to dinner to celebrate. Anywhere you guys want." He runs out before they can respond.

After they finally decide on a restaurant, Alex drives back to his dorm to change into something nicer than day-old scrubs. The only nice thing he has is his blue suit from the dance. Why the hell not?

He takes his blue and pink striped flag pin off his coat and puts it on his blazer lapel. When he and Mark lock eyes at the expensive steakhouse, Mark laughs. He steps out of the way to reveal Sarah in her fall formal dress and a pair of navy stilettos he's never seen before.

Alex has never eaten at a restaurant nicer than Applebee's, so this is sort of a culture shock. The restaurant is downtown, and a modern-looking crystal chandelier drips from the ceiling in the foyer. An attendant seats them the moment they walk in, past mostly old white men in suits and the occasional young couple. The light is low, emanating from lanterns that dot the restaurant, floating just above everyone's heads.

They sit at a cozy booth in the corner, their server attending to their every need. They're probably the loudest table, excitedly chatting over each other. When the bill arrives, Elizabeth chokes on her drink before putting her debit card in the check holder. Mark has to pat her on the back awkwardly. Sarah's head is resting on Alex's shoulder, and their hands are intertwined under the table.

"Hey, Alex, where can I get one of those pins?" Mark asks between bites of the chocolate cake their all sharing.

Alex nearly forgot about it and blushes. Pretty much everyone knows he's trans, although he and Sarah have never expressly discussed it.

"My mom found it on Etsy," he replies, keeping his eyes on Mark. "It's, um, the trans pride flag."

Mark nods. "Yeah, I know. I've been looking for something like that for a while. Can you have your mother send me the link?"

"I should get a bi one," Sarah says. "Oh, and a lesbian one for Gabby! Do you know if they have those?" And just like that, the tension is gone from his shoulders. Alex texts his mom for the name of the Etsy store, and she responds when they're standing by their cars, parked next to each other in the fifteen-dollar garage that Mark paid for them to be in. They ogle the pins, and Mark ends up ordering a bunch for what seems like everyone he knows. The night is cold, so Sarah is wearing Alex's suit jacket. The city is filled with the energy of the thousands of people that live there, and the electricity makes Alex giddy.

Sarah rides home in Alex's car, hand on his thigh and head on his shoulder, although it can't be comfortable with the console between them.

When they're caught at a light just before the interstate, she leaves a feather-light kiss on his neck. "I love you, Alex," she breathes.

His heart stops, but the light turns green before he can say anything. It's a Saturday night, so a car honks at him when he hesitates. As he pushes his foot on the accelerator, merging seamlessly onto the busy highway, he replies, "I love you, too." He's never said that to anyone before, not in this context, anyway. The fire inside him blazes, and sparks out of his fingertips the same way it does when he gets back to the city after summer, the same way it does when he manages to pass all his end-of-year exams.

She places the softest kiss against his neck, her hot breath giving him goosebumps. His eyes well up with tears, but he doesn't let them fall. God, he's so emotional. He keeps his eyes on the road and gets her home as quickly as possible.

Yesterday had been the worst day of his life. Somehow, though, today is the greatest. Funny how that works.

# CHAPTER THIRTY-SIX
## Gabby

GABBY HAD BEEN ELATED WHEN SARAH CALLED with the news about Helen's capture Saturday night. Throughout the rest of the evening, she'd sent pictures of her and Alex hanging out, so Gabby hadn't felt terrible about not being there. With all the updates, she had practically been with them.

Now, though, she's an anxious mess. The entire drive back to St. Louis on Monday evening, Kelly's words play over and over in her head. *I don't think we should date anymore.* Kelly had come to the hotel just to tell her that. Tears stream down Gabby's face, but her parents don't look back to check on her. As long as they don't see her falling apart, she'll be okay.

The trunk of the car is filled with as much of Rudy's luggage as they could fit—he's coming home next weekend, so their parents thought it would be more efficient to bring some of his stuff back now.

What if Gabby ruins him? She's been an absolute disaster lately, and his hospitalization had been from being around other people's volatile minds. Her's isn't exactly stable.

That's ridiculous, though. She tries to convince herself that he will be okay around her. They can balance each other out, like they always have.

*Shouldn't date anymore.*

There's a text on her phone, one she's refused to open but hasn't deleted. *I'm sorry. I think you and I both knew this wasn't going to work out.* Of course Gabby hadn't known that. Why would she be in a relationship with someone she isn't certain about?

She can keep her semblance of control. She has to. When she gets home in twenty minutes, she can hide upstairs and sob like usual. Not here, though. She opens a relaxation app on her phone, one Sarah recommended last weekend when she'd caught Gabby having an anxiety attack in the bathroom. It's supposed to work her through breathing exercises, but it doesn't help. She scrolls through Instagram, but it's no different than the last time she checked it seven minutes ago.

Panic claws at her like a beast in a cage, but she keeps her distance. She wishes that this were a healthy method of staying calm, but it just drains all of her energy used to keep out other people's emotions.

*Just keep it together until we get home. The house is only sev-*

*enteen minutes away now. It can't be that hard.*

Moments after they cross into the city, the traffic comes to a stand still. Not only does this lengthen their journey, but Gabby is flooded with the emotions of the people in the nearest cars. Instead of flashes and hints, there are full-on attacks. Hot anger from someone too impatient to wait. Frustration. Sadness. Fear. Sickness. Anxiety. Anger, anger, anger. So many angry people.

It's hours before they make it. They're mere miles away, but it's late when they get to their neighborhood.

When they pull into the driveway, she's shuddering, and can her stomach keeps clenching and unclenching. She has to jump out of her dad's pickup so she doesn't puke all over the leather seats. Instead, she throws up in her mother's be-loved year-round dandelions, which change color with the season. Now that the days are shorter and the temperatures are lower, they're a pale, icy blue, and she's vomiting on them. Ruining them. Like she ruins everything.

Her parents leap out of the truck, but she can't focus on them as tears blur her vision. She can't breath, because every time she tries to take in a breath, her stomach empties again, and it doesn't feel like it's ever going to stop, and she's on her knees in her favorite—now ruined—gray sweater dress that she wore to their fancy lunch earlier this afternoon. The night brings with it a frigid cold, so she's trembling, barely holding herself up.

For the first time since Gabby came out as gay, her mother

wraps her arms around her, rubbing her back and assuring her that she's going to be alright. Gabby wants to hug her mother back, but she's viscerally aware that she's covered in the contents of her stomach, and Mom shouldn't have to wear ruined clothes, too.

"It's hard, Mama," she says. Her voice is scratchy from the acid, and her tears now run freely, fat and frigid.

"I know, sweetie, I know. It's going to be okay," Mom whispers back. "Everyone is on edge. It's over now, though."

"Kelly broke up with me." A sob bursts out of her when she says it out loud. It hasn't been real until now, until she gave it a voice.

Her mom pulls her in tighter. "I'm so sorry. That must be hard." Her tone isn't forced or distant, and Gabby lets herself cry in her mother's arms, just like she used to when she was little and scraped her knees or got a splinter.

After a few minutes, the cold has numbed them both, and Gabby shakily stands, a fawn finding its legs. Her father leads her into the downstairs guest bathroom, and when Mom gets back with a robe and towels, she helps her wash the puke out of her hair, like when Gabby was just a kid and she'd be up all night with the flu. Gabby isn't even embarrassed about her mom washing her hair while she sits in her bra and underwear under the hot water—she can't remember the last time Mom touched her.

"It's going to be okay," Mom says again, massaging her scalp with water.

"No, it won't," Gabby whispers. "Everything is going to shit." She doesn't usually curse in front of her parents, and this would normally earn her a light smack upside the head, but nothing about this is normal. They've barely had so much as a conversation for months.

Mom sighs and takes her hands out of Gabby's hair in order to turn the water off and grab a towel. The entire room is fogged up, and she gives her fragile daughter a kiss on the forehead before leaving. A final shudder runs through Gabby, but she's done freaking out for now. She dries off as well as she can, leaving all her clothes on the floor for now as she wraps herself in the soft black bathrobe hanging off the back of the door.

Out of the hot water, she feels vulnerable, like the darkness suffocating this city—especially St. Merlin's—is reaching and clawing, getting closer and closer to her.

No. Helen is gone. Captured. She can't hurt anybody else. *It's fine.*

She sits on the toilet seat, wrapping her arms tight around her stomach. Of course it's not fine. Two girls are dead, and one is in the hospital. And Kelly is gone. Out of her life in the span of an afternoon. The air goes thick and heavy, pressing her down and into herself. It's sticky, like a hot summer day that leaves her dripping with sweat, except she isn't actually sweating.

She has to call Sarah, or Alex, or someone. This feeling is absolutely unbearable, and she can't be alone right now.

She just can't. After looking over the counter, she remembers that her phone is still in the car. She tightens the bathrobe around herself and grabs the door handle. If she can just call somebody, she'll feel better. This dark stickiness will go away.

The handle won't budge.

She double checks, and then she triple checks to make sure it isn't locked.

Her breath catches. She wants to call to her parents for help, but the calmest presence she's ever felt—no, not calm, empty—sips all her panic away in a moment, washing it down the drain with her soiled bath water.

She turns her eyes to the foggy mirror. The reflection isn't her own.

A dark figure with a mane of red hair stares back at her, but she can't make out the features. She drops the door handle and reaches to the sick reflection, and the hand in the mirror, fingers far too long, reaches back. Another tear rolls out of her eye, and then another.

Ice trickles down her spine, and she understands, logically, that she should be terrified, but the presence in the room is too calm, too empty, and it's stealing all her emotions and leaving her with its emptiness. It's the absolute opposite of her empathy, taking things out of her head instead of putting them in. When her fingers brush the mirror, it explodes, glass shattering everywhere.

When the emptiness breaks, she finally screams.

# CHAPTER THIRTY-SEVEN
## Alex

WHEN ALEX'S PHONE RINGS, IT'S NEARLY MID-night. He scrambles toward his phone, but after a moment he remembers that he's not in his dorm, but in Sarah's bed. He has to dig around the blankets while trying to not wake her, and a photo of Gabby's smiling face is staring at him from the screen. He clicks the answer button but doesn't speak until he's out in the hallway.

"Hey, what's up?" he says, shivering in his thin pajamas, which he'd grabbed from his dorm earlier this evening. The heat hasn't been turned on yet, so he tries to focus on using his fire to warm himself internally. Gabby's breathing is heavy, but she doesn't say anything. He goes to sit on the couch, his eyes drooping with exhaustion. "Gabby, are you there?"

A broken sob barely makes it through the phone. He sits up, all his senses heightening at the sound. The fire in him is on high alert, ready for anything.

"Gabby, what's going on?" he demands, his voice hard. He can't let her know how scared she's making him. If she'd just answer, maybe his heart wouldn't be trying to beat out of his chest.

"I don't know," Gabby finally replies, her voice meek and shaky. He switches his phone to the other ear. After a long pause, he's about to ask what she means, but she continues, "I don't remember. I got home, took a shower, and then...." The line goes quiet once again. Something is so wrong about this moment—perhaps it's the chill in the air, or the darkness pressing in, but Alex stands to leave.

"I'm on my way. Wait right there." He glances into Sarah's room, where she's still asleep, her bare shoulders just peeking out over the top of the blanket.

"There's broken glass everywhere. I don't—" her voice cuts as another sob comes out. He can picture her curled up and crying, and he can't stand it.

"I'm gonna bring you back to Sarah's house. Elizabeth is a psychic. She can help you figure it out. It's gonna be alright." Leaving Sarah alone for even a moment is eating him alive, gnawing at his stomach.

He has to, though. Gabby is his friend, too, and she needs him. She needs both of them. Sarah is safe, and he won't be gone more than a couple hours.

He places the gentlest of kisses on her forehead, glancing at her one last time before walking out the door, but she doesn't even stir.

GABBY'S PARENTS HELP HER OUT THE DOOR when Alex arrives, her mom carrying a backpack. Gabby is looking around wildly, as if waiting for something to get her. She sits in the car and holds the backpack to her. A thin red mark is sliced across her cheek. She had mentioned broken glass on the phone.

"Keep her safe," her mom tells Alex before giving Gabby a kiss on the forehead. "It'll be okay. It's probably just your anxiety. Like with Rudy? And he's okay now. It'll be okay." Alex wonders if maybe she's just trying to convince herself. Did Gabby break something? Is that what this is about? "We'll call someone to fix the bathroom mirror tomorrow."

"It'll be alright," he assures them both. "Elizabeth should be able to figure out what's going on." His voice doesn't betray his own fear. This isn't normal. Destroying a bathroom and then forgetting it happened? That doesn't sound like something that Gabby would do. With all of her anxiety problems that he's witnessed, it doesn't seem like she's ever just forgotten something.

A darkness hovers around the edges of the neighborhood, though. Sticky and oppressive. It isn't just in her mind. There's something out there. Watching. Waiting.

He has to remind himself that Helen is in police custody. They're safe.

The thoughts don't reassure him.

While he drives, he keeps an eye on her as well as he can, gauging her state. Her hair is up in a tight bun, and she keeps chewing her nails, but they're already worn down to the quick. She isn't even wearing her usual acrylics. As an empath, she can feel others' emotions, but she can also sometimes project her own, and fear is rolling off her, tightening Alex's gut and breaking him out in a cold sweat. His fear is then projecting back into Gabby, so they're a complete mess by the time they're on the interstate, headed back north. On a normal day, the drive would take at least an hour. Without traffic, though, he goes as fast as he's willing to risk.

Gabby takes his hand in hers, and he squeezes. He's trying his best to be comforting, but his heart is still pounding out of his chest, and his breath is caught in his throat. The winter air should feel dry, electric, but it just feels sticky, like it's trying to slow them down. He doesn't look in the rearview mirror, mostly because he's afraid he'll see someone in the backseat who shouldn't be there.

*Gone. She's gone. We're safe. It's over.*

"Almost there," he whispers when they pass the exit that would take them to St. Merlin's. One of the lights along the interstate flickers and then goes out, and his hand tightens on Gabby's, betraying his ever-growing fear. He isn't even sure if she heard him—the Ford sits low to the ground and rattles when it goes over sixty, and one of the windows isn't sealed quite right. The car is loud as he speeds through the autumn city.

They have to wait at the stoplight off the exit in Chesterfield, and he can almost feel the gooey blackness approaching, ready to eat up the car and swallow them whole. *There's nothing there.* He checks over and over, and there isn't anything to be afraid of.

A police car pulls up in front of them, lights and siren blaring. Sarah's house is quite a ways off the interstate. This means nothing. Nothing at all. The car is going far over the speed limit, and Alex uses this as an excuse to speed up—not quite enough to keep up, but enough to keep it in sight.

It turns right at the stop sign where Alex always turns.

His phone is ringing, but he doesn't recognize the number. He sends it to voicemail and speeds up. Everything is fine. It has to be.

Gabby's phone rings, and when she shows it to him, it's the same number. She doesn't answer.

"We're almost there," Alex says, keeping his voice carefully light. "Everything is fine."

His phone rings again. Gabby answers it for him.

"Who is it?" he asks at a normal volume. There's no reason to yell, to panic. Again, he turns onto the same street as the police officer—Sarah's street.

She holds up a finger and listens.

"Okay," she says, her voice suddenly serious. "Thank you for letting us know." She hangs up and tells Alex, "Speed up. You won't get pulled over."

"What's going on?" He asks for what feels like the thousandth time tonight. The speedometer is reaching a dangerous high, but he doesn't slow until he has to slam on his brakes to turn into the driveway.

Gabby leans forward in her seat, squinting out the windshield. The police car is in front of the house.

"Helen escaped," she says, her voice not more than a breath.

Alex's heart drops, and his fingers run cold. He puts the car in park as soon as he's close to the house, running in behind the cop, who's speaking with Elizabeth and Mark in a very serious tone. Sarah had been in a dead sleep when he left, so she might not have heard all the commotion.

He swings Sarah's door open, ready to relieve his fear by seeing her sleeping peacefully in her bed, Arthur at her side. When his eyes adjust to the darkness of the bedroom, her bed is a mess, blankets strewn half on and half off. A breeze wraps around him, and the curtains flutter. A shudder runs through him.

Sarah and Arthur are gone.

# CHAPTER THIRTY-EIGHT
## Sarah

WHEN SARAH WAKES UP, A FAMILIAR FAERIE song is playing. She stands, wrapping herself in a quilt that Mark gave her to keep warm as the temperature plummets overnight. Alex is no longer in her bed, but he should be back soon. Where could he have in the middle of the night, anyway?

Lights dance through the trees, as clear as they ever were now that the protective spells have been taken down. It's not like they need them anymore now that Helen is out of the way. She pulls on a pair of fleece leggings and a heavy knit sweater. She has to follow the lights, to find the party once again. Something in her heart is telling her that that's where she'll find Alex, just like last time. They will have come full circle—strangers their first time, in love the second.

Rather than going through the front door and risking

waking Mark and Elizabeth, she slides her window open and quickly pops the screen out. The revelry only gets louder when she lands on the ground, the soil of Mark's garden soft under her hiking boots. Her skin tingles with excitement. She walks slowly through the yard, a small smile on her face as she goes to meet Alex.

The moment she crosses the iron fence line, all sounds cease to exist. The music and rabble from the party are gone, and there aren't even birds or insects making noise. The moon and stars have disappeared behind a sudden thick of clouds.

She moves to turn around, to go right back to her room and get Elizabeth or Mark or someone. Something in the air isn't right. As soon as she begins to turn, though, all the air is sucked out of her. She tries to breathe in, but her lungs aren't working, no matter how hard she gasps. Her heart pounds, and her head spins. Her chest is sharp with pain as she desperately tries to take in air.

"She who intervenes must be the last to die," a syrupy voice says. She looks into the trees, clutching at her throat. Helen is standing there, hair in a braid, clothed in a pair of jeans and a long-sleeved black t-shirt. She looks so normal. Her face is encased in shadow, hiding the one feature that scares Sarah the most. From here, she looks just like the woman who'd given Sarah cake for breakfast for her birthday. The woman who taught her to ride horses—to really ride them, not just pony behind her on Dad's old gray mare.

Helen takes another step, and her black eyes are revealed. Unlike Alex's pooling dark irises, the blackness encapsulates all of Helen's eyes—the pupils, the irises, and the sclera. Sarah falls to the ground, holding herself up just enough that she's on all fours like an animal.

"Come with me," Helen commands. Her voice is just as Sarah remembers from her dreams—not the ten years of excitedly announcing their trip to Chuck-E-Cheese's for Sarah's birthday, not the whisper telling her to make a wish, which always came true, as she blew out her candles early in the morning. It's the voice she remembers screaming at her to go away as she tortured the unicorn. A twisted darkness that Sarah has only heard from this woman.

When Sarah tries pulling away, the invisible hold tightens around her neck like a noose. When she falls forward, it releases just enough for her to gasp in the hint of a breath before she's suffocating again.

She drags herself forward so that she can breathe.

"Good girl," Helen says, helping Sarah to stand. Tears prick at her eyes, but she doesn't let them fall. "If you listen, it will all be over soon. It won't even hurt."

She doesn't want to die.

Oh, god, she's going to die.

If she keeps walking forward, she's not going to make it out of this alive. Still, she keeps walking. It's either that or suffocate. Maybe this will at least buy her some time.

Helen follows her through the woods, directing her

where to go. All the while, Sarah is straining to project her mind to anyone who could be listening. Where is Alex? He should be able to hear her if she projects loudly enough. He couldn't be gone, could he? No matter how far she reaches, though, she feels nothing.

Except Arthur.

She's used to only feeling his feelings, seeing his memories, but this time, she pushes for him. She tries to communicate the danger and urgency, but it's complicated since she's worried about whether or not her next breath will come to her. The trees reach out to them, the brambles dragging her along as she stumbles across the suddenly unfamiliar landscape. She flinches at every touch—she can't tell if it's the jagged branches or Helen's sharp claws brushing against her arm, her back, her neck.

When Arthur sends her the color red, she responds by picturing Alex and Elizabeth and Mark and Gabby as strongly as she can. If this works, he'll go get them. They'll know something's wrong. She concentrates so hard that she doesn't see the river until she's ankle-deep in it.

"Get in the boat," Helen says. "Careful, it's unsteady." She helps Sarah in, her nails digging into Sarah's forearm, a steep contrast to the false kindness in her words. After the whisper of a spell, the boat takes them downriver at a breathtaking speed. Soon enough, Sarah will be completely out of range. In one last burst of desperation, she sends Arthur everything she can see right in front of her—the hull of the boat, Helen's relaxed face smiling at her like a chiding mother, the river as they head West.

"It's a lovely evening out," Helen says, leaning against the side of the boat. What would happen if Sarah pushed her over? She considers is, but the risk of suffocating is too great to attempt it. "I should've brought a sweater. Silly me, forgetting everything." The voice is wrong, so wrong. With it comes that same sticky darkness, prodding and pulling at Sarah's hair, her clothes, her skin. The words dig into her, scraping and making her raw.

When the boat slows toward a dock, Sarah's vision goes black. She lets out a little gasp, reaching out to grab anything she can. Helen helps her slowly stumble out of the boat and onto a dock. She leads her into the back of a van, by the sound of the doors and the bare metal floor. If she could see, she'd get the license plate in order to....something. Project it to Arthur? Call for help? There's nobody around to help her. She's on her own.

"You might get some sleep," Helen suggests. "It's going to be a long drive home." The door slides and slams shut, and, as soon as the van starts moving along the bumpy ground, Sarah falls to the floor, her cheek resting against the cool metal.

Not long after the start of the drive, the vehicle stops. The familiar sounds of a gas station comes in through the thin metal walls, and the corner where her head is lying vibrates just a little when Helen starts filling the gas tank.

She turns her body enough that her feet are touching the far wall, and she kicks it as hard as she can. A mistake.

Her body freezes in a convulsion, a shock running its way through her, paralyzing her. Her muscles contract, and she tastes blood when she bites the tip of her tongue. The electricity only lasts a moment, but the agony stays. She has to cough and sputter to get the blood out of her mouth, but it just keeps coming.

Minutes tick by, and the van doesn't move. Eventually, the driver door opens again. Sarah's tongue has stopped bleeding, but her face is in a small pool of blood, and she retches. Her stomach only has a little water and acid in it, and it all ends up in that same pool. Tears spring to her eyes, and a sob bursts out of her—the first vocal response she's allowed herself all night.

"Try something like that again," Helen says, her voice poison, "and I will take much longer killing you. Besides, the van is completely soundproof. You hurt yourself for no reason." The last sentence is sickly sweet once again.

Another sob breaks out of Sarah, and the lack of air makes her choke. This time, when she heaves, nothing comes out of her. She wishes she could stop crying, but she's in so much pain that she can't stand it, and her death is going to be terrible. Nobody is coming to save her.

She can't stop thinking about it. The pain that she'll feel when Helen carves those ghastly symbols into her flesh, the stinging of knowing that nobody is coming to save her. It takes a few minutes for her to sense that she's not alone—not just in the van, Helen's predatory essence emanating from the front seat.

This in her head. There's something else there, just the hint of the unfamiliar. It's like how she felt when the dragon in the forest called to her, or Hawthorne at the zoo, or the unicorn in the woods, or even Arthur. This one, though, is more subtle. Quieter, somehow. Focused.

Human.

Once she snags its presence, she focuses on it, away from the dull pain in her muscles, from the cold metal floor, from the pool of fluids that she may never be able to get away from. She moves toward it, picturing herself holding a red thread to the source. The further she walks along that thread, the less she can hear the highway passing beneath her, and the more the pain fades.

She walks until she's completely enveloped in the darkness, where nothing can hurt her. She turns to look back where she came from, and the thread pulses with a heartbeat—her heartbeat, grounding her to her body—all the way back and back and back into the darkness. When she faces forward again, Elizabeth is standing only a few feet away. Close enough to touch.

"Sarah," she says, her voice quiet, not a whisper, but a distant call even though she's right here. It's eerie, like listening to a horror movie from the other room. "I need you to open your eyes."

And, because Elizabeth tells her to, she can. When she forces her eyes open, she can see everything around her once again. Her senses are back full force, but that means the pain has returned, every ounce of it beating through her body. She forces herself to a sitting position, just enough that she can see out the passenger window. All she has to do is find some sign that indicates where she's being taken. Anything that can be used to find her.

In the distance, flying so far away that she only spots it when it passes in front of the moon, is a dragon.

# CHAPTER THIRTY-NINE
## Gabby

WITHIN MOMENTS OF DISCOVERING SARAH'S disappearance, Gabby is helping set up a scrying bowl on the open floor of the newer living room. Along with police, Alex and Mark are searching the forest for any sign of her, casting spell after spell in an effort to track her. They're supposed to call when they get anything, even a hint of where she could have been. So far, nothing.

She fills a deep wooden bowl with a thick, dark liquid that Elizabeth has in her closet. "Are you sure this is safe?" Gabby asks. Her voice shakes despite herself. Scrying is something that requires a lot of skill—it's banned from being taught to anybody under the age of twenty-one.

Elizabeth ties her hair up in a loose bun. Wearing holey sweatpants and a workout tee, she doesn't look like a psychic about to perform a spell—if anything, she looks like an Instagram star preparing a gross type of facial soup in her pajamas. "Relatively." The liquid sloshes around as she moves it closer to her. "I mean, so long as I'm grounded, my soul *shouldn't* wander too far to come back."

That is not even a little bit reassuring.

There are no other options. Everyone else had been killed without anybody noticing, and Gabby had been targeted in her bathroom with her parents closeby. The police shouting spells into the woods will do nothing unless their plan is to find Sarah's body after she's been killed.

After giving Elizabeth a leather watch strap to bite down on, Gabby takes her hands and closes her eyes.

"Just a warning," Elizabeth says, "I can't control a lot of what's about to happen. You might put up a shield. Just in case." She doesn't elaborate, doesn't explain what could happen.

"But you've done this before? Properly?" When she shrugs noncommittally instead of a reply, Gabby mumbles a spell for a physical shield as well as a mental one. Better to be safe.

Alex comes in, the door clicking shut behind him. His comforting campfire scent is immediately recognizable, although now it's mixed with the cool pine of the forest. "Sit," Elizabeth says. "And listen hard."

"Listen? For what?"

But before he's even finished asking, Elizabeth's emotions snap right out of Gabby. They're just gone. As if she isn't even there. Gabby opens her eyes to make sure she is really holding Elizabeth's hands. The sight before her sends a chill down her spine. Warm, electric Elizabeth is near unrecognizable, her eyes open, pupils completely dilated—Gabby can't see a trace of her green irises. Her jaw is slack, but the rest of her body is rigid as a board.

Alex joins them on the floor, his stress driving into Gabby's mind. She grits her teeth, and he rests a hand over Elizabeth's, his eyes fluttering shut.

"Tell me what you hear," Gabby says, but her voice is too spooky for her liking, like they're in a horror movie. Someone always dies in those. She clears her mind of all thoughts about death.

The room is silent for what feels like an eternity, but the clock on the dresser only ticks thirty seconds. Like he's been struck by lightning, Alex jolts up, his hand still clutching Elizabeth's. "I see her," he whispers.

At that moment, Mark walks in the room, his hair ruffled and clothing scuffed with mud and thorns. "What do we know?"

Alex's voice is distant. He's talking to them, but not looking at anyone. His eyes flick behind his lids. "She found her. We have to go. Now." He speaks the words to a tracking spell over and over—seven times total.

Mark carries Elizabeth outside, and, although the SUV is bigger, he puts her in the passenger seat of the much faster Pontiac. Alex slides in lithely behind her, so Gabby scoots behind the driver's seat.

An officer stands in front of their car, holding a hand up. He can't be more than twenty-two, and his eyes betray his fear. "We can't let you leave until we've searched the premisis," he says, his voice shaking.

"Move or I will move you," Mark replies, his voice deeper and more serious than it's ever been. Gabby can't imagine that he can actually do anything about the officer. Nobody would choose to be a math teacher when they could pick something magical. He revs his engine. Thunder crashes overhead, although it isn't raining. "Tell your captain to do whatever he can to get us out of the city as fast as possible." A blue spark leaps out of his fingers, and Gabby's eyes widen.

The cloud cover has begun to dissipate, the full moon just visible through the trees. Still, lightning crashes into the wide oak tree that hovers over the yard. The officer scrambles out of the way, and the car peels out of the driveway, slamming Gabby against the back of the seat.

"I'll be in trouble for that later," Mark comments, and Gabby slams against the side when he turns out of the driveway whilst going far too fast.

Alex mumbles directions, his fingers digging into Elizabeth's shoulder. He curses every time they make a wrong turn, and Gabby braces herself along the backseat. How Mark hears Alex over the roar of the engine is beyond her, but he doesn't take any turns that Alex doesn't tell him to.

The interstate is practically empty this late, so the car flies along the dark lanes.

"A long drive home," Alex mumbles. "She said it's a long drive home. What does that mean?" It seems like he's speaking to himself, and Mark ignores everything he's saying. Alex's fingers nervously snap on his free hand, pulling up a flame as though he's clicking a lighter. If she's not careful, Gabby will get burned.

In that moment, she has an epiphany. She Googles Helen Jackson on her phone, but, for the first time since they've started researching, she makes sure to subtract the word "missing" or "wanted" from the results.

Instead of hundreds of news articles from the past few weeks and a few from six years ago, only a couple sites come up. The main one is a social media page that has been inactive for years. Jackson Equine Training Center. The logo is the silhouette of a unicorn, its head held high and proud, a spiral horn protruding from its forehead. When she clicks it, the last post sends her heart racing.

The photo is a selfie of a woman with wild red hair and a huge grin, her arm around a ten-year-old girl. The child is unmistakable—Sarah. She was so small, so carefree. Completely different than the anxiety-ridden teen that Gabby knows now.

*Can't wait for my favorite niece to come visit! I'm sure she'll be a better trainer than me when she's older!*

She clicks the About section, and there, in tiny plain letters, is an address in Arkansas a few hundred miles away.

She pulls it up in her phone's GPS, and when Alex's next instruction confirms her suspicions, she speaks up.

"I know where she's taking her."

Elizabeth still stares off into space, her body not reacting to any of the movements of the car, but Alex gets even more tense.

"We have to hurry," he whispers, his eyebrows bunching. Mark speeds up, the needle climbing into the triple digits. When they aren't making a wrong turn every twenty miles, they get further a lot faster. Somehow, nobody pulls them over. Gabby whispers a thanks to the police captain, although there's no way he can hear her.

When the tank runs empty, Mark is hesitant to stop, but they'll only end up stranded if he doesn't fill up the car. Based on Alex's barely intelligible muttering and his pained expression, they're gaining on Sarah and Helen anyway.

*Not fast enough,* Gabby thinks, but she won't say anything negative out loud. Alex isn't the only one familiar with faeries and speech-based magic. She knows just how powerful words can be when spoken aloud. She won't give her fear anything to grasp onto.

Mark fills the car as quickly as he can, the gas station sitting right next to a Waffle House that smells like it's been doused in oil and cigarette smoke and sadness. The lights of the gas station are too bright, like it's trying too hard to act like daylight, although with a quick glance around, the area they're in looks like a place that may try to rob them.

SMOKE AND MIST

While the gas station is modern, the surrounding buildings are outdated and dim. Mark is clumsy with fear, and, even inside the car, Gabby can smell the gasoline that splashes across the ground when he pulls the spout out too early.

It isn't until Mark is back in the car that Elizabeth screams.

An instant later, Gabby's nails dig into Alex's arm as she holds on for her life, the pain digging into her arm.

# CHAPTER FORTY
## Sarah

SARAH KEEPS HER EYES FROM FOCUSING, AND she doesn't look around when the van pulls to a stop and the back door opens. The sky is utterly black, and the lights of the van are off by the time Helen gets around to opening the back door, but she still recognizes her surroundings instantly. The barns may be crumbling, and the house may be a rotting husk, but she knows.

The scent of the outside air brings her back. The midnight cold, the absolute stillness, and something new that takes her a moment to place.

Rot.

There is something decaying about this place, something that had once been very much alive. Not a creature, but an energy. The emptiness of the world around her presses in, like all the warm magic has been sucked away and replaced with this dark, throbbing energy that sticks to her clothes, a burr that just works its way in the more she tries to shake it off. It's stronger here than anywhere she's been. Her ears pop at the rapid pressure changes as the darkness pulsates around her.

Helen wraps a talon around Sarah's ankle, the closest part in reach, and yanks her out. Sarah lets out a cry as her head slams on the bumper and then the ground, and the wind is completely knocked out of her so she can't breathe again. Still, she's careful. She doesn't look in Helen's direction, and she keeps her focus soft as to not arouse suspicion. Helen has to think that she's still blind. They'll be here soon. She just has to last a little longer. A couple hours at most.

"Get up," Helen orders. She doesn't say it again while she waits for Sarah to clamber to her feet unsteadily. She doesn't have to fake her disorientation—her head throbs, and a wetness drips onto the ear that hadn't been in the puddle of bile earlier.

As soon as she's steadied herself enough to stop swaying, Helen grabs her by the wrist and drags her over to the barn. She almost thinks that she's going to take her inside and let the building collapse on top of her, but she stops short and tosses Sarah to the ground like a rag-doll.

Sarah doesn't fight.

She knows she should. Logically, she should try to hold Helen off for as long as possible, to increase her chances of being rescued. Right now, though, she's just tired. Her eyes are wide open, but her entire body is painful and heavy and it doesn't seem worth it. Even if she gets away, Helen will come back for her. "She who intervenes must be the last to die," Helen says once again. "You stopped me from completing my ritual. Now, it's finally your turn to die."

Even if Sarah goes back to St. Louis, there will still be two dead girls and one who will never be the same, and it's her fault.

No, it would be easier to just die for this. Her head throbs and she moves to the edge of unconsciousness. Does she have a concussion? Does it matter?

When the knife buries itself into her skin, everything becomes razor-sharp.

# CHAPTER FORTY-ONE
## Gabby

GABBY BELIEVES THAT PAIN THREE TIMES REMO-
ved shouldn't be so bad. That it should be dulled down through the filters of each person that it passes through, like water being cleaned until everything dangerous has made its way out.

Pain is not like water, though.

It's electricity, zipping through each host without pause until it makes its way into her. She grabs the first thing she can get to—Alex—and holds on to keep from losing herself in the agony. Other than a scratch on her cheek, she wasn't hurt when Helen's darkness showed up at her house. Now, she feels every ounce of the pain that she would have— worse, still, knowing that this isn't her pain to claim. She isn't the one who's dying.

She keeps her jaw clenched shut, but she can't help but let out a thick groan every time the invisible knife returns.

Elizabeth has stopped screaming, but Mark hasn't started driving yet, too concerned for his wife's well-being. The plethora of emotions from everyone in the car floods through her along with the pain, and all she wants is for it to go away. She wants to stop feeling everything around her so acutely.

With the next strike of the invisible knife, she snaps. She just can't take this anymore. A yell leaps out of her, a warrior cry, and she forces everything out of her mind. Anything that doesn't belong to her is destroyed by a fire that rampages through her, taking down anything in its path. She isn't just a vessel for other people's emotions. It isn't her job to feel everyone else's pain or happiness or anything else for that matter. Not if she doesn't want to.

For the first time in her seventeen years of life, Gabby's mind is completely her own. A landscape ravaged by flame and hurt. Her entire life, she's been forced to work herself around the emotions of everyone else, to be careful. No more.

Although distant, the fire still rages inside her, pushing against the emotions still trying to invade. She won't let them in.

"Get in the fucking car," she growls. Now that she has a moment to herself, she's filled with red-hot anger. Anger at her life, at her anxiety. Mostly, though, her anger is for Helen. How dare she destroy so many lives? How dare she take Gabby's best friend away from her.

She sets her phone in the holder on the dash so she can watch the GPS. Elizabeth has gone from screaming to whimpering, and Mark moves her to the backseat so that Alex can sit up front.

It's a good thing her sister taught her to drive a manual last year. The instant the doors are closed, she burns out of the parking lot, jumping on the interstate and heading south. The car jets past the few cars and big rigs plowing down the interstate this late at night. No, not late at night. When she checks the time, it's early in the morning. She speeds up, her foot to the floor.

When they finally arrive, the property is only vaguely the same as the photos online. The front gate, once turquoise with swirling metal leaves and vines, is brown with age, overgrown with thick foliage. There's no longer a metal sign hanging overhead that announces where they are, although a large hunk of crumpled metal is lying on the ground a few yards away. The car dies the moment they get too close, the engine simply cutting out as the steering wheel jerks out of her hands. The silence is deafening. She has to muscle the car to the side and slam her foot on the brake for it to manually stop.

Elizabeth shakily climbs out of the car, her eyes distant but pupils no longer dilated. "I lost her," she whispers. After a moment of wallowing in the silence, she holds her hands up in front of the gate. "There's a barrier. Something strong."

"Can you get past it?" Alex asks, eyes locked on the gate and voice hard.

Tears fall silently down Elizabeth's cheeks. "No."

Gabby shudders, nausea churning inside her. Her hands are clammy. After an hour and a half of keeping everything out, she's can barely hold herself together, and little things start to seep in. Alex's guilt, Elizabeth's pain, Mark's anger.

"We have to," she says, setting her jaw. She turns to them and keeps her ton authoritative. "Okay, so everyone has to take one side of the barrier and throw everything you've got at it. These types of things are generally big circles, right?" She pauses, chewing her lip. Then, she says, "Elizabeth."

Elizabeth's eyes snap up to her, her mouth making a little "o" at Gabby taking charge.

"You stay here on the East end. Mark, you take the West." Mark immediately starts walking, setting their current location on his phone. "Alex, I want you on the Southern side. Do what Mark's doing and take note of where we are so you know when you're there. I'll go North."

Alex follows Mark to the right, and they're quickly out of sight.

When she's in place, she starts a conference call with everyone and sets her phone on the ground, shivering in the December chill. "Alright, let's go. Hit it as hard as you can as often as you can. And if you get through, find Sarah."

"If you get the chance," Alex says, his voice breaking up over the shoddy reception, "kill Helen. This ends today."

Gabby doesn't know many offensive spells, so she uses a basic attack—a thin wisp of magic that's made to burn its target like acid. She goes through the movements in quick succession. Her phone is on the ground, and Mark is mumbling a spell followed by the crashing of thunder, and a loud whooshing sound must be Alex's fire. Whatever Elizabeth is doing, she's completely silent.

*We're coming for you, Sarah. Just hold on,* Gabby thinks even though her friend can't hear her.

# CHAPTER FORTY-TWO
## Sarah

HELEN IS SPEAKING AS SHE CUTS. NOT A SPELL, but mad ramblings that Sarah tries desperately to ignore. "He doesn't even love you. He's under a love potion that I gave him. It was so he would stay near you, and the tracking spell I added is nearly undetectable."

No, it's not true. Helen is lying. She has to be.

"It's really a shame that you take so many photos of your friends. It made it so much easier for me to choose the remaining ingredients for my ritual," she says.

Sarah's phone. It hadn't been found. The attack on Kendall was her fault. If she hadn't kept the pictures from the dance, if she hadn't left her phone in the woods...

*Cut.*

Her throat is raw as another scream comes out, although her eyes are out of tears now. She keeps her eyes to the sky, which is hinting at the beginnings of a sunrise.

Then, as the tip of the knife grazes the top of her sternum, another scream pierces the air.

Sarah knows what it sounds like when a dragon is screaming, ready to attack, to dive down on its prey and rip it to shreds. She's been educated on that sound her whole life. And, mere months ago, she heard a similar scream from a different dragon, a scream of pain. This is utterly different, and it penetrates down to her bones. This isn't a creature in pain, begging to be saved. This is a creature determined to kill.

It plummets from the air above them, and Helen drops the knife in shock when she turns up to see it. A green arrow diving through the morning freeze.

Sarah half thinks that it's after her, coming to put her out of her misery. But then, when it slams into Helen, she sees the red feathers raised on the back of its neck.

Arthur tears and snaps at Helen, but she's cunning and capable of holding him off. With years under her belt training animals, it makes sense that she can keep a juvenile dragon from ripping her throat out, even if he is sixty pounds. Still, he claws at her arms and bites anything he can, pulling out small chunks of skin and tearing at her clothing.

And, Sarah realizes after a few moments of dazed thought, keeping her distracted. She stumbles to her feet, but collapses to her knees as the world spins around her. She looks to her arms for the first time, and the same symbols that have haunted her for years are now carved down her arms. All but the one on her chest. She could vomit. Blood is streaming down, pooling in the crevices of her elbows.

She forces herself to stand once again, and Helen tries to chase her, fingers clawing the air inches from her face, but Arthur is upon her once again, gouging at her every chance he gets. Her face still has the same blackened, wild eyes and pale skin, but from her collarbone down are stains and splashes of red, similar to those marring Sarah's body.

The fastest Sarah can move is a sort of walk-jog toward the dilapidated house, her head still trapped in dizziness, either from the blood loss or the head trauma.

The house isn't the greatest plan, but if she can hide long enough, then she will be rescued. With every beat of her heart, she loses more blood, and just the sight of it is making her faint, but she keeps going.

One of the steps breaks beneath her, and she has to catch herself on the porch to keep from falling in toward the ground. When she pulls her leg out, her calf scrapes against a nail that's sticking out, and it buries its way into her flesh. A shooting pain rips its way up her body, and she has to stifle a scream. She glances behind her, and Arthur is going after Helen's legs, and Helen's black eyes embed themselves into Sarah's.

After carefully unhooking the nail from her skin, she limps into the house, and, aside from the musty smell and the layer of dust, nothing has changed from that night six years ago. The ceramic coffee mug Helen had been drinking from is even sitting in the same place she left it, resting on the counter, waiting to be picked back up. Footsteps—recent ones—trail through the dust on the hardwood floors. So Helen has been in here, then. A good deal of the footsteps lead to the basement, and the visceral stench of rot that weaves through the evening is stronger in here. She shudders.

When she slams the front door shut behind her, she goes to sit at the kitchen table to stifle the bleeding. Hiding will be useless if there's a trail leading right to her. She takes a pair of kitchen scissors out of the knife block and cuts all the way up the leg of her pants, then rapidly chops around in a circle around her thigh. The skin is torn, and a chunk of fat hangs out of the hole. She gags, but she has to do this if she wants to make it out of here. How did she think, even for a minute, that she would be able to bear the pain Helen would put her through?

She puts the scissors in her mouth and carefully wraps what is now a long strip of cloth around her calf, covering the hole three times. When she ties the knot tight, she groans against the cold metal in her mouth, a dull pain throbbing up her leg and into her torso. She takes a coat of the rack by the kitchen door, covering the markings on her arms. That will have to do. She rinses her hands in the sink for just a moment, but Arthur can't hold Helen forever.

Now, all she has to do is hide until help arrives. Thunder

echoes in the distance. She uses the sound as an opportunity to sprint up the stairs before sneaking through the hall, avoiding any soft spots in the wood. She goes into the guest room, locking herself in the closet and burrowing deep under a pile of musty blankets and pillows. She whispers as many spells as she can think of—protection spells, her favorite barrier spell, even a sound muffling charm. Anything that will give her even a second of extra time. It all seems so flimsy in the face of Helen's darkness.

Just as orange morning light begins to seep in through the cracks in the slatted door, Helen's footsteps make their way into the house. Sarah is tempted to send a mental call for Arthur, to find out if he's okay, but it may be a beacon straight to her position if Helen catches the telepathy.

Helen stomps through the rooms—she wants Sarah to know she's there, wants her to be scared. The worst thing is, it works. While her leg throbs and her arms sting, Sarah freezes, holding her breath for as long as possible to make no sound. She can still feel sharp magic weaving its way through the cracks in the floorboards, and she only hopes that it can't tell Helen where she is. The entire house is holding its breath along with her, waiting for her to slip up so that Helen can hear her. It doesn't make even the faintest of creaks, despite its disrepair. It wants Sarah to be found, so she has to be better.

At the same time that something heavy thumps on the roof, the shelf that's been tirelessly supporting Sarah's weight cracks, the sound utterly deafening in the silence.

The stomping makes its way to the bedroom, and her spells dissipate instantly. The closet door is ripped off its hinges, and Sarah cries out. When she's uncovered, Helen drags her out by her hair. Sarah kicks and screams. She sends telepathic cries to Arthur, begging him for help. This time, she will not go quietly. Her head throbs and her wounds ache, but she will not take this. Helen drags her all the way through the house, down the stairs and out the front door.

"Running just made it harder for you, sweetie. It's going to hurt a lot more now, you know. You really have nobody to blame except for yourself. You're the one who ruined everything that night and made me do this the hard way." Her voice is still sweet, but with hints of bitterness.

Sarah thrashes and bucks, kicking and grabbing for something to keep her from being taken back outside, back to the bloodied spot on the ground that has never quite healed from the dark ritual Helen performed all those years ago. The grass is black, and her mouth is filled with the coppery taste of blood.

She fights as hard as she can, her energy somewhat restored from a combination of decreased bleeding and increased adrenaline. Still, it isn't enough. Still, she's pulled along like nothing more than a little dog on a leash. No matter how hard she fights, she isn't going to win.

When Helen flings her to the ground, back to the spot where her blood is now frozen to the Earth, she cries. There's nothing dignified about it—she doesn't want to be hurt anymore, but no matter how hard she tries to save herself, she's still not going to make it. Nobody is going to save her—that much is clear by now. A weak whinny sounds from the direction of the barns, which once used to house some of the most expensive horses and unicorns in the world. Sarah turns her head, and, just past the first barn, her eyes catch the glint of an opalescent unicorn horn, although the animal it's attached to is faded and malnourished, its features hollow. This isn't the same one from before—this creature wasn't lucky enough to escape.

"After you're gone," Helen says, her breath hot in Sarah's ear, "I can finish what I started." She picks up the knife gingerly, like someone might pick up a dropped phone. She inspects it, although Sarah can't think of why she'd need to. "I was hoping to get you after I killed you parents, but I was too weak back then."

The accident. The truck driver had insisted that he didn't remember a thing. That there was no way he could have done it. That he must have been possessed. *Of course.*

She considers begging for her life, but that won't help. Helen doesn't care about her. "Why, Helen? What made you hate us—hate me—so much? Why are you summoning demons? You were so good. I loved you so much." Sarah whispers.

A dissonant laugh scrapes out of Helen's mouth. "Helen? She hasn't been around in years. You know, she gave up fighting me so easily. She begged me to spare you. If nobody else, she wanted you to live. But that just isn't possible."

Everything clicks in that moment. The sudden change, the black eyes, the darkness that pulsates around her. This was never Helen. It's someone—some*thing*—else. So there's no hope for Sarah to reason with her.

With it.

She leans over her legs, holding her head in her hands. Tears stream down her face. This isn't a dignified way for her to die—covered in blood and tears and snot—but she can't stop.

"No," she moans, mostly to herself. Her shoulders rack with pain and tears, and she says it again, a little louder. "No." It isn't a whine, more like a command. Something she'd tell Arthur when he's caught chewing on her bedspread. The tears keep falling, but her voice only gets stronger. "No."

Helen grabs her by the wrist and laughs. "Yes," she hisses. "Don't worry. It's almost over. I'd say that you'll see your parents again, but your soul won't even exist anymore."

She draws the knife up to Sarah's chest, and just as a tiny bead of blood trickles down her chest, Sarah screams, the word coming out with a power that she's never felt before.

"NO!"

It bursts out of her, a shout of defiance. A white light shoots out in all directions, blinding her. Everything around her burns cold, her skin blistering. It hurts. The pain is so much worse than everything else. Worse than the accident, worse than her leg injury in the woods, worse than her head, worse than the markings...

The thud of the knife falling into the dirt is the last sound in the entire world.

# CHAPTER FORTY-THREE
## Alex

WITH A FLASH OF NUCLEAR WHITE LIGHT, THE barrier is gone. One moment, Alex is throwing all the fire he can at it, and the next, it sheds away, flaking like ash. The one thing he can say for certain is that this has nothing to do with the futile magic they've been throwing at it. This destruction had come from inside.

He doesn't question it—he just runs, blind for a moment as he sprints through the sparse woods on his side of the barrier. He focuses his telepathy on the center, searching for any sign of life. It's only a minute or two before he sees the house—or, more accurately, what used to be a house.

His heart races as he slows at the treeline. Everything here has been shorn to the ground, like a bomb went off in a bubble. One of the barns is nothing but wood and metal past the first horse stall, and that path of destruction follows all the way to the tall oak that still stands just behind the collapsed home. He searches the center of this destruction, anything that could explain what happened, when he sees a heap right in the middle, a girl with short brown hair lying on the ground in blood-soaked clothes.

He dashes toward her, falling to his knees behind her. She doesn't move at his arrival. He counts to ten, hoping beyond hope for just one breath, but nothing comes. *Not again. Please, not again.* He wants to touch her, but he's isn't sure he can survive what he'll find if he turns her over.

Holding his breath, he leans down and gently rolls her onto her side. Her eyes are shut, her face peaceful. He puts his fingers gently against the side of her neck to feel for a pulse. If she's breathing, he can't see it. His hand is shaking too much to find anything in her veins that might show him she's alive.

"Please," he whispers. "Please be okay." A drop of water drops on her face, but it's not raining. There aren't even any clouds. It takes a moment for him to recognize the tear as his own.

He brushes her hair out of her face and tries checking for a pulse again.

"Sarah, where are you?" Gabby's voice calls from the woods across from him. She emerges from the trees, Arthur dragging her by her sleeve as he hovers in mid-air. She freezes the instant her eyes land on Alex's, her face paling.

He looks back to Sarah, who still hasn't moved.

"It's alright," he says, choking on his words. "We're gonna get you home now." He picks her up and caresses her. The least he can do is carry her back. If he hadn't left her alone earlier, maybe this wouldn't be happening. He has to believe he would have been powerful enough to stop Helen when she came for Sarah at the house.

"What's going on?" Gabby asks, her voice desperate and close. He doesn't look at her, doesn't answer. He won't put words to his fear. That would make this moment real. If he doesn't speak, Sarah still has a chance.

While his eyes rest on her face, he catches the slightest flutter in her eyelids.

He stops breathing.

She opens her eyes.

"You're alive," he says, the words coming out in a rush of air. His knees go week, but he can't fall over. He still has to get her to help.

He looks at Gabby, who has tears welling in her eyes. "She's alive," he says louder.

# CHAPTER FORTY-FOUR
## Sarah

SARAH IS ONLY IN THE HOSPITAL FOR A FEW DAYS, but she doesn't return to St. Merlin's. She's been ordered to remain on bedrest for the rest of the semester, and a psychologist comes to the house once a week. At first, she doesn't talk—not about anything that matters, anyway. She discusses Arthur, her new room decor, her favorite shows, but not the incident.

After a few sessions, though, she opens up, words tumbling out of her faster than she can think of them. The doctor collects them into a glass ball, and Sarah can finally breathe again.

Alex and Gabby are at the house every single day, and they even spend most weekends with her. They help her with her homework and keep her updated on all her classes.

"Mr. Thompson put me with Lionel Schmidt in Potions,"

Alex tells her, rolling his eyes. "She's literally the worst."

One of the perks of having a guardian who's a teacher is that Sarah is excused from attending classes easily, as Mark seems to know all the rules and paperwork and loopholes to exploit.

The marks carved into her arms are wrapped in bandages so she doesn't have to look at them, and, when they've healed into angry red scars, she covers them with long-sleeved shirts. Before he goes home for winter break, Alex gives her an oversized grey sweater as a birthday and solstice gift, which she wears every day to stave away the loneliness. It smells smoky, like a campfire, so she suspects that it has some sentimental value. He promises to return as quickly as possible, and he video chats with her every night until she falls asleep. She doesn't ask about the things Helen—no, the demon—told her.

Over break, she doesn't see Gabby as much as she'd like, but she knows that her family is acclimating to having Rudy back in the house after his time in the hospital. At least Sarah has Mark and Elizabeth, who shower her with attention. For her birthday, they spend the afternoon at the zoo, lying in the false summer field of the dragon aviary while Arthur frolics with the other dragons. They marathon bad Hallmark movies throughout December, and they even open presents under the plastic tree that Elizabeth brought home one afternoon for them to decorate together.

Carefully, Mark asks, "Do you want to try seeing your

aunt in the hospital today? Since it's a holiday?"

The room goes from jovial to serious in an instant.

Twelve bodies had been recovered on the property, all girls around Sarah's age with the horrible marks embedded in their arms. Some had decayed, others hadn't.

Helen was found as well, comatose beneath a portion of her home, but still alive. According to Detective Gonzales, the demon possessing her had been collecting the original bodies to gain strength, but the demon was expelled by Sarah's powerful psychic outburst. The detective hadn't commented on the ritual it seemed to be performing, and not knowing what it means keeps Sarah up at night.

"I think another day, maybe." Sarah's whisper is scratchy and high. Tears prick at her eyes, and she controls the temptation to scratch at her scars. Helen may be innocent, but her face still haunts her nightmares and wakes her up screaming. No, it's better that she stays away for now.

NEW YEARS EVE, THE WOODS ARE SINGING. SARah isn't asleep, but Arthur jerks awake at the crooning. He weighs more than her now, so she doesn't let him sleep on her chest at night, although the weight of his head lying on her helps to alleviate the nightmares.

The night she was taken, how had she thought that the singing in the woods had been faeries? Now that the real thing is here, she can't understand how she'd believed Helen's—the demon's, she corrects herself—lie. It had been sick, twisted with the magic that stuck to her clothes. This, though, is pure. Melancholy and sweet. She sees that now.

Because the demon is gone—really gone this time—she's free to come and go as she pleases. She gets dressed in her nicest winter dress, a lavender one Elizabeth had gifted her, Alex's grey sweater, and a white winter cape that goes down to her hips. It would look better in the snow, but it's an unnaturally balmy night for December, and her boots get sucked into the mud as she tromps through the woods, Arthur drifting along in the sky over the trees, his shadow a comfort as it blocks out some of the pale moonlight.

When she walks into the party under a hill she's never seen before, her eyes are caught by a beautiful boy. The dark-haired pyromancer is waiting on the edge of the dancefloor, a smile lighting up his face the moment he sees her. Next to him stands a tall girl with thick, curly black hair and freckles across her dark skin.

They meet at the center of the dancefloor, and Alex gathers Sarah in his arms, pulling her into a deep kiss. For the first time since before the incident, she loses herself in it, although his lips are careful against hers at first.

After they pull away, Gabby wraps her in a hug, grinning.

They dance until the sun rises, and Sarah lets the music pound her eardrums into a blissful oblivion.

# ACKNOWLEDGEMENTS

A S IT TURNS OUT, WRITING A BOOK IS REALLY hard. Ridiculously hard. I did a lot of this book on my own at the start, because I felt like I had to. However, in the past year or so, I've gotten so much help that I didn't think I deserved. It's been a long journey, but I'm so happy that this book happened the way it did.

My readers are so important to me. The fact that you're willing to take time out of your day to read my words is absolutely incredible. If you have the time, I would love it if you could leave a review for this book online!

For working on this book, I'd like to think Monica Borg. The cover illustration is absolutely gorgeous. You truly brought Sarah and her dragon egg to life. It's more than I could have imagined.

I also want to thank Ren Hutchings. You were the first person to lay eyes on *Smoke and Mist*, and you took great care of my baby novel when it was still fragile. Your revision notes meant more to me than you can ever know—it was the first step in me being able to publish this book. I couldn't have done it without you.

Eilis Barrett, this whole thing started with a project we worked on for like half a day in 2014. I can't believe where it's gone from there.

Kristy Nicolle, your support means so much to me. You've been so much help, and I wouldn't have had the confidence to self-published without your encouragement. I really think this is the best path for me, and it's all because of you.

Some other writers I'd like to thank are Sarah Glenn Marsh, who showed me that girls are allowed to be bi on page, and Gwen C. Katz, who was the first published author to take me seriously.

Mrs. Olivares and Mrs. Sanders, my high school English teachers. You were the first people to read my creative writing, and the first to tell me that my writing was any good. Your encouragement kept me from giving up. (Also, Mrs. O, sorry I said "shit" in front of you at Walmart that one time. My bad).

Madelyn, you're going to do great things. Don't let the bastards get you down. You are in control of your future, and nobody can take that away from you.

Andrea, you've always been there to talk. You've helped me through some of my hardest days these past couple years, and your friendship means the world to me.

Katrina, you're my closest friend. I'm so glad we ran into each other after work at Scholastic. Your friendship is so important to me, and your editing services are phenomenal. I'm so glad I found an editor with the kind of cold-hearted precision I need.

Virginia Wilcox has always encouraged me to follow my dreams. My mom is the best anyone could ask for, and she's done everything possible to allow me to pursue my passion without judgement. Mom, you taught me what it's like to be unafraid of what people think. You also taught me that sometimes, on the path to success, people will think you're a bitch. I'm so glad you raised me with a backbone so that I could stand up for what I believe in.

Finally, Jacob. You're my best friend, my rock, and my husband. My favorite person. You taught me what true love really means after years of toxicity in my life. You've been there for me through everything, and I couldn't have written this book without you. Also, you're the first person to write fanfiction about my work. I won't forget you when I'm famous.

KATE HALL is a full time traveler, dog owner, artist, wife, and reader. She believes in wild
things like love, magic, and basic human decen-
cy. Some of her least favorite things include self-
ish people, eating fish, and tornados. *Smoke and
Mist* is her first novel.

www.KateHallBooks.com
Twitter @KateHallAuthor
Instagram @KateHallAuthor

*  9 7 8 1 9 5 0 2 9 1 0 3 8  *